The Woman Next Door, was a No.1 ebook bestseller, while the follow-up, *In a Cottage in a Wood*, was a *USA Today* bestseller and a *Sunday Times* top ten bestseller. She is the writer in residence at East Barnet School and teaches courses in Writing for Children at City University and Crime Fiction at City Lit. She lives in London with her family.

 @CassGreenWriter

Also by Cass Green

The Woman Next Door
In a Cottage in a Wood

DON'T YOU CRY

CASS GREEN

HarperCollins*Publishers*

This novel is entirely a work of fiction.
The names, characters and incidents portrayed in it are
the work of the author's imagination. Any resemblance to
actual persons, living or dead, events or localities is
entirely coincidental.

HarperCollins*Publishers*
1 London Bridge Street
London SE1 9GF

www.harpercollins.co.uk

This paperback edition 2018
1

First published in Great Britain by
HarperCollins*Publishers* 2018

Copyright © Caroline Green 2018

Caroline Green asserts the moral right to
be identified as the author of this work

A catalogue record for this book is
available from the British Library

ISBN: 978-0-00-828721-4 (PB)

Typeset in Sabon by Palimpsest Book Production Ltd,
Falkirk, Stirlingshire

Printed and bound in the UK by CPI Group (UK) Ltd,
Croydon, CR0 4YY

MIX
Paper from
responsible sources
FSC **FSC™ C007454**
www.fsc.org

This book is produced from independently certified FSC™ paper
to ensure responsible forest management.

For more information visit: **www.harpercollins.co.uk/green**

Readers: I'm so grateful to each and every one of you.

1

Nina

The sun still blasts through the restaurant windows at seven pm, showcasing dust on the red plastic table cloths and monochrome movie stars on the walls. Even Sophia Loren is looking the worse for wear as she smiles down on my table-for-two, her picture yellowing and wrinkled in the unforgiving light. Two large ceiling fans churn the soupy air, bringing no relief.

The initial, barbecue-novelty of this heatwave has long passed and most of the passers-by now share the same shiny, bad-tempered patina. There's a fraught, irritable energy in the heavy air. Earlier, on the bus into town, a young woman had unleashed a barrage of swearing at an old man she accused of hogging all the space on their double seat. Physical contact with strangers is even less welcome than it ever was.

I pluck at my neckline to let in some air; sweat is gathering under the seams of my bra. Because I've been living in vest tops, baggy old shorts and flip-flops after work lately, I feel imprisoned by this outfit. I don't even like this dress that much, nor the sandals that supposedly go with it, which seem to be made mainly from barbed wire and sandpaper.

I bought the shoes and the dress from a shop I normally avoid because it's so expensive, deciding I needed to be bolder, braver, in my wardrobe choices.

Making any kind of decisions the day after your husband of fifteen years moves out of the family home and in with his new, younger partner, isn't, it transpires, the brightest idea.

I picture her; reasonable, smiling Laura with her huge, moist eyes and her, 'I really hope we can become friends, Nina.'

Friends.

Ian posted a picture on Facebook today; the two of them looking tanned and happy outside a pub. Laura's face was turned to him like a heliotrope seeking sunshine. He seems to have dropped ten years in that picture and it stung, I can tell you. If that wasn't bad enough, Carmen, my supposed best friend, had liked the post. It was as though she'd forgotten all that stuff about being 'better off without him'. Forgotten about my broken heart.

So, I'd bashed out a furious private message to her. She'd claimed it was 'difficult' because we all 'went back a long way' and a load of other rubbish that finally made me snap. I'm pretending not to see the missed calls and four texts she has sent since then.

It's fair to say that it has been a shitty day.

I usually love this time of year. The thought of six weeks away from the comprehensive where I work as an English teacher should be something to relish. All those weeks without lesson planning, marking and having to mop up hormonal teenage angst. Lots of time to hang out at home. The extended summer holiday usually includes some lesson planning and a couple of meetings, but for now it stretches ahead of me. That is the problem, in a nutshell.

Last night, my twelve-year-old son, Sam, went off to stay

with Ian and Laura before travelling with them to visit Laura's parents, who live in Provence. I've seen the pictures of where they're going. It's all turquoise shutters and tumbling wisteria. Idyllic. There's even a small pool. But the icing on the cake is the resident dog, a shaggy-haired golden retriever. Sam has always wanted a dog but Ian's allergy to pets meant it was a no-go. I can't help enjoying the thought of Ian spending the whole holiday sneezing. Maybe I'll get the biggest, hairiest dog I can find while they're away. That'll show him.

I pretended to be excited for Sam, however hard it was to mould my mouth and face into the required shapes for a response. I want him to have a lovely time. Of *course* I do, but the idea of rattling around the house on my own, picturing them all together as they amble down sun-sparkled lanes surrounded by lavender fields, causes a panicky emptiness to swell inside my chest.

Must snap out of this. I take a swig of my tepid white wine and blink hard. I wish I had thought to bring something to read, or at least my iPad. I'd been watching something on Netflix in the bath, and I left it on the side. Ian disapproved of this and now I do it as often as possible in a pathetic act of rebellion.

I look around the restaurant.

There aren't many other customers. Whether it's because it is still early, or there is no air conditioning here, it is hard to say. A couple with two small children stoically attempt to eat with one hand each, while simultaneously pushing rising offspring back into highchairs, wiping mouths and occasionally tapping at their phone screens with the other. I remember those days all too well, but how quickly they go. People told me this but I didn't really believe it then.

I still think a Starbucks might have been a better choice

for this blind date, or whatever it is. When he suggested this unprepossessing family Italian restaurant, Gioli's, it had thrown me a bit. Feels like more of a commitment; harder to make a getaway anyway, should the need arise. But Carmen is always telling me to be bolder, to 'get back out there again,' and so I agreed. The man I'm meeting, Carl, is an acquaintance of Stella at work, who assured me he was a) clean b) not mad c) quite good looking, in that order. The order of importance might have been different twenty years ago.

My attention is drawn now to the back of the restaurant, where the manager, a rotund moustachioed man, is having an intense conversation with a waitress who appears to have just arrived. She is tying an apron around her narrow waist, and looking sourly over his comb-over'd head. Taller than him by several inches, she is willow-thin, with jet-black hair only a few midnight degrees up from natural judging by the Celtic paleness of her skin. Her hair is tied up in a tumbling ponytail. Her large features and smokily made-up eyes remind me a little of Amy Winehouse.

As the manager turns away, grim-faced, I shoot her a tentative smile of sympathy. The young woman lifts her fingers and makes a shooting gesture at her own head, which makes me laugh out loud.

The restaurant door flies open then and a man enters with much bustle and energy, carrying one of those foldable bikes. He manoeuvres it past a table, catching a chair that almost clatters over. I hear a murmured grumble.

He's tall, balding, slim. Not bad looking. Carl, I'm sure of it. I offer a smile but he regards me with a furrowed brow. Like I haven't quite matched up to expectations. Something deflates inside me.

'Are you Nina?' His voice is a little curt. He still isn't smiling.

4

'Yes,' I reply, feeling my own friendly expression sliding off my face. He bobs his head in greeting and begins fussing with the folded bike, trying to wedge it next to the table up against the wall. This all seems to take an age and he looks increasingly annoyed.

I'm starting to squirm a little in my seat by the time he finally does look up. He manages a brief smile, warming his eyes for a moment like a light flicking on and then off again.

'Sorry,' he says. 'You must think I'm rude. I'm Carl.' He holds out his hand and I'm aware that mine is a little damp in his oddly dry one.

'That's dedication,' I say with a grin, 'cycling in this heat. I almost melt in a puddle just walking anywhere!'

The frown's back. Maybe I've said the wrong thing, or the thought of me sweating is repulsive to him. He picks up the menu and says, rather abruptly, 'So. Are we eating?'

No, we bloody aren't, I think, *not if you're going to be like this*. But he's calling Amy Winehouse over and within seconds he has ordered a chicken salad and a Diet Coke.

My eyes dart to my glass of white wine and I take a large, defiant sip.

'Anything for you?' the waitress asks quietly, her voice deep and soft. She has a bumpy rash of spots around her chin smeared in concealer. She looks like she needs to eat more fruit and vegetables. A plastic name badge says 'Angel' on the breast of her white shirt.

What a pretty, unusual name.

Carl is tapping the Fitbit on his wrist and staring into its face greedily. Heaven knows when he finds time to go walking, what with all that cycling.

This isn't going to work. But I'm too well brought up to simply get up and leave. On any other day, I'd have probably made a plan for Carmen to ring with a fake emergency. That was out, obviously. I'm just going to have to deal with this on my own. I'm not staying much longer, that's for sure.

'Just some olives, thanks,' I say. 'And a tap water. With ice.'

Carl looks at me curiously.

'Ate earlier,' I lie. I'll finish my disappointing glass of wine, eat the olives and then pretend I've had a text calling me away. Decision made, I feel myself relax slightly.

As the waitress writes down our order, I spot what look like fingerprint bruises circling her delicate wrist, but it's just a glimpse. She moves and a trio of cheap metal bangles cover the spot with a tinkling sound.

'So, Nina,' says Carl, pulling my attention back, 'you aren't a cyclist then?'

'No,' I say, 'well, not unless you count using an exercise bike once, before guiltily stuffing it in the garage.'

He regards me blankly.

'You're keen then?' I say, a bit weakly.

Oh yes. He is.

He proceeds to talk at length about the cycling club that saved him from a serious bout of depression. He tells me how many 'Ks' he does every weekend and about his plans to enter some race or other in the summer. I tune out and finish my wine miserably, while surreptitiously dragging my handbag onto my lap in readiness to receive the fake text.

He doesn't even stop talking when the food arrives. I drain the glass of water then robotically pop olives into my mouth, waiting for the best moment to pretend my phone is vibrating.

'You should try it,' he's saying now. 'Literally saved my life.'

'Yep. You said.'

He stares at me then, an odd expression on his face. His cheeks redden a little.

The next thing he says is in a lower tone and I don't catch it at first.

'I'm sorry?' I say, sliding the last olive into my mouth.

He clears his throat.

'I'm not very good at this sort of thing,' he says, sotto voce, 'but do you want to come back? For sex?'

I stare at him for a couple of seconds, unable to believe what I just heard. His cheeks are now flaming. A mental picture of him attempting to peel off Lycra shorts in a seductive manner comes into my mind and a surge of hysterical laughter rises in my throat. I inhale sharply and the olive shoots backwards, covering my windpipe. I try to cough it away but my throat just spasms uselessly, silently, failing to budge it. The olive is a solid mass at the back of my throat. There's a split second of disbelief before I accept that I'm choking. My pulse thunders in my head and there's a whooshing in my ears.

I can't breathe . . . I can't breathe.

'I don't think it was that funny,' says Carl, his face sour now. He doesn't understand that I'm dying, I'm actually dying *right here*, in this shitty restaurant.

Slapping my hands against the table, I stagger to my feet, panic blooming in hot waves as my body strains for air. I try thumping my own chest but nothing changes, nothing shifts. The olive feels vast in my throat as my lungs strain and pull uselessly and my face is wet with tears.

Carl's mouth opens and closes, fish-like, his shocked eyes wide.

Why isn't he helping me? *Why isn't anyone helping me?*

My vision begins to smear, the floor shifting under me. My mind blooms bright with Sam's face and I strive even harder to make the air come. But it's no good.

I'm going to die.

And then arms encircle my body from behind. It feels unbearable to be touched and my panic ratchets higher and higher again. Then a hard fist under my diaphragm jerks upwards – *again* – *again* – *again* – and the olive shoots out of my mouth onto the table, where it sits, glistening with spit.

Air rushes into my lungs. I start to sob uncontrollable tears of relief. I can't stop them.

There's a hot hand on the bare flesh of my arm and I'm looking into the face of the waitress, who says, 'You're OK, you're OK.'

It takes me a few moments to find my voice and then I manage to croak, 'Thank you, thank you so much.' It's the strangest feeling but, in that brief moment, I love this waitress a tiny bit.

I wish I could stop crying but I can't. Carl stands awkwardly in front of me, arms dangling by his sides, and the other diners stare as one.

Thank God, I'm finally out of that place and on the way home.

I pretend to root in my handbag to avoid the curious eyes of the cab driver framed in the rear-view mirror. I know I look a state, with eye make-up migrating down my cheeks and skin all blotchy from crying.

Every time I think about how it felt, my eyes well up again. The precise texture and taste of the terror keeps coming back to me in waves. It was all-encompassing; a drenching horror I'd only ever experienced in my worst nightmares.

I have never come close to dying before, not really. I was in a car accident when I was a teenager, when a boyfriend misjudged a bend and wrote off his car. But all I got was a bit of whiplash.

This was the most frightening thing I have ever experienced, worse than the most intense bits of childbirth when I thought nothing could be as bad. Or the time when I lost Sam at the Natural History Museum for twenty whole minutes until there was an announcement calling for me. I'd thought then that it was the most intense terror I'd ever experienced, but it was nothing like the feeling that I was about to die.

For a moment, standing in that crummy restaurant, I really thought my life was over. I'll never forget that hot panic and the desperate fight for air, not for the rest of my suddenly-precious life. Oh, here we go again. I swipe my nose with a piece of kitchen towel I find in my handbag. So humiliating too. For this intimate thing to happen, being reduced to my basest self, with all those strangers.

Carl . . . well, I hadn't been wrong about him. After a lukewarm, 'Alright now?' he had lingered awkwardly as I sat down again and attempted to get myself together.

Perhaps he felt slighted. His bald offer of sex having, after all, almost killed me. Hopefully he'll sharpen up his chat-up lines before his next date, unless I've frightened him off for life.

This, almost, is enough to make me smile inwardly.

The life-saving waitress had been monosyllabic, as if what she'd done was no big deal. Afterwards, she just asked me if I wanted a cab and, gratefully, I'd accepted, hoping there wouldn't be a long wait. We'd quickly split the bill; Carl throwing down more than enough in his hurry to get away. After he had gone, I had sat there, deflated and wrung out, gazing out at the street and wishing I'd never come out tonight.

When the cabbie arrived, I asked him to wait a minute and hurried to the far end of the restaurant where the waitress was talking to another, older woman who had just arrived. They both regarded me curiously as I approached.

'I'm sorry. Excuse me,' I said. 'I just want to thank you again. You saved my life!'

The waitress hadn't replied. Flustered, I hurried on. 'I wish I could repay you in some way. Look, let me give you something. An extra tip.'

I found myself thrusting a twenty-pound note at her. The waitress looked up sharply, a little suspicious, almost as though she was being tricked in some way.

She took it with only a small nod of thanks.

Just before I left, vowing to never come back to this restaurant, I reached out and touched her thin, pale wrist.

'Your name is apt,' I said. 'I can never thank you enough.'

I sniff now and the taxi driver eyes me again.

Please don't make conversation.

I hadn't been able to face the bus. My car is in the garage and, even though it feels extravagant to get a taxi all the way out of town to mine, I just want to be home so I can close the door on this terrible evening.

More than anything, I want to grab hold of Sam and squeeze him for all he's worth. But that's not going to be possible.

What a disastrous day. I can't wait for it to be over.

2

Angel

Angel's phone buzzes like an angry insect against her thigh. Over and over again. Text after text. They just keep coming, each one a variation on the same pattern.

Im sorry babe. Can we talk l8r?
i luv u. u know that right???????
Pls?
Get bck here Ffs.
U R actually fcking with me now.
I luv u???

It's embarrassing.

Even though she has always communicated with him in the same language, it isn't a novelty any more. Pathetic, that he can't write properly, or use punctuation. He's not fourteen. He's a thirty-year-old manager of a pub.

It used to be a strange kind of draw, that he hadn't had the same sort of schooling as her – had any kind of schooling, probably. Once she teased him about his lack of education and he hadn't liked it one bit.

She rubs her wrist and winces, thinking about earlier.

She didn't know why she always did it. Picked fights. She simply couldn't help it sometimes. Had always been that way. When she was small and The Bastard was in one of those volcanic moods, when you could see the fury building up heat inside him, she hadn't made herself smaller and quieter, like her brother had. No, she had made herself even more of an irritant, added more friction to the situation, even though she knew what would follow.

They'd had a perfectly decent evening, by any normal person's standards. But maybe that was the issue.

Time was, they'd party until six am then sleep into the afternoon, only waking to eat, fuck and smoke. Lately though, Leon had been saying stuff like 'Maybe we should stay in and have a quiet night' or complaining about being tired all the time, or too broke to go out.

Last night they'd spent the whole evening watching telly with ready meals on their laps. Angel could feel something bitter fermenting inside her. She'd barely spoken all evening and Leon had kept asking her if she was alright. Eventually, getting no real response, he'd gone into a sulk and slunk off to bed early. Angel had finished another bottle of wine, alone, barely taking in what she was watching on the television.

This morning she had woken with a feeling of clarity, despite her clanging head.

She'd looked around at the bedroom, and suddenly hated the smelly sheets and lack of proper curtains. The overflowing ashtray next to the bed and the sticky glasses and mugs crowding the bedside table. It had turned the dial on her hangover, making it more technicolour and nauseating.

Angel had watched Leon slide out of bed and pat his naked belly in a self-satisfied way. She'd hated him then. So, she'd picked a fight – hard to even remember what it was about, but it didn't really matter because it had quickly escalated. She'd thrown some stuff and tried to scratch his face. He'd twisted her arm behind her back and called her a mad bitch. He'd looked like he wanted to cry as he said it. Idiot. Then he had stormed off to work.

She feels strangely cleansed now. It's over. He can go ahead and burn her stuff if he wants to. She's got what she needs right now in her rucksack.

Before she had left though, some strange impulse had driven her to do one last thing.

Leon was vain about his looks. He spent a lot of money on shirts, lining them up in the wardrobe by colour, so they ranged from white through the pinks and purples to blues and patterned varieties at the other end. Before she left the flat for good, she found herself with a pair of scissors in her hand.

Snip, snip, snip.

It felt good.

For a little while, anyway.

Angel pushes the memory away.

She'll get to the end of this shift, pick up her pay for the week and then Ron, with his manure breath and his clammy little roving hands, can go fuck himself. He won't even know until Saturday, because she has a day off tomorrow. And then she'll get on a bus and go away for a bit.

Scotland, she thinks, picturing the landscape of watery green mountains and lacy mist. The air is cleaner there. It will sort of scour her on the inside. She can start again, and leave all her mistakes behind her. A fresh start.

Lucas comes into her mind then; a cloud across her positive thoughts. She'd like to see him properly before she leaves. Make things right.

She never really meant what she'd said to him. There was no need for him to cut her off like this. She's been trying to catch up with him for weeks and he never responds to her texts, WhatsApps or calls.

Well, if he's going to be like that, she doesn't have time for it.

This, rather than anything else, is what drags at her now. He doesn't really need her any more. When they were small they'd clung to each other like the inhabitants of a sinking lifeboat but maybe those days have gone.

That's a good thing.

It is.

Angel idly watches the choking woman fussing about getting her stuff together, flashing small grateful smiles her way. She's glad she could help. Learned how to do the Heimlich Manoeuvre years ago, when she'd thought about being a nurse. Never had to do it before though. The woman looks beleaguered, and almost blurry at the edges, like she is trying not to take up any room in the world. She's actually really pretty, with those big brown eyes and curly auburn hair. Bit frumpy, maybe. She definitely has potential, but it's her expression that's off-putting. Mouth turned down. Sad eyes. It's depressing, looking at her.

Angel doesn't want to end up like that.

It's definitely time to make some changes.

3

Nina

People say two things about where I live: 'What a great house' and, 'How do you stand living next to *that*?' Not necessarily in that order.

I live at the far end of a country road that runs parallel to a stretch of dual carriageway on the outskirts of the city of Redholt. The road has an unusual name, Four Hays, which often confuses people because it sounds like a house, not a street name. There are only two properties – mine and my immediate neighbour's, which has been empty and for sale since my elderly neighbour died six months ago. The main road makes it feel less isolated, but we still don't let Sam walk home alone.

When we first moved in, I thought I might never get used to the constant traffic, which throbs and pulses all day and all night. Now, I barely register the sound of the cars and lorries that thunder past twenty-four hours a day.

Proximity to the road was one of the reasons we could afford to buy this in the first place, one of a pair of red-brick semi-detached cottages, originally designed for railway workers. The railway line running towards the back of the property is now defunct, only a small portion remaining at the bottom of the steep bank that borders our back garden.

Inside the house I gratefully kick off the offensive shoes and peel off the dress, pulling on a shapeless vest top and a loose skirt. I examine the sore, red patches on my heels glumly and for a moment contemplate what it would have been like if I had taken Carl up on his offer. It hadn't felt like much of a compliment, considering he hadn't shown the slightest sign of being attracted to me before this outburst. Maybe he thought I looked desperate.

Grimacing at the prospect of revealing my overweight forty-five-year-old body to a fitness evangelist like him, I go into the kitchen, hesitating only a moment before opening the fridge and eyeing the bottle of white wine in there.

When Sam is around and I'm ferrying him to swimming, judo and Scouts, I barely touch a drop of alcohol on week-nights. But on these evenings when I'm alone in the house, it's too easy to numb myself with a glass of something. I'll stop next week. Designate week-nights as alcohol-free nights. Maybe I'll even invest in a Fitbit like Carl and try not to be a boring git about it.

I take the wine and my laptop outside to the patio chairs and make myself comfortable there.

The evening sun is kinder now, the brutal intensity of the day finally having burned itself out. I breathe in the sweet air, scented with the jasmine creeper that Ian had diligently trained up a trellis on the back wall. The low droning mumble of bees in the plant is soothing.

Then I turn on my laptop.

It's impossible to resist. In seconds, I'm back on Laura's Facebook page, looking at the smiling couple. I almost relish the pain it brings. This is what masochism is, I'm sure, but I can't stop myself from scrolling through Laura-related posts. I seem to be making a habit of this self-destructive behaviour.

It feels like they have everything to look forward to.

Ian has told me that she wants kids.

The other day, I somehow found myself mournfully looking through Sam's old baby clothes in the attic. Pathetic, really.

I'm not friends with Laura on Facebook – even I'm not that much of a mug – but she hasn't made much effort to keep her profile private. She is an enthusiastic selfie-taker, and her timeline is packed with images of her and various friends gurning into the lens against a variety of backdrops. She's ten years younger than me and Ian, whose birth dates are only a few months apart, and has some sort of job in marketing for a sports clothing chain.

I scroll to a picture of Laura and Ian at a skating rink with a group of other people who are clearly Laura's friends. Ian looks a bit sheepish. Skating, for heaven's sake . . .

Then I click on the photo to enlarge it, studying my husband's familiar face.

Ian used to claim that I was 'at least two leagues' above him when we were young. His mates would tease him he had struck lucky. Pretty ironic.

Something seems to have shifted now we are middle-aged. All I can see is the weight that clings to me now; the wrinkles and the sagging bits. He, on the other hand, has grown into his age. His short grey hair suits him, more than it ever did when he was young and strawberry blond. He's comfortable in his skin, the angular gangliness of youth replaced by a sturdier build.

The gym membership had been one of the changes he made after his mid-life epiphany, or whatever it was. I get to the swimming pool now and then but that's about it. I know I should do more. Would it have made a difference, if I had joined him at the gym? Or had he been unhappy for years? These are the questions that plague me in the middle of the night. Trying to find the piece of thread that came loose and unravelled a whole life.

Was it as obvious as last year, when Ian had a semi-breakdown? Or earlier?

Ian's depression was precipitated by the death of his long-time boss and friend, Adam, whose cancer took only weeks from diagnosis to his death. Ian works for a medical software company that sells packages to the NHS and other healthcare providers and he and Adam had worked together for over ten years. I never got on that well with Adam's wife, who seemed to have stepped out of the pages of a 1950s housewife manual. She was one of those competitive mothers, always banging on about tutors and violin lessons and asking my advice 'as a professional' about whether the expensive school their child attended was basically ruining him for life. We didn't tend to socialize as a foursome much, but Ian took Adam's death very hard. After he had lost weight and not slept well for several weeks, I suggested he try some counselling.

It had worked, at least in terms of helping him get through his depression. Unfortunately, it also prompted him to decide that his life was too short to – what was it again? – 'Waste it in a marriage that isn't working any more.'

I genuinely never saw this coming. When he said it, I actually burst out laughing. It sounded so fake. So staged. Not like the things people really say. Married people. Friends.

Maybe that was the trouble. OK, so we spent a fair bit of time apart, and we didn't have sex that often any more. But wasn't that like most marriages, when people had been together half their lives? Well, clearly it was more. I hadn't realized the cracks were signs of serious stress until the marriage broke in two.

18

Oh damn it, here I go again. My eyes are leaking all on their own, without any warning that it was about to happen. Was this what Ian was like, privately, in that dark time? Maybe I'm having a breakdown too.

I picture Sam, my quiet, serious boy, lying in his unfamiliar bedroom. He had been quietly fretting in his usual way about the upcoming holiday. Even with the promise of access to a dog, he'd been worried. It had taken some gentle cajoling to get him to talk, then I'd been able to reassure him that the boat wouldn't sink, and that Laura's parents wouldn't force him to eat frogs' legs. He's always been a worrier, ever since he was a tiny boy who would stand watchfully at the playground while others climbed like happy monkeys. For a hot, shameful moment, I hope he will be too upset to go tomorrow and that Ian will bring him home.

This feels like a new low.

My arms prickle now and I look up, aware suddenly I've been out here for some time. The air feels alive with the prospect of rain. The setting sun has disappeared behind a dark band of gathering cloud. For a moment, I contemplate stripping all my clothes off and standing in the coming rain to feel the cool freshness on my skin. It would be wonderful after all the nights I've spent lately, twisting in sweaty sheets.

I could do it if I wanted, too. The house next door has been empty and for sale since my elderly neighbour died. No one would see me. Isn't this the sort of thing I should be relishing now I'm alone? Dancing naked in the rain? Not giving a shit?

But I'm already starting to feel a little cold, so I gather up my things.

I'm stepping through the back door as the first fat drops

begin to fall, releasing the sharp smell of ozone, hot brick and parched earth.

Inside, I tip the last of the wine into my glass before curling onto the sofa and turning on Netflix on the telly. There's a trashy American comedy I've become mildly addicted to.

We used to hoover up all the crime series and Scandinavian dramas but now, alone in the house, stories about murder are less appealing. There are enough shadows in real life.

It feels like this is yet another thing that has been taken from me. Ian is no doubt enjoying 'educating' Laura, whose tastes had previously, he once let slip, extended only to reality TV and soaps.

Without even knowing I've slept, I'm somehow being pulled awake. Groggy and confused, I squint at the clock on the mantelpiece and see it is two am.

For a moment, I think I'm hearing the sound of thunder.

Then I realize someone's hammering on my front door.

4

Lucas

Rain dashes into his eyes and mingles with tears and blood, stinging his cheeks and dripping off his chin. The burden he carries seems to be getting heavier by the minute. Sometimes, though, he imagines there isn't anything there at all and his chest swells with panic. This doesn't make any sense. But he stops and checks anyway, peering awkwardly inside the neck of the coat that's sucking in water like a sponge and making him move twice as slowly as usual.

Reaching a brightly lit mini roundabout he stops, disorientated, and has a moment of confusion about which way to go. Right? No, left. It's left here. He's sure of it.

He hurries on but this place is not designed for pedestrians. He is forced to huddle at the side of the slip road, his stomach swooping as a car blares an angry horn, and then he reaches the narrow grass verge. Lucas stumbles along next to the main road, cars roaring past, so close he could stretch out his fingers and lose an arm.

But he welcomes the terror, the biting cold and the pains in his face and ribs. These sensations are too powerful to allow contemplation to creep in. He almost wants to keep moving forever but the tiredness is getting to him now. For a second he pictures himself taking two steps to the right and stopping it all, but he knows he can't do it. And it's not just about him, is it?

Not far now. But what will happen when he gets there? Lucas stops for a moment, breathing hard.

This whole thing is a terrible idea.

But it's the only one he has right now so he stumbles onwards.

5

Nina

Sam. It's the only thought in my head as I run from the room, punishment for my earlier, wicked wish.

I wrench open the front door so fast I almost fall over and am too stunned to react when the cold, wet figure pushes past me.

'Sorry, sorry. I need to come in.'

I rummage in my brain but somehow can't locate the necessary words as I take in the bedraggled woman standing there, dripping onto the wooden floor of my hallway.

It's the waitress from earlier. Angel?

She's wearing a thin raincoat over a short turquoise dress made from towelling-like material. Her long pale legs – knees reddened and scuffed looking – disappear into battered grey ankle boots. She's holding a massive leather handbag – the sort that is like a sack with handles at the top – and a bulging rucksack, which she lowers with a grateful little 'Oof' sound.

'Why are you here?' I say. It's the only thing *to* say, I realize.

But Angel is off, stalking down the hallway with long strides. She disappears into the kitchen so fast I almost have to run to catch up.

When I get to the kitchen, I see she has picked up a damp tea towel and is now rubbing her face and hair vigorously with it. Pausing to give it a smell, she grimaces. This finally switches me from numbness and shock to the correct response – outrage.

'That's a tea towel!' I say. 'Why are you *here*? What do you want?'

Angel regards me; thick, dark eyebrows raised as though this question is wholly unexpected. She throws the towel onto the table and chafes her arms.

'You said you wished you could do something to thank me?' she says. 'After the whole . . .' she makes an almost comical choking gesture, hand at her throat, eyes boggling.

I can only stare back at her. It seems like the sort of thing Sam did when he was in single digits. I find I'm colouring in shame all over again, despite the bizarreness of this situation.

'But I didn't mean . . . *this*!' I manage to squawk. 'I meant . . .' I fumble for words. 'I don't know what I meant. How did you know where I *live*?'

Angel hesitates and I realize.

'Oh.' I'd told her the address myself, earlier, when she ordered the taxi.

Angel moves smoothly to the kettle on the side and starts filling it with water as though this is the most natural thing in the world. My head is still muzzy with wine and sleep. The right, obvious way to handle this is just out of reach.

I must take control of the situation. Right now.

'Look, Angel.' I try to keep my voice steady. 'It's two o'clock in the morning. I don't know you. You can't just walk into my house and start making tea. Do you understand?'

Angel is suddenly very still. Her face is without expression as she looks back at me. But although she isn't moving,

24

a strange energy seems to crackle around her. I have the uncomfortable thought that she is somehow *coiled*. Waiting. Belatedly, I experience a real sense of unease.

She points a long, pale forefinger at me, its nail bitten. When she speaks again, her voice is low and quiet.

'I saved your life. You *said so*. You *said* you wished you could thank me.'

'Yes, but . . .' I manage a short bark of laughter at the absurdity of this logic. 'I didn't expect you to turn up at my house in the middle of the night!'

'I know. But . . . *fuck it*.' Her shoulders round.

My maternal instincts must kick in because I suddenly feel aware of how pathetic she looks. She is shivering all over, soaked from the rain I can hear flinging itself at the windows.

'Look,' I say, 'are you in trouble? Should I call the police?'

'No,' she says, eyes widening. 'Not the police. Please.' She swallows. 'I just need help.'

I let out a long, slow breath as I remember the bracelet of bruises I thought I saw earlier. Her arms are now covered by the tattered sleeves of the raincoat, sleeves scrunched over her hands like makeshift gloves. What if Angel is running away from someone who has been hitting her? I wouldn't be able to forgive myself if I chucked her out into the night and then something bad happened.

'OK,' I say, resignedly. 'Wait here a minute and let me get you some dry things. Help yourself to tea, as you already . . . well, help yourself.'

I hurry out of the room but, in the hallway, I grab my mobile from my handbag under the hall table, and stuff my purse at the back of the drawer in the table. There's something about her that feels . . . off. Not least the way she has come barging into my house like we are old friends. But didn't she save my life? Don't I owe her something if she is in trouble?

Ian would be furious. He would have kicked Angel straight out the front door again. But Ian isn't here, is he? And there's no Sam at any potential risk. It's just me. I used to be a kind person, who gave money to homeless people before Ian got into my head with his talk of how I was 'only helping them to an early grave'. I'm always saying I ought to do some voluntary work now I have all these weekends with hours tumbleweeding through them. This can be a start. I will let this obviously vulnerable young woman get dry, give her some tea and send her on her way. It's the least I can do after what happened earlier, however strange the circumstances.

When I come back into the kitchen, Angel is sitting at the table.

There's a coffee cup from earlier there, plus some newspapers. Sam's school bag, not yet stowed away since the end of term, takes up the chair at the end. Angel stares down at her phone, a deep groove between her eyebrows that makes her look older. In the café, I thought she was early twenties but now I think maybe she is older, twenty-six or twenty-seven.

I hand her a bath towel and some dry clothes, warm from the airing cupboard. It was hard to decide what to give her, especially in a hurry. But after a quick search through piles of clothes that would never fit, I opted for a soft stretchy dress that's a bit tight on me, one of my hoodies and some thick woollen socks. Angel accepts the pile of clothes with a short nod of thanks.

'I'm so much shorter and fatter than you,' I say. 'But I hope this will do?'

Angel stares down at the clothes for a moment and then begins to undress on the spot, shucking off the dress in one fluid movement. I look away quickly, but can't help noticing that she wears no bra. Her small breasts have large, chocolate-brown nipples that are stark against her pale ribcage. She pulls on the dress, which is more like a baggy top on her long frame, then the hoodie. Removing thin, bony feet from the boots, she hops on one foot at a time as she puts on the socks.

I can only wait politely, not knowing where I should place my gaze.

'Thanks,' says Angel and dumps her wet things on the kitchen table. She pulls her hair from the collar of the hoodie and rubs it with the towel. 'Do you have a dryer you can stick those in?'

'Um, no. Sorry, I don't.' I fold my arms in an attempt to appear more assertive but evidently this doesn't work. I'm aware that I'm doing that *thing* – that Carmen picks me up on so often. Saying sorry for something that doesn't require an apology.

'Hang them up for me then,' says Angel. 'Just to get the worst of the wet out.'

I hesitate. How long is she thinking of staying?

I somehow find myself scooping up the clothes anyway and taking them to the short corridor that runs along the side of the house. We use it as a cloakroom and utility room in one and it is filled with boots and trainers, raincoats and household stuff. I hang up her stuff on a clothes horse and hurry back into the kitchen.

Angel is sitting again, now furiously tapping at her phone screen, face scrunched in concentration.

'Are you telling someone you're here?' I ask. 'Is someone coming to collect you?'

Angel holds up a hand to silence me and I now feel a thrill of anger pulse through me. I'm suddenly very tired. This is all too strange. I just want this young woman out of my house now. There is something decidedly off about

27

her, even if she is running away from someone bad. The feeling of unease creeps back. Maybe this was a mistake.

'Look, Angel,' I say. 'I need to know what you want from me. You're going to have to—'

Angel gives a sort of rev of frustration in her throat and looks up, her eyes now dark and intense.

'Shut the fuck up, will you?' she says. 'I can't hear myself think.' She dips her gaze back to her phone.

I buzz with outrage at this. I can almost see sparks.

'Look, just because you helped me in the restaurant earlier, that does *not* mean you have any right to come to my house! I'm sorry, you're going to have to go.' I draw a steadying breath for my next salvo and remove my phone from my back pocket. 'Or I'm going to have to call the police.'

'Oh, for fuck's sake!' The volume of her sudden shout stuns me like a slap to the face.

Giving me a dark look, she bends down and rummages in her rucksack. Thank God. She's going to gather her things and leave.

What happens next is such a shock, my brain can't seem to accept what I am seeing.

Angel is pointing a gun at me.

'I'm going to need you to give me that fucking phone,' she says.

6

Nina

Terror is a solid bolus in my throat. I throw the phone across the table and then lift my hands up, slowly, palms up in placation.

'I don't understand,' I manage to squeeze out. 'What is it you want?'

Angel continues to stare down at the mobile, ignoring me. She places the gun in the pocket on the front of the dress. I spend approximately one second contemplating whether I could wrestle it off her, but swiftly conclude that this would be pointless and ridiculous. This woman is taller than me, younger by at least fifteen years, and – crucially – clearly a bit unhinged.

'We just want some space,' says Angel when I had already given up on a reply.

We?

Then her expression softens slightly. 'Look, you seem like a nice woman,' she says. 'I'm not coming here to bring you a load of grief. But you said you wanted to help me and that's what I need right now. Help. From someone with no connection to us. Do you understand me?'

No, I don't understand any of this. I can feel my knees

knocking together and shivers running up and down my arms. I have to clench my jaw to stop my teeth from chattering with the shock.

Think.

'The thing is,' I say after a moment's silence, 'my husband is asleep upstairs. He was very tired after . . . working late. He'll wake up soon.' Shit. I'm a terrible liar. But I force myself to meet Angel's gaze evenly. 'He won't be happy about this.'

Angel half smiles, almost sympathetically.

'I know there's no one else here,' she says.

'How?' Anger rises, hotly, inside. 'How can you possibly know that?'

Angel gestures towards the kitchen surfaces. 'One plate, one cup. Ready meals in the recycling bin. I think you have a kid, judging by all the . . .' she waves her hand at the fridge, where various school letters and pieces of art work are pinned with magnets, '. . . but the kid isn't here. Or the father. Are you divorced?' She pauses. 'Was that your new bloke?' She says this last bit with genuine curiosity, as though we are two women having a chat.

'None of your business,' I reply. I pull out the chair and sit down again. 'And no,' I add, despite myself. 'He was . . . no one.'

Angel makes a face. 'Good,' she says. 'Because he was a tosser.'

A laugh almost slips out before I remind myself that this strange, probably unstable, young woman invading my house has threatened me with a *gun*. Having one aimed at me in my own kitchen doesn't feel quite real. Yet it still manages to be horribly frightening.

'Look,' I say, going for calm and trustworthy. 'What do you want from me? Do you want money? Is that it?'

Angel looks up from her phone, where her thumbs have

been a blur of motion, and stares at me. She has extraordinary hazel eyes that are almost golden. Quite cat-like. But it is impossible to read what she's thinking; her expression is as flat as a pool of still water again. She seems to slip in and out of this state. As though other conversations are buzzing in her head at the same time and she has to tune in to hear me.

'Yeah,' she says, 'I think so. And a car.'

I let out an exasperated sound.

'My car is in the garage,' I say. 'And I've got about a tenner in my purse.'

'Oh fuck, really?' Angel's dismay is palpable. 'That's a pisser about the car.'

She drags a hand through the bird's nest of her hair and then an old-fashioned bell ringtone comes from her mobile. She snatches it up and holds it to her ear. Getting to her feet, she says, 'I'm coming.'

Hope spasms in my chest as I hurry after her down the hallway. Maybe someone is here to pick her up. I can just shove her outside and lock the door.

But before I have time to do anything, Angel is pulling another stranger, a man, through the front door and into my home.

7

Nina

He is slightly built, shorter than Angel, with wet, black curls plastered to his face and dark eyes sunk in shadowed sockets. He's enveloped in a long tweed coat that's reminiscent of the sort me and my friends bought from charity shops in the eighties. He smells of wet dog, with another, staler smell underneath it. The coat seems to hang on his frame oddly, as though he is fat and thin all at the same time. He bulges around the middle, but his thin neck and narrow, white wrists protrude. It's like a tall child wearing a grown-up's clothes.

Angel touches his cheek, tenderly, and he visibly shivers.

'Come on through,' she says in a practical sort of tone. 'You look freezing.' She bolts the door then lifts the keys from the bowl on the hall table before locking the door and pocketing them.

I don't even know where to start with this.

Angel almost drags the man by the sleeve down the hall towards the kitchen. I find myself following, mutely, torn between trying to escape and the dangers of leaving these two strangers here.

In the kitchen, Angel mutters something to the man, who

is trembling so violently now that he looks as though he might collapse. He listens with his eyes closed as though receiving instruction. They stand over by the sink. I hover by the doorway, trying to work out what I can do.

I catch him say, 'The blood. There was all this blood,' which makes my stomach clamp like a clamshell, but then Angel shushes him and I don't catch the rest.

'Who are you?' I say finally, in my boldest voice. 'What do you want?'

The boy – man – I should say, drops his head, avoiding my gaze. Angel turns to me and I almost take a step back at the ferocity in her expression.

'This is Lucas. He's my little brother and he needs a bloody minute.'

Little brother.

Lucas looks only a few years younger than Angel, maybe early twenties. His face is much finer-boned than his sister's, his shoulders hunched and narrow. He's slightly built but looks like he has a wiry strength. His eyes are what frighten me the most though; they're wide and staring as though he is watching something playing out in his mind and doesn't like what he sees.

Lucas murmurs something then and that's when I become aware of another sound, coming from somewhere about his person. It's a sort of creaky *puttering* noise; familiar but so out of context I can't place it. I move a few steps closer, drawn to its source, and that's when I see what is causing that odd bulge in the coat.

'Oh Jesus!' I cry out.

Tufty, reddish hair pokes up from a head the size of a grapefruit.

The baby stretches its neck backwards, revealing a scrunched face. It's so small; surely only a few weeks old; possibly new-born. The little twist of a mouth puckers and forms a square and the unhappy creaks turn into an ear-splitting wail.

All instinct, I cross the room and reach for it, hands outstretched.

'Get back!' Lucas yells and flails his arms and I stumble back. Lucas's eyes are wide and a little unfocused. Is he on something? He lifts his hands up and says, in a strangled voice, 'Just give me space! Don't crowd me. I just need space, that's all!'

'Get away from him,' shouts Angel. 'Can't you see what a state he's in?'

She has the gun in her hand again now and is waving it around wildly, horribly close to the baby's tiny head. Barely breathing, I peel my gaze back to Lucas and the shrieking bundle in his coat.

He wipes his face with a hand that's battered and cut, the knuckles raw. I can see what looks like dried blood on his fingers and the backs of his hands. His nails are rimed black. When he places a filthy hand on the baby's tiny head, I experience an internal mushroom cloud of pure horror.

The blood. The gun. The baby squirming visibly at the opening in his coat. Any combination of these things is wrong.

'Lu babe,' says Angel over the wailing. 'Are you hurt?'

'What's wrong with you?' I shout then. 'Don't you care more about that baby?'

'The kid looks fine to me,' says Angel sharply.

'Oh, you know that, do you?' I say. 'Because I don't think that's a given right now.'

Angel stares at me and, for a second, she looks unsure.

She gives her brother a slight smile. 'It is *OK*, isn't it? Lucas? Can I just . . .?'

Lucas is breathing heavily, almost panting, as she approaches him, her movements slow and careful. When she reaches out he whimpers and steps back. But with shushing, comforting sounds she begins to open his coat. The baby is straining hard against the makeshift sling, which appears to be made from a man's shirt. The sleeves are tied around Lucas's back, the back of the shirt bagged into an unsatisfactory pouch. One of the baby's legs, encased in a white sleepsuit, protrudes and dangles awkwardly.

Lucas closes his eyes as Angel reaches behind him and tries to unknot the sleeves. The baby screams on, jolting downwards with every tug of Angel's arms. It is unbearable to watch. I bite back helpless tears and wrap my arms around myself. I can't stop shaking.

'Please,' I whisper, 'be *careful*.'

Somehow, I know this baby does not belong to either Angel or Lucas. So where is its mother?

Angel now has the baby, who is puce-faced, drawing knees to chest. She looks like she is carrying a bag of sugar rather than a squirming child and she places it on the table, not exactly roughly, but with little care. Then she peels off Lucas's coat, speaking in a quiet, fussy tone all the while, before dropping it onto the floor.

I can't stop myself from lunging for the child. But Angel is faster and with a yell she slaps me, hard, around the face. My cheek rings, hot with pain. Tears spring to my eyes and, for a moment, Angel looks almost contrite.

'Look, it doesn't have to be like this,' she says, defiant again. 'I don't want to have to hurt you?' She pauses. 'But I will if I have to. Do you understand me?'

I nod dumbly, holding my cheek.

Angel sighs and says, 'Oh for fuck's sake.' She snatches the baby up. 'Happy now?'

She holds the hot, angry face to her shoulder, as the baby shrieks on. Lucas emits a small moan and wraps his arms around himself, rocking gently.

Somehow, I find my voice again. 'Please, please, Angel,' I say. 'I won't do anything. Just please be careful! Can't you see how little he is?' I'm sure he is a boy.

Angel meets my eyes, her expression toxic with resentment. 'It's all going to be fine if you don't do anything fucking stupid, alright?' She begins to jiggle the baby a little roughly, and then, in what is presumably an attempt at a softer tone, says, 'It's OK, it's OK.'

The very words said by Angel in the restaurant after she saved my life. It seems so long ago.

Who, *what*, have I brought into my home?

The baby isn't showing any signs of quietening.

'Please make it stop?' Lucas's voice is plaintive, his accent more plummy than Angel's flat London vowels. 'I can't stand this fucking noise! It won't stop. It's getting inside me!' He presses his fists against the sides of his head and lets out a moan of despair.

Dread throbs through me. What is wrong with him? Whether it is drug-induced or simply how he is wired is unclear. But it doesn't really matter which. What matters is that baby not being injured in any way. I look at the blood on his hands again. I desperately want to examine the child to see if it's hurt but must tread carefully. Neither of the other two adults present seems to be stable.

'Come on, babe,' soothes Angel. 'It's just pissed off. Babies are always grumpy, aren't they? It'll settle soon, you'll see.' Her tone is gentle, cajoling, and it seems to work because he moves his hands away from his head.

'Now get those wet things off, right?' she says briskly. 'Then we can all calm down.'

Lucas shucks the wet black T-shirt over his head and stands there shivering like a whipped dog. His chest is almost concave, delicate, like a boy's. He has bruises on his ribs. The shape of him reminds me of Sam but the sharp, fearful smell of sweat is adult.

'Where can he get dry clothes?' demands Angel. 'Which room?'

It seems challenging to think of the right answer to this question.

'What, oh uh . . . upstairs, second door on the left,' I say, then, 'Shall I go?'

But Angel shakes her head. 'No, not you,' she inclines her head at Lucas. 'Find all the landlines while you're at it, yeah?' As he begins to walk out of the room she calls out again. 'Hey?' He turns to look at her.

'Wash your hands up there,' she says gently, then gives a small, tight grin. 'Your pits too. You stink.' Lucas's mouth twists and he leaves the room.

The baby screams on, hoarse now with misery. Every nerve end cries out to take over as Angel jiggles it roughly and says, 'It's OK,' over, and over, again in a voice lacking any warmth at all.

8

Angel

Angel has seen her brother at his lowest ebb before, but this is something different. It is beginning to scare her now, the desperate look in his eyes. She hasn't seen him for months and now this?

If he'd only tell her the whole story. She hasn't had all of it, she knows that. It's something about the way his gaze keeps sliding away from hers, like he's frightened to meet her eyes full on.

When he'd rung earlier, Angel had been on her way back to a mate, Liz's, where she'd intended to kip until the next morning. Then, bright and early, she planned to be off into London where she'd blow her money on a ticket to Inverness. She was really going to do it, too, this time. Make a fresh start in the clean sweet air, away from all the crap.

When her brother's name had appeared on her screen she'd had the briefest moment when she contemplated not answering. It would serve him right for his recent lack of contact.

But she couldn't do it. She could never really say no to Lucas.

When she heard the state he was in, she'd known straight away that this was it, a turning point in her life, albeit not the one she had been hoping for. He'd been incoherent with gasping sobs. As Angel tried to get him to calm down and tell her what had happened, it felt like everything inside her was swirling helplessly down a plughole. Whatever this was, it was very bad indeed.

She'd finally managed to extract the barest details from him and, while they'd sounded terrible enough, they hadn't been everything. There was something missing.

It feels like he doesn't trust her and that is beginning to piss her off. Hasn't she always been the one to protect him? Didn't she promise to do that very thing when they were kids?

Whatever he has done, they can find a way through it. How bad can it really be?

He just needs to calm down. Then they can make a proper plan and get the hell away.

The baby is on the table, next to her, screaming its head off still. The noise road-drills inside Angel's skull. She shoots a look at the squalling creature. Tiny babies are so *weird*, with their jerky little limbs and crumpled pensioner faces. Strong and delicate all the same time. God knows she doesn't want to have to hold it.

Angel's disobedient brain immediately lobs an unwelcome image into her mind, like a shuttlecock over a net.

Her skinny sixteen-year-old legs with blood running down them, and the awful pains slicing across her stomach. The unsympathetic way the people in the hospital had spoken to her, about how she only had herself to blame and that she may have done some 'permanent damage'.

Lucas keeps gazing at the baby, mournfully. It isn't even his. But Angel knows her brother and has a strong suspicion that he isn't going to agree to leaving it and getting the hell out of here. Why even bring it in the first place? It's *insane*.

She pictures the bus to Scotland, weaving its way between soft green hills. Travelling far, far away from here.

9

Lucas

For the moment, he's still bubble-wrapped against the pain.

Getting away had been a good distraction. Pounding down those endless country roads, across rutted fields and along the side of the dual carriageway in the rain, feeling the bouncing squish of the baby inside the coat, had taken every bit of his resources.

But a juggernaut of guilt is bearing down on him and he won't be able to out-run it for long.

Lucas recognizes this feeling. He wonders whether everything in his life has been a series of wobbly stepping stones from there to here.

'I've found somewhere,' said Angel when he'd rung her, almost incoherent with shock. 'It's not ideal but it's all I can think of for now. A place with no connection to either of us.'

She knew only the bare facts and hadn't pressed for more. But she will. And Lucas can never tell her the truth. He can picture all too well how she would look at him if she knew what he'd done. No, he needs her too much right now. His sister is the only person in the world he could have called. If *she* abandoned him . . .

Angel had been almost calm on the phone. But Lucas knows this is how she deals with the really big things. For all her dramas, she's capable of going to a quiet, still place in a storm. That's what he needs right now.

'Whatever has happened, we'll get through it. Together,' she'd said, then, 'Hey, do you remember Grandad's? Remember what I said?'

How could he forget? It was what he'd been thinking about all the way to this woman's house.

Their safe place.

The sharp animal stink and the prickly, itchy straw in the barn. Lying on their bellies and peering down, pretending no one could find them. Eating Grandad's weird old-school food. Pies and tinned peas. Custard creams and cocoa.

Laughing at his crap jokes, and playing with Boris. Lucas having to be prised away from him every night at bedtime. And even then, the old sheepdog would find its way onto his bed and Grandad would pretend not to know anything about it in the morning. He'd say things like, 'It's the funniest thing, but Boris's bed looks quite untouched. I can't understand it,' and pretend to shake his head, while Lucas vibrated with suppressed giggles and hugged the dog harder.

Angel doesn't know about the photo he keeps in his wallet, soft now with age and handling. Marianne is in it, grinning at Angel, so Grandad must have taken it. His sister is standing on one leg and making a daft face. Lucas leans against Marianne, with one hand on Boris's head.

'It's OK,' Angel had said in a harsh whisper. 'I'll look after you, Lu. I'll always be the one who looks after you best.'

He looks at himself in the mirror in the small bathroom

now, forces himself to meet his own eyes. He almost flinches at what he sees there, the burning shame.

Leaning his head against the cool glass, he tries to slow his breathing down.

He wishes the baby would stop crying.

10

Nina

The water pipes rattle, telling me that Lucas is using the bathroom upstairs. I try to summon the most benign expression I can muster but my face is stiff and mask-like. It feels like an impossible thing, to make this horrible situation better.

The pure disbelief – that this really is happening to *me*, ordinary me – is beginning to pass now. I've finally stopped shaking. But every time I look at the baby I'm overwhelmed by an instinct to grab him and just run for my life.

'Look,' I say gently, 'Angel. I think the baby is too hot under all those layers. Can you please let me hold it and help? I'm not going to do anything stupid.'

Angel regards me warily. 'I wouldn't.' She lifts her chin. 'You have to know that the kid isn't important to me. It's Lucas I'm bothered about, alright?'

'Yes, yes.' I know I'm nodding a bit too vigorously. 'I get that . . . please? Can I? I might be able to settle him.'

Angel pulls in a long suck of breath and then thrusts the baby towards me like an unwanted parcel. I cringe at her lack of gentleness and quickly take hold of him. The baby hesitates, contemplating this new location and then, presumably finding it still isn't the desired one, continues to wail.

'It's OK, little chap,' I croon gently, looking around.

I need somewhere soft to put him down.

When we had the large kitchen renovated, we made the decision to hang onto a battered old mustard-coloured sofa we'd had since first getting together. It sits at one end of the room and is covered in a fleece blanket. I cross the kitchen and grab the blanket, fashioning it into a mat with one hand, while I hold the tiny boy over my shoulder with the other.

Then I lay him down gently, murmuring the sort of soft nonsense words I used to say to Sam; a time that feels both near and yet very long ago. The baby pauses and for a moment I think it's me, I've performed the magic of making him calm, then the room is filled with a powerful smell.

'Oh my God, that's disgusting,' says Angel holding her wrist delicately towards her nose, her face scrunched. 'Has it done a shit?'

The baby is now grumbling, rather than giving full-throated cries. I ignore Angel's theatrical complaints.

'You just needed a poo, didn't you?' I sing-song, 'and now you feel better, don't you?'

The little boy stares up at me. His eyes are a dark blue, which might be on the cusp of turning brown. It gives them a look of being bottomless; alien and other.

How am I going to change him? There haven't been any nappies in this house for years and years. And what about when the child becomes hungry?

He starts to cry again, his little face scrunched in pure misery as I try to unpeel the suit. I'm terrified of hurting him, of being too rough. All the hours I put in with Sam as a baby seem to be for nothing; I have entirely lost that ease with small babies. There is apparently no muscle memory for this practical role. I feel an irrational but powerful disappointment at this.

'Can you fill the washing up bowl with warm water?' I say to Angel. 'And bring me the kitchen towel roll?'

Wrinkling her nose, she moves around the kitchen and mechanically follows instructions, bringing bowl and paper towels to the table. Then she steps back and lights up a cigarette, standing with her smoking arm resting on her other. I will deal with that later, I think, peeling off the white sleepsuit. It all feels so unfamiliar. I have forgotten about bending tiny limbs in and out of clothes and the fear of causing accidental hurt. I used to do this ten times faster, when it was part of my everyday life.

Angel is now pacing the room, darting glances at her phone screen and occasionally mumbling under her breath.

It's like having a small electrical storm in the kitchen, whirling around me. She positively crackles with a malign energy that makes me instinctively want to hold the baby as close as I can. Would she hurt him? Maybe. I wouldn't put anything past her right now.

I finally release the small nappy and the smell intensifies. I was right. He's a boy.

Mustard-coloured shit is smeared up to his belly button, which is still new enough to be swollen with a small scab nestled in the folds. This baby was clearly born very recently. Far too tiny to be away from his mother. Where *is* his mother?

I quickly check him all over for injury, but, thank God, he seems unharmed. As I then carefully wash around the scrawny little legs and the nub of the penis, he releases a thin stream of urine in a perfect arc I just manage to dodge. This makes Angel laugh – a quick, sharp bark of mirth – and I snap her a look before continuing with my task. The little boy is now hiccupping miserably. I try to fashion a nappy out of clean kitchen towel but it's hopeless. All I can do is wrap it around his bottom, awkwardly.

'Does Lucas have any of the baby's things?' I ask, but I already know the answer. He arrived with only that coat as far as I could see. A too-big coat and a too-small baby.

'No,' says Angel, distractedly, looking again at her phone. 'We're just going to have to make the best of it.' I wonder if she is waiting for a message from someone.

A thought suddenly chills me; maybe they have kidnapped this child and are waiting to talk terms with his parents.

I swallow, trying to quell my queasy stomach. What the hell have I become caught up in? The baby grumbles and I stare down at him, feeling all at sea for a moment until I pull myself together. I have to look after him the best I can. I'm all he's got tonight.

That's when I remember my self-indulgent time in the attic the other day. Maybe it was meant to be.

'Look,' I say, trying to sound calm but firm. 'My son's baby clothes are in the attic. I can find them easily if you'll let me get them. There might be a bottle there too, which we can at least use to give him a drink of water.'

There's no 'might'. I know exactly what's there because I thought, 'Why am I keeping *this*?' before shoving it back into the bag the other night.

Angel narrows her eyes through a stream of smoke. 'I don't want you leaving the room. Can't you do something else?'

I want to scream in frustration, but I must stay calm. I'm conscious of how odd and unpredictable she is.

'What exactly do you suggest?' I say after a moment.

'I don't know.' Angel casts her eyes about the kitchen and spies the towel she used to dry herself with. Then she starts opening cupboards and comes back with a handful of tea towels, which she thrusts at me.

'Do something with these.'

47

I'm awash with incredulity now. I can't help my sharp retort.

'Don't be so ridiculous!' I want to grab this feckless creature and shake her by the shoulders. Breathing heavily, I say, 'If you want this child to stop crying he is going to need to be clean and comfortable. And he's very possibly dehydrated. Babies can get sick if they are dehydrated.'

She gazes back at me and shrugs, defiant. Doesn't she even care if he gets sick? Can she really be that callous? I force myself to be calm, to think of something that will actually matter to her.

'Look,' I say, trying to quell the shaking in my voice, 'he's just going to scream even more if he's uncomfortable or unwell.' I pause, letting that sink in. 'I can quieten him down if you let me get the stuff out of the attic.'

Eyes still narrowed, Angel regards me carefully. Lucas comes back into the room, now wearing a shirt of Ian's. An old, tatty one. All his good ones were packed up and taken away a few months ago. He hasn't picked up everything yet – apparently Laura's flat isn't big enough for that. He said this with an apologetic air that made me want to scream.

The shirt swamps Lucas, although oddly enough Ian's jeans almost fit; Lucas is all legs, it seems. His eyes dart around the room, never settling on any of our faces for long. He walks over to the kitchen window and peers out cautiously, before moving towards the back of the room again.

I turn my attention to the baby, who is mewling miserably now, gathering his resources. His skin is hot and dry to the touch as I hold him to my shoulder, the awkward nappy bundled up, cringing at the scratchiness of it against such delicate flesh.

'Look, for God's sake,' I say now. 'This baby could die

without a proper drink of water! At the very least we can do that for the poor little thing!'

Angel and Lucas exchange looks. His eyes seem to communicate something.

'Alright,' says Angel. 'Let's get the stuff out of your attic. You can get him what he needs, alright?'

'What he *needs* is his mother,' I mutter. 'That's who he should be with.'

Lucas screws the heels of his hands into his eye sockets.

'Where *is* his mother, Lucas?' I say, addressing him directly for the first time. My heart flutters as he pulls his hands away and meets my eyes. His are filled with a kind of hunted despair.

In a hoarse whisper that's barely there at all, he says, 'She's—'

'Lu!' barks Angel, cutting him off. 'Remember what we agreed?'

What was he going to say?

11

Nina

'You don't need to know anything.' Angel directs this at me. 'It's better that way, OK?'

I think of the blood crusting Lucas's hands when he arrived. My mouth floods with saliva and I swallow again, forcing the sickness and panic down. I see then that Angel has put the gun on the table and I think for a mad moment about making a grab for it. But this isn't some crime drama on telly. I'm a middle-aged English teacher. I've only ever fired a gun once before, at Sam's Scout camp on the rifle range. And I don't want to see what happens if Angel or Lucas start to panic. I make myself breathe slowly, in and out, in and out, until the nausea subsides.

'Can we please just get these baby things?' I say tightly. 'We can all stay calm if we can get him comfortable.'

Angel probably imagines people like me always know where to find things in their attics.

The truth is that if you had asked me a week ago to find Sam's baby stuff, we'd have been in trouble. But I found myself up there just after Ian told me about the baby, and almost ripped the place apart trying to find the blue canvas holdall I knew was there somewhere.

I'd spent an hour in tear-soaked reminiscence, smoothing out the small sleepsuits and dungarees, shuffling my pack of memories. Later, I somehow got through three-quarters of a bottle of wine and almost fell over on the way to bed.

It had been a bit of a low point.

I pat the squirming baby in my arms now and try to make reassuring noises as I gaze up at Angel's long legs above me on the stepladder. I direct her to the bag near the entrance.

She calls for me to mind out of the way, and throws it down.

Back in the kitchen, Lucas is sitting at the table, hands flat against the surface. He is apparently just staring into space, but his right leg jiggles up and down as though keeping time to some crazy beat inside his head. He watches silently as I begin to dress the baby. Thank goodness for this bag of stuff.

The best find is a swim nappy that somehow ended up in the bag. It is a little bit too big, but a definite improvement on the kitchen towel, which has already almost disintegrated from handling and the movement of the baby's kicking legs.

There is a vest with poppers at the bottom that is almost the right size and a small pair of leggings that will do, rolled up. I'm so relieved to see the baby bottle there. At least I can get some water into this little chap now.

One-handed, I fill the kettle to the brim with water. I will have to boil this bottle in a pan, and I'll use the rest of the water as a drink, once it's cooled enough.

The baby is still chuntering miserably throughout this process. I can't tell if he is lethargic. He does feel hot, but despite the rain, the air still feels thick and warm.

Lucas now sits with his hands buried in his hair, head down. Angel is furiously flicking through something on her phone. She pauses once only to say, 'Fuck,' and then, ignoring Lucas's plea to show him what she is looking at, she keeps on scrolling, shaking her head slowly.

It is still raining outside; I can hear it. I stare back at my reflection in the black window, my face a pale oval and my eyes wide and frightened looking.

The baby bottle rattles loudly against the side of the pan as it boils. Will five minutes be long enough? I never did it this way in the past. I used a machine instead, which has long since gone.

The lack of milk looms large in my mind. What are we going to do about feeding this baby?

The windows are misting up with the water boiling on the stove now; combined with the heat of the night, it feels claustrophobic in here. I hesitate for only a moment before leaning over to open the top of one of the windows, feeling four eyes drilling into me as I do it. What do they think? I'm going to haul my body out of that tiny window and escape?

When I turn back, Angel is frowning, chewing on her thumbnail, apparently deep in thought.

'So,' says Angel. 'We need money. You have to get it for us.'

'I'll happily give you money,' I say, carefully. 'But I already told you. I only have about ten pounds here.'

'Cashpoint,' says Lucas, coming alive suddenly. 'Where's the nearest one?'

'There's one along the dual carriageway,' I say. 'A Tesco garage.'

Angel and Lucas exchange a glance, then look back at me. It's unnerving, like twins communicating silently, despite the difference in age.

'I'll give you my PIN number,' I say. Angel shakes her head vigorously.

'No,' she says. 'They have cameras on ATMs. I don't want them taking our pictures. You have to go and get it yourself.'

My heartbeat quickens. Surely, they won't just let me go? But then I'd have to leave the baby here with them. The two thoughts collide unpleasantly.

As if sensing this, Angel says, 'We'll keep the baby here.' She glances at the wriggling child in my arms and says, 'You know we don't want it to come to any harm.'

The open-ended way she says this is chilling and I realize I'm holding the baby too tightly. He squirms.

I'm grateful for the distraction of the bottle, still rattling in the pan. The water in the kettle must be cool enough now.

'I need some help with this,' I say curtly.

Lucas looks at me for a moment. I force myself to meet his eyes, which are the same golden-toffee colour as his sister's, thickly fringed with black lashes. I realize, belatedly, that he is quite beautiful, despite the hollowness of his eyes and sallow complexion. Much better looking than his sister, whose features are similar but have a heaviness to them. It must have been hard for Lucas to be the prettier of the two. Then he turns his face away from me, pointedly. Right, so no help will be forthcoming there then.

With a theatrical sigh that any of my Year Elevens would be proud of, Angel comes over and says, 'What should I do then?' in the tone of one who has been horribly inconvenienced.

The baby starts to wail again and a look of pure distaste passes over her face.

'Wash your hands carefully,' I mutter. 'Then take that bottle out of the water and fill it with water from the kettle. Put it on the windowsill to cool off.'

She follows these instructions well enough. I watch her all the time, as I murmur to the baby. He is rooting at my shoulder now, small mouth pursed, trying to find a breast. Water is not going to be enough. I hope to God the Tesco garage has formula milk.

The craziness of this whole scenario hits me again. I shift the position of the baby boy, so he is lying on my forearm, stomach down. I remember an afternoon when Sam wouldn't stop crying, and the health visitor had arrived to find us both inconsolable. She had shown me this move and it had worked magically when Sam was grumpy with colic.

But it's not working now. The baby screams on. I hurriedly rearrange him back on my shoulder. He's becoming surprisingly heavy, the longer I hold him, especially in this heat.

Finally, the water, the bottle and the teat are cool enough. I instruct Angel to put it all together. When I hold the bottle to the baby's lips, he sucks greedily with noisy slurps. The hydration calms him for a moment, but it doesn't take long for the realization to come that this isn't what was wanted.

He starts to cry again, a miserable mewl. I look up, anxiously.

'Look, he needs milk. I'll go to the garage and get your money. I won't tell anyone. But please, please be careful with him. He's so little.'

Angel looks at Lucas and then back at me.

'He'll be fine,' she says flatly. 'But that's entirely in your hands.'

When he has drunk as much of the water as he seems prepared to take, I reluctantly hand the baby over to Angel. Then I go to find outdoor shoes and a light jacket, watched by Angel the whole time. I'm trembling as I pocket my wallet and a small torch. I'll need it for the darker bits of the road.

'Right,' says Angel, when I am ready to go. 'You had better think very carefully about contacting anyone while you're out, do you understand me? I mean it. I've told you I don't care about this baby. Do you *understand*?'

'Yes!' I snap, then, 'Look, you know I can only get a limited amount of money from a cash machine, don't you?'

'Three fifty,' says Angel. 'That's the daily limit. That will have to do.'

She pats the baby's back, her eyes cold. Is she too rough? It's hard to tell. I feel like a tuning fork, vibrating with every sign of possible aggression around this vulnerable infant.

My instincts scream at me that I can't, mustn't, leave. But what choice do I really have?

Angel unlocks the kitchen door and then says my name.

'It's three am now,' she says. 'I think, what, forty-five minutes is plenty long enough, don't you?'

'There might be queues,' I say, a thread of desperation running through my voice. 'It's always busy in there. And it's a good ten-minute walk too.'

Angel regards me, her eyes cold.

'Fifty minutes,' she says. 'If you're not back by then, we're going to have a problem.' She holds the baby away from her, considers his face and says, 'Aren't we?'

Then she pats her pocket and her meaning is clear. I can see the outline of the gun through the fabric.

12

Angel

There is a loaded pause of a few seconds and then she can't hold it in any longer.

'What the *fuck*, Lucas?' she says and her voice is too loud even to her own ears. 'Why the shitting hell did you bring that *baby* here? Are you actually insane?'

He doesn't reply, merely hangs his head and Angel is suffused with a mix of intense frustration, fear, and love that makes her cross the room and hug him fiercely.

She feels him wince and he doesn't reciprocate. A bit stung, she drops her arms and turns away.

'Well, we'll just have to work something out,' she says and there is a tremor in her voice now. She wants to cry and she hates crying, so she swallows the feeling down like a bitter drink.

It's only now that she remembers she hasn't eaten anything apart from some garlic bread on her shift earlier. Her limbs feel weak and watery, her head filled with cotton-wool.

She goes to the fridge and begins gathering items of food, suddenly ravenous.

Lucas moves to the table and sits down, burying his

hands in his curls, and closing his eyes. Angel glances at her brother as she puts houmous and cheese onto the table.

She feels a burst of resentment that he hasn't answered any of her messages for ages, then presents her with this hot mess. But when she sees the tremor in his hands as he runs them through his hair her heart contracts.

'You know I love you, whatever, you big drama queen,' she says.

Lucas looks up and is surprised into a weak smile.

'I love you too,' he says and then something about this exchange causes a shift and he suddenly jumps up and begins to pace up and down the length of the kitchen, scratching at his arms. It hurts to watch. It's like he's trying to escape from his own skin or something. He used to do it when they were little and Marianne once made him wear gloves in bed.

'Stop doing that,' says Angel and he stops abruptly.

The baby over on the sofa starts to cry again. God, the sound of it is unbearable.

'I hope she won't be long with the milk and stuff,' she says. 'He's doing my bloody head in.'

Lucas tears his gaze away and sees the radio by the sink. 'Try putting the radio on,' he says. 'See if that helps.'

Angel darts him a startled look at this but says nothing as she moves to the counter. She switches on the radio and pop music burbles out. Angel twists the dial so for a minute it drowns out the sound of the shrieking baby lying on the sofa.

The baby is evidently startled by this and he stops crying. She gradually turns it back to a more comfortable level.

'Well, aren't you the expert,' she says drily.

'Angel, don't,' says Lucas, much more sharply than he intended.

Angel slaps her hand on her thigh. 'For God's sake, Lu! Why won't you tell me what really happened? Don't you trust me or something?'

Lucas stares at his sister and for a moment she thinks, this is it.

'Why would I call you if I didn't trust you?' he says in a weak voice. 'Anyway, I have told you everything.'

The siblings stare at each other across the kitchen while in the background Little Mix sing about shouting out to exes.

'Right,' says Angel, turning away. 'Sure you have.' She wants to slap him. 'Why don't you go and lie down or something,' she adds as she goes to hunt for bread in the cupboards. 'This could be a long night and you look like shit.'

Lucas hesitates for a moment and then silently leaves the room.

13

Nina

The air is pleasantly warm outside, but shock must be catching up with me. I start to shake, so hard my knees almost give way, and I'm forced to stop, panting lightly, hands resting on my thighs.

I can't believe this is happening. It's all so surreal. Her barging into my home like that. Then him arriving, covered in blood. And that tiny baby . . . Oh, the baby.

As the shivering becomes less violent, I start to walk, glancing over at the cars on the bypass, which are present even at this time. I wish I could get into any one of them and be carried far away from this situation.

I could do it. Or at least flag down a car and ask for help. But what if the police go storming in there and the baby gets caught up in it all?

I picture again the blood riming Lucas's nails and think about his reaction when I'd asked about the mother. What has he *done*? And what might he be capable still of doing? That's not even taking Angel into account. She feels utterly unreadable to me.

It's a strange sensation, to be walking away, ostensibly free, but yet trapped all the same. I hurry on, reaching the dark part of the road, and then follow the bobbing light of the torch. The road feels so long in the dark. Like it is never-ending. I would usually be scared, walking here at night. But I only feel frightened of the dangers currently in my home. What an irony it would be, if I was attacked tonight, of all nights.

When I finally reach the end of the road, I turn left at the roundabout there and start walking along the side of the bypass. Obviously, it isn't designed for pedestrians, so I am forced to walk in a semi-ditch at the side. Cars thunder past now and then, so close I feel the gusting force blowing into me. I've never walked along here before; never had any reason to. My heart leaps every time a car passes. I'm intensely conscious of my breakable body, so close to speeding weapons of steel and rubber.

The long, wet grass whips and clings at my lower legs and my shoes are soon soaked through.

I wonder whether a police car would stop if I was seen walking along such a dangerous road. It might even be an offence. I don't think I'd be able to stop myself from blurting out the whole sorry story, if they did pull over.

I turn my ankle in a hidden dip in the grass and swear. Sweating from both effort and stress, I finally see the welcoming lights of the garage ahead. It seems no distance in a car but it's much further than I realized. I look at my watch and hasten my pace.

Thank goodness, the garage is on this side. Hopefully I can get in and out, quickly.

It's surprisingly busy, for the middle of the night. But this road is a main artery leading, ultimately, to London, so I guess the traffic never stops.

There are two cars and one van filling up as I emerge onto the forecourt, blinking at the sudden harsh lighting. The normality of it, white light reflecting off wet car roofs, a man yawning widely as he walks briskly from the pumps, a snatch of grime music drifting from an open car window, brings sudden tears to my eyes. I have a fervent longing to go back to my life before tonight. It seemed so complicated, but it was so simple, really. Why did I complain? Things weren't so bad, were they?

I'm suddenly overwhelmed by a hot urge to run into the centre of the forecourt and yell at the top of my lungs, 'I'm a hostage! I need help!'

But even as I picture myself doing it, another image comes to mind: the outline of the gun in Angel's pocket. Even if she wouldn't actively hurt the baby, I picture her panicking and dropping him onto the stone floor, his unfinished skull cracking like an eggshell. This thought makes me shudder and I hurry to the cashpoint first, which is located outside the shop. But my hands shake and I fumble the PIN number. There's a second of total panic that I can't remember it. The thought of going back with no cash makes the world spin for a moment until the four digits float, blessedly, into my mind. I tap them in and opt for three hundred and fifty pounds in cash.

This done, I enter the shop and scan the shelves for baby products. The section is small and there are only nappies for ages three to six months and toddlers. Even the smallest packet is going to swamp that tiny body. But they will have to do.

When I spy the small selection of ready-prepared formula milks, including two cartons for new-borns, I feel quite weak with relief. A thought floats into my head from nowhere and I pause, then realize how ridiculous it was. For a moment there, I had worried about giving the baby formula when he may be conditioned to his mother's breast. As if that was important, now.

Who is his mother? This question keeps coming to me,

over and over again. *What happened to her?* Why did Lucas have blood on his hands?

Have to focus. I place both cartons in my basket, then grab a Snickers bar, suddenly craving a hit of sugar. Maybe it will stop me from shaking. I look around, anxiously, sure I am conspicuous, that eyes are roaming and picking over me, even though I know logically that people are just going about their business, bleary with fatigue and their own problems.

When I join the short queue, I become aware of a commotion.

There is only one till, where two girls are arguing with a middle-aged man in a Sikh turban.

The white girl has blonde hair in a ponytail so tight that her thickly mascaraed eyes almost bulge from her face. She is in a skimpy dress, stretched tight over rounded hips and thighs. Her black friend is almost bursting out of jeans and a crop top that finishes above a roll of flesh. Her hair is dyed a brassy ginger with a heavy fringe almost meeting her eyelids.

'Yeah but what's your problem?' says the white girl. 'There's no need to give us all this fucking grief, is there?'

'You get out of here with your filthy mouth,' says the garage attendant in a raised voice. 'I'm not selling you cigarettes without ID.'

'Didn't we just give you that, towel-head?' says the black girl and she and her friend dissolve into giggles that make them sound five years younger than they look.

The man behind the counter is shouting now.

'You give me your fake bloody ID and I give you a trip in a police car! You think you like that, *hn*? Get out of here, you little sluts, before I call the police. And stop doing that!'

'You sexually harassing us?' says the white girl, who is

now holding up a mobile phone in a silver sparkly case. 'I need evidence.'

I shift from foot to foot, uneasily. Please don't call the police. Please let this nightmare end so I can get out of here.

There are three other people in the queue: a young man who is studiously avoiding getting involved by staring into his phone screen, an elderly woman clutching a loaf of bread and some beans, and a suited man about my age, sighing with irritation. The old lady casts her eyes around and tuts at intervals. She throws a few disgruntled looks at the man behind her but this obviously doesn't satisfy her because she then manages to snag my gaze before I can avoid it.

'Disgusting way for girls to behave,' she says. I nod briskly and look away, out at the forecourt, which now has a queue of cars forming at the pumps.

'Shut your mouth, you old cow,' says one of the girls as they barrel past, laughing hysterically.

Several more people now join the queue.

Anxiety throbs in my veins. How long have I been gone? Glancing at my watch, I see it is now 3.35. The thought of the baby's hunger and distress tears at me. It is literally unbearable to think about. I find I'm tapping my foot against the floor, unable to stay still.

The old woman is at the till now. She is clearly a regular because she is asking after the health of several people whose names I don't catch as the man rings through her purchases. He still looks ruffled after his altercation with the girls but dutifully answers all her questions, finally managing a small smile.

The woman is about to pay when she says, 'Oh, give me one of those Instant Lottos, Ajay. Bloody waste of money, but you never know. I quite fancy a little trip to the Bahamas, don't you?'

Ajay joshes along with her now as he painstakingly selects

63

the scratch card and rings it in. All this seems to take an agonizing amount of time. It takes everything I have not to scream, 'Come *on*!' until my throat aches.

Finally, the old woman is done. As she moves past on her way to the door, she shoots me a curious look. Is it obvious that something is going on with me? Can everyone tell? I feel as if my anxiety is leaking through me like visible steam. Maybe you'd get burned if you stood too close.

The man in front is served quickly and, finally, I'm able to place my purchases next to the till, sighing with a mixture of relief and impatience.

'Any petrol for you today?'

'No,' I say. 'Just these things.' There's a clock just behind the man serving and, on seeing it, my heart speeds up again. I have exactly fifteen minutes to get back to meet Angel's deadline. Flustered, I miss the man asking if I would like a carrier bag the first time. He repeats the question and, blushing, I accept, before handing over my debit card.

'Contactless alright for you?'

'Yes.' *God, yes! Just bloody hurry!*

After what seems like half an hour in there, I am out of the door. I turn to cross the forecourt and go back to the main road when someone touches my arm.

'Mrs Bailey?'

With a start, I turn to find myself looking into the fresh, smiling face of a teenage girl. Familiar, but her name is just out of reach.

'It's me,' says the girl, 'Hannah Bannerman? You taught me English last year?'

'Hi Hannah,' I force the words out, painfully. 'Bit late to be out, isn't it?'

My brain is turning over and over. Is bumping into someone a sign that I should tell someone what is happening to me?

Hannah, who is looking at me a little uncertainly now, says, 'We're going on holiday. Catching an early flight to Paris.'

She is now joined by an older woman, who looks like the horsier, wider, version of Hannah in about thirty years' time. The blonde-haired, Barbour-jacketed woman is smiling broadly at me. I picture myself climbing into the back of some huge SUV and being cradled by it all the way to the police station. The decision is taken from my hands.

'Oh, are you the famous Mrs Bailey?' she says in a loud voice. 'I believe we have you to thank for Hannah's A star last year, don't we, Hannah?' Her voice seems to thunder in my ears.

Hannah grins and nods enthusiastically.

'Hannah is at Warwick now,' says her mother, 'and she's having a great time, aren't you, darling?'

'I'm having the *best* time,' says Hannah, drawling the word 'best'.

I'm nodding along and trying to smile but I can't think of a single word in response. What can I say? *'Lovely to see you, only, I have a hostage situation back at my house and a tiny baby might be in danger. Bye then!'* Normal etiquette seems to have entirely abandoned me. Being with two unhinged misfits all night has somehow robbed me of my own manners.

Both of the other women are looking at me oddly now, clearly expecting a response. Casting about inside myself, I finally find something to toss back at them.

'That's wonderful,' I say. 'That's absolutely wonderful to hear. And a holiday! In Provence!' I realize straight away I've said the wrong place, but they are too polite to correct me. When a sufficient number of seconds have passed, I say, 'Well, I'd best . . .' but Hannah is holding onto my arm again, blushing slightly.

'I just want to say that I couldn't have done it without you, Miss. You really helped me through . . . well, you know.'

I stare back blankly and a strange expression passes over Hannah's face, a kind of disappointed horror. Then it comes to me and I feel *sick* for forgetting.

Hannah's dad died at the beginning of Year Thirteen and for a while the talented student had, understandably, lost her focus. I lost my own mum in my teens and so I just got it. I spent a lot of time talking to Hannah after lessons and gently encouraging her not to throw away her opportunities.

'God, yes, yes, of course. I'm sorry, I—'

From nowhere, tears bead my eyelids. I try to blink them away, but the two people in front of me fracture into a watery blur. The memory of Hannah's distress, coupled with the heartfelt thanks, are more than my bruised emotions can handle right now.

'Are you alright?' says Hannah's mother. She must now notice the nappies bulging in the thin carrier bag because she bursts out with, 'You've not had . . . a *baby*?'

This is it. This is the moment to tell them.

But I can't do it. I can't risk harm coming to that innocent child because I'm not brave or strong enough to help him. I'm all that little boy has right now. I take a small breath in before speaking again.

'No, dear me, no!' My attempt to sound chirpy and friendly comes across as shrill and deranged now. 'But my, er . . . my . . . friend is staying. In fact, I'd better get back! It's been so good to see you, Hannah! And you too, Mrs . . .' but it's no good, the surname has gone again, 'and you too.'

I hurry across the forecourt before either of them have the chance to detain me any longer, feeling their curious eyes on me as I go. They must be wondering where the hell my car is too.

I know I've come across as a total fruitcake, but I have no time to worry about that now. Two damaged, possibly violent people are currently in charge of a tiny, innocent life. At their very best, they are rough and incompetent, even if they aren't about to inflict any deliberate damage. Heaven knows how they are coping with the screaming, which must surely be getting worse as hunger bites deeper. All the very worst stories about child cruelty on the news tickertape through my mind now; babies with burns, babies with tiny broken limbs, babies in bins . . .

I start to run.

My breath is tight in my chest and my skin bathed in sweat in the muggy air as I get to the roundabout and negotiate my way back to Four Hays. Carl bobs into my head and I picture him running alongside me with precise, economic strides. It does not help.

And now my stupid, *stupid* brain is unhelpfully filing another thought: Ian jogging alongside Sam the first time Sam rode his bike without stabilizers at the bottom of this road. Why think of that now, for God's sake? But I can see it so clearly; the pale pink blossom from the apple tree in our garden blowing in the breeze like confetti, Sam's delighted shrieks of, 'Look at me! Look at me, Daddy!' The shared look of love between Ian and me. The memory has a honeyed, golden glow. It's pleasure and pain all mixed together and I cling to it as I slow down.

My knees ache and I can't get my breath, so I stop and walk; small, panicked sobs punctuating my gasps as I struggle to fill my unfit lungs with air.

It feels like someone has played a terrible joke and made my road, so familiar I notice the tiniest change in vegetation over the seasons, twice as long as usual. But at last I see the lights of my home and force a last surge of energy to get myself to the back door, where I hammer the flat of my hand against the wood, almost doubled-over with exhaustion.

The door flies open and Angel stands there, looking down at me.

'Took your time,' she snaps, eyes flashing with fury.

14

Nina

The first thing I notice when I come inside is that the baby has stopped crying. Is this a good thing or very bad indeed? The radio that lives by the sink is playing some sort of generic pop.

Lucas is not in the kitchen. I see the baby lying on the makeshift mat on the table, fast asleep, arms at right angles by his head. His tiny ribcage is rising and sucking inwards in that speeded-up way of the very young. It unnerved us so much when Ian and I were new parents.

Suddenly wrung out, I place the milk and nappies onto one of the kitchen surfaces. Then I lean my hands against the cool granite and try to catch my breath.

'Why were you so long?' Angel's voice is whingey, behind me. 'You were fucking ages. We were starting to think . . .'

'I'm sorry, but there was a queue and then . . .' I pause, 'it just took longer than I expected, that's all.' I had been this close to saying I'd run into someone I know, but I'm sure that would be a mistake. I must try and appear calm in the hope that they will follow my lead and not do anything stupid.

'Well, it felt like forever.' Angel's voice is quiet. 'We had to put the radio on to stop it screaming. Thought you were never coming back.'

This seems to be entirely at odds with the calm scene before me and I shoot a look at her. But her head is down again, eyes plugged into the screen of her phone.

It looks as though Angel has been raiding the fridge in my absence, judging by the mess of bread, cheese, houmous and ham at the other end of the table. A knife has fallen out of the houmous and left a slick smear on the surface.

Angel licks her fingers and stares back at me.

I turn away, realizing I will have to sterilize the bottle all over again to feed the baby. I'd forgotten what a faff it is, feeding infants. But thank God for the milk.

I go to the kettle and switch it on. It's all so long ago, when I could do this stuff in my sleep. More or less did, sometimes.

The radio burbles on in the background. It is a local station; one which Sam likes because one of the morning DJs makes him laugh. I get a sudden, vivid mental picture of my son shovelling in Weetabix and giggling like a maniac at the kind of high jinx I find irritating first thing in the day. This sends a spasm of pain through me and I think, *At least he's not here.* It's some small comfort.

Lucas coughs, from the sitting room, I think, and we both glance in that direction. Angel's expression is soft, but there's something else there too. Fear? It's hard to tell.

'You're very close, aren't you?' I say gently. Angel's gaze snaps back to me, suspicion tightening her face again. 'I mean, you're lucky,' I add quickly. 'Lucky to have that relationship.'

Angel gives a bitter laugh then her face becomes serious again as though mulling these words over more carefully.

I press on. 'Not all siblings are like that, you know. I have nothing in common with my brother at all.'

This is true. Steve is a successful insurance broker who lives in a virtual mansion in Wimbledon. He has a long-term girlfriend called Clare, who always looks as though she has a bad smell under her nose. We only meet at Christmas at Dad's place in Yorkshire, or at family weddings. I don't think about him much in my everyday life.

At first it seems that Angel is not going to reply but then she finally responds.

'Had to be,' she says quietly. 'No one else to look out for us.'

Wondering how far I dare go with this, I lean back against the sink and regard Angel, who has a faraway look.

'What about your mum and dad?' I say, after a moment. I immediately think I've blown it because Angel looks at me with narrowed eyes. Then she sighs deeply and yawns unselfconsciously, revealing surprisingly white teeth.

'You don't want to know,' she says. I can feel the moment slipping away, but I soften my voice and try again.

'Look, Angel, I can tell that you are a good person,' I lie. 'After all, you saved my bloody life earlier!' My forced laugh falls flat in the atmosphere of the room. But I press on. 'You must know this baby needs to be with his mother, or his father. I don't know what has happened and, honestly, I don't even want to know. But why don't you two get on your way and leave the baby here with me? I can take him to the police and say I found him on my doorstep or something. I won't tell them anything about you or Lucas.'

Even as I'm saying it, I know how lame it sounds.

Angel pulls at her bottom lip and appears to be listening, though. My pulse quickens at the thought of this ending easily; safely. I picture myself telling people about it all after the event; my weird night as a hostage in my own home. What a story it will be.

'It's all too late for that,' says Angel, rubbing at a crumb on the table with her finger, eyes cast down again. Disappointment cuts deep and we both go quiet.

On the radio, the station goes to the hour and the local news comes on. I'm only half listening when the presenter starts to speak.

Then it is as though every inch of my skin has been electrified.

'*Police are asking for witnesses,*' says the sombre female voice, '*after the vicious murder of a young mother in the Foxbury area of Redholt this evening and the kidnap of her six-week-old baby. The twenty-eight-year-old woman was stabbed multiple times. If you have any information about this please call 0333 563334.*' There's a pause and then, '*Now for traffic news . . .*'

Angel lunges to switch off the radio and turns to me. I can hardly breathe.

She turns to me and her expression darkens when she registers the horror in mine.

'Don't you dare judge him,' Angel hisses through teeth that are almost clenched. 'Don't you fucking dare. You don't know him. You don't know anything at all.'

15

Lucas

It's raining again.

Lucas lies on the sofa, listening to the soothing pattering against the windows. The room is dark, save for the pale wedge of light against the wooden floor coming from the hallway.

He can hear the low murmur of conversation between Angel and the woman. He's forgotten her name . . . if he ever knew it. He wonders what they are talking about and hopes Angel isn't saying anything stupid.

Mainly, he's thinking about Marianne. Curling up, cosy, inside a memory that turns into a light doze.

Early summer in the kitchen. Buttery yellow light.

The radio is playing 'Hotel California' by the Eagles. Marianne is up to her elbows in suds at the sink. Lucas is at the table, drawing, and he and Angel are waiting for the cakes to come out of the oven, barely able to hold their excitement. Lucas's leg is jiggling under the table. It does this sometimes when his feelings want to spill out but it's OK today. He won't get smacked for fidgeting. He is away.

Angel is nagging about how long they are waiting. Marianne throws a bit of foam at her and tells her to 'hold her horses'. This could be enough to send Angel into a tantrum on another day and for a moment he clenches inside, hoping she won't spoil it. But Angel giggles, infected by the atmosphere, and he relaxes again. There won't be any shouting today. No one will be hurt, or sad. He won't get the horrible cold feeling in his stomach when things go bad.

Lucas is thinking about how they might decorate the cakes. His tongue pokes out the side of his mouth, as it does when he is concentrating. Angel teases him but he can't really help it. It just pops out of its own accord.

He's drawing a design in crayon, a smiley face with yellow hair and blue eyes. He hopes Marianne will recognize who it is. He could never make it as pretty as she is though.

She's not like other mums. No one else looks like her. No one else's mummy lets their child call them by their first name either, or sometimes lets them stay off school on a sunny day so they can go for a picnic.

Secretly, Lucas only wants to call her Mummy. But he can't tell Angel this because she will say he is a big baby.

Angel starts to join in the singing in her funny tuneless voice. Marianne goes to her and then Lucas, taking their hands in her wet, soapy ones. Lucas giggles like a maniac. He can't stop. He thinks he might pee. It's almost unbearable, the happy feeling.

He's eating the cakes now but he can't really taste them so he crams more and more of them into his mouth. Something has shifted and everything feels cold.

With a queasy lurch Lucas comes to, his heart beating fast. His ribs hurt and when he goes to move into an upright position, he discovers new places that are sore too.

He can't believe he actually dropped off, even though he still feels a deep exhaustion in his bones.

Alice.

She fills his head now. He squeezes his fists into his temples as if he can physically grind the memories away.

Alice in her leotard and that soft, fluffy cardigan that did up in a complicated way across her narrow ribcage. She always wore it to do her stretches. He would watch, from the garden, as he dug and weeded and cut grass, calmed by her movements, but a little frightened too about what he was doing. He had never seen anyone move as gracefully as her as she bowed and dipped, her limbs flowing through the air with a languidness that made it look as though she were in water.

Alice, lying on her back on the kitchen floor, arm bent at a strange angle, eyes sightless. Bright blood pooling from her stomach.

He's dimly aware that the baby is crying again in the other room. The woman speaks to it in a high-pitched, sing-song tone, a bit panicky. He can't see how that would calm anyone down.

He pulls a cushion onto his head, squashing it down to try and deaden the sound.

16

Nina

The baby starts to cry again, a piercing wail that increases the tension in the room even further. Angel mutters, 'Fuck's sake,' and I rise quickly, ready to go to him, but she is faster.

She scoops him up and almost shoves him against her shoulder, her face sour. Every harsh pat she lands against the baby's back sends a thrill of worry through me. I want to beg her to be gentle with him, yet I'm scared of winding her up even more. That sense of her being like an unexploded device seems even keener every time the baby cries. I find that I'm taking such short, stressed breaths that I'm almost panting and I force myself to try and calm down. I'm no good to anyone like this.

Lucas comes into the room then, hands raking his hair, his face scrunched.

'Shit,' he says, 'I dropped off.' He slumps back onto the sofa and looks ahead with a desolate expression. He seems unaware of the miserable sounds still coming from the infant.

'The baby needs milk,' I say, averting my eyes from him. I don't want to look at him. Don't want to think about what he might have done. 'It won't take long.'

I busy my shrieking mind and shaking hands with getting the milk bottle and teat into the pan to boil again. Soon the kitchen is filled with two sounds only: the baby's plaintive cries and the hard rattle of the plastic bottle against the pan.

Lucas gets to his feet and reaches for a half-eaten piece of bread and houmous that lies on the end of the table. He winces and touches his belly experimentally, watched as ever by Angel. I look away again. I can't stop thinking about the words, 'stabbed multiple times' and 'kidnap'. I wonder if he has made a call in the other room, setting out demands for the return of the child.

I try to focus on the right-now, staring at the bottle rattling in the pan, but all I can see in my mind's eye is a young woman lying bleeding on the floor while her baby screams. I think again about the blood that had caked Lucas's hands on his arrival. The victim must be – must *have been* – someone with money. Why else would the baby be kidnapped?

At last I can fill the hot, sterilized bottle with the pre-prepared milk and swish it around, hoping the warmth of the bottle will permeate the liquid inside. I fret briefly about whether to microwave it or not. Is it still too cold for him to drink? All this knowledge feels somehow beyond my reach. It's like the early days of parenthood again, when we would look at the small bundle in his bouncy chair with something akin to terror. But then familiarity began to kick in and soon everything felt like second nature. It strikes me that the whole business of parenthood is a kind of loan. I'm too tired and upset to work out whether this is profound or the kind of naff thing you might see on a greetings card.

Anyway, the baby is too frantic for me to wait any longer.

'Do you want to do this?' I say to Angel and she gives a little shudder and says, 'God, no,' just as I hoped.

She holds him towards me like a bag of potatoes and I carefully take him into my arms. Making gentle soothing nonsense sounds, I sit on the sofa and position him into the crook of my arm. His lips enclose the teat and he gulps and slurps greedily, fathomless dark eyes trained on my face. I can both feel and hear the thin buzzing of air in the bottle as the milk leaves and the air enters. I really had forgotten how heavy small babies can be. My arm is quickly aching.

It doesn't take long for him to drain the bottle. I lift him over my shoulder and rub his back in small circles. When the loud burp comes, I feel a sense of satisfaction. I've finally done the right things for this small, helpless person who has somehow come to be in my care.

In no time, he has dropped off to sleep.

I close my eyes, suddenly tearful at the thought that he has no mother. And to actually be there, as I presume he was, when she was murdered. Hopefully he is just too young for it to mean anything. Unless a mother's safety is hard-wired into a baby's brain somehow.

Glancing over, I see Angel and Lucas in deep conversation over by the sink. He seems to be refusing to do something because I catch an anguished 'No, no,' but Angel is emphatic, her large eyes wide and cheeks flushed.

She seems to be the brains of all this, if you can call it that. She constantly looks at her phone. Maybe she is waiting to discuss ransom.

Murder, kidnap, ransom. The words seem to clang inside my head like the pealing of a furiously rung bell. I cannot believe these concepts have become part of my life. Panic feels near again and I make myself take slow, deep breaths, counting to six as I do so. I can't freak out. If I'm in control, there is more chance that they – those horrible people – will be too.

* * *

78

Carefully, I lay the baby down on my lap, head at my knees, his feet touching my stomach. I can feel the heat coming off him.

My mind buzzes. Must find a way to alert someone about what is going on here. But how?

Then I remember something and my head shoots up sharply, I can't stop myself. But neither Angel nor Lucas is looking at me, thankfully.

I've always liked the thought of acting, but didn't expect it to happen like this. I'm in charge of the school plays and that's as far as it goes. Ian used to try and get me to join the local AmDram club, but I'm far too shy.

This, though, will require all my skills.

Come on, I think. *Have to make this work.*

I lower my head and let out a small groan. After a few moments, I sense eyes on me from across the room.

'What's wrong with you?' says Angel finally.

I look up with a grimace.

'It's my stomach,' I say quietly. 'I don't feel well.'

Angel regards me and then looks around the kitchen. 'Are you going to throw up? D'you want a plastic bowl or something?'

I shake my head and lower my eyes. 'It's not that kind of upset,' I say, in a small, ashamed voice. 'I . . . I need to go to the toilet.'

Angel sighs and gives a small twist of her lips.

'Right,' she says, 'come on then. I'll have to come with you. Lucas, watch the baby.'

I reluctantly lift the sleeping child and hand him to Lucas, whose pale hands tremble as he takes him from me. I try not to look at his fingers, now scrubbed clean.

Angel and I climb the stairs in silence. When we get to the bathroom door, I gesture as though asking Angel to go in first.

'Fuck off!' says Angel. 'I don't want to watch you take

a shit, thanks very much. I think it's probably alright to do this on your own.'

She peers into the bathroom and gives it a cursory once-over and my heart stops for a moment. Then, miraculously, I am inside, alone.

Gently, I pull the small bolt across. It's only been there for a few weeks, added because Sam had begun to complain lately that we had no bathroom lock. It's so new it glides into place almost silently.

It's a relatively new thing, this modesty. I still remember when he would run around the upstairs rooms after his bath, shouting, 'Nudie! Nudie!' at the top of his lungs. Then he would collapse in a heap in my arms, giggling, and I'd wrap the lanky, bony limbs in a fluffy towel and kiss his sweet-smelling neck. But now he is becoming self-conscious about his body, and even though he hasn't hit puberty yet, it won't be long until the metamorphosis into sullen teen begins, I know.

Inside the bathroom, I reach for the iPad under my dressing gown on the stool. I'd forgotten to turn it off earlier, but there's still plenty of charge left.

What can you do *online* in an emergency? There's no virtual 999 that I can see after a quick search. You can report a crime but when I load the Met Police page I see that it is not for anything urgent. There are about twenty questions and I have no time.

What to do? My mind is coming up blank. Facebook? Everyone would think I'd gone mad. And that might cause a friend to come over and put themselves in danger too.

I could email someone. But none of my friends are likely to spot emails that quickly. And Ian will be in holiday mode, so not checking.

Think, Nina.

I tap on Twitter and look up a local news site, quickly finding mentions of the crime at Foxbury.

Victim's husband is the famous war correspondent Nick Quinn, I read on one tweet. *He has asked for the public to pass on any leads about his missing baby son, Zach.*

I know him. He was a familiar face for many years on the BBC, reporting from various conflict zones. I think he might have a new book out because I saw something in the paper the other day.

Zach. That's the little mite's name. For some reason, knowing this drenches me with sadness. I force myself to concentrate.

The sharp rap at the door makes me almost cry out.

'Are you nearly done in there?' Angel sounds impatient. There's no time . . .

'I think so, sorry,' I say. Hastily pulling down my shorts and knickers, I pee, simultaneously hunting for Quinn's profile on Twitter, which I quickly find.

@NQuinnWarReporter

I tap out a private message. Even though he doesn't follow me, it seems I can.

Your baby is here. I am also hostage, They have a gun.

I'm just typing out the address with panic-clumsy fingers as Angel bangs on the door again.

'You're very quiet in there. What are you doing?' The door handle turns and Angel gives a bark of indignation as she discovers it is locked. 'Hey, open this door right now!'

'Sorry! Just coming!'

I shove the iPad into the bathroom cupboard and flush as Angel begins to pound on the door.

Washing my hands quickly I hastily unbolt the door. Angel almost falls through, face flushed and expression sour.

'Why did you lock it? What were you doing in there?'

she says petulantly. I force myself to look her squarely in the eye.

'You said yourself you didn't want to watch me taking a shit, Angel.'

Angel studies me for a moment, makes a grumpy sound in her throat, and turns away.

'Well, I hope you've got it out of your system now.'

'Yes,' I say quietly, 'I think so.'

17

Nina

The baby is asleep, making the kind of grunty, snuffly sounds I remember from Sam's early days.

One night we couldn't stop laughing because our son appeared to be neighing like a horse. It hurts to remember this. All the good memories – and there are many of them – feel rinsed in dirty colours now, their innocent happiness tainted. Since Ian left I have been turning them over in my mind, endlessly asking myself whether I should have seen the signs of what was to come earlier.

My mind unhelpfully flips to a night a month or so before he told me about Laura. It was a Friday evening and Sam was on a sleepover. We were a bit tipsy on gin and tonics. I was cooking, and we were playing lots of the eighties indie music we bonded over in our early days. Ian had been quiet and sad lately, but he seemed happier that night. As I watched him singing tunelessly along to 'In Between Days' by The Cure, his eyes scrunched in bliss, I had felt such a sense of peace and rightness with the world. Now I think maybe he was picturing himself in bed with her the whole time. A fresh wave of pain assaults me and something else too. Anger. How dare he mess everything up.

This should be the least of my worries, right now, anyway. Ian seems far away, part of another life where I took the most basic things – like being safe – for granted.

The little boy – Zach, he's called *Zach* – has his arms thrust out, bent at the elbows, his face turned away towards the back of the sofa. His chest rises and falls at speed. For a moment, I wonder what would happen if he became ill here. Would they allow him to go to hospital?

Lucas has retired to the sitting room again. I saw him as I'd passed, clenched into a comma shape on the sofa. His chin was tucked into his chest and I could see only his dark curls, his face hidden. He looked vulnerable like this, barely more than a teenager. But that doesn't mean he isn't capable of terrible things.

I go to the kettle yet again and fill it with water from the tap.

'Do you want a hot drink?' I say, flatly.

Angel says, 'Do you have any vodka?'

I shake my head. 'I have some gin,' I say. 'Or wine.'

'Yeah, go on, I'll have a gin,' says Angel and then yawns luxuriously, her thin arms stretching above her head, so her bangles click together as they fall. When she speaks again her voice is restricted by the last vestiges of the yawn.

'You got anything to go in it? Tonic?'

I clench the muscles in my jaw and silence the sarcastic response that forms in my mouth: *Fevertree alright for you?*

I'm too tired to work out whether giving Angel alcohol will make things better or worse. I just pour the drink and make it neither weak nor generous. After adding tonic, I place the glass on the table in front of Angel, half expecting a request to come for ice and a slice. But Angel grabs it with a small grunt and takes a long drink, her eyes closed for a moment.

84

I make myself tea and watch her surreptitiously as she gets out her phone and scrolls through it, occasionally taking sips of her gin and tonic.

She is so striking, with her large eyes flicked with thick black liner and her strong Roman nose. The full lips, which she is currently chewing, her face suddenly tight and anxious about whatever she is reading on her screen.

I bring my cup of tea to the table and sit at the opposite end.

'Dickhead,' says Angel quietly, evidently to her phone. I sip my tea before replying.

'Something wrong?' I say carefully, aware how strange it is to be asking my jailor this question.

Angel looks up and I see, with surprise, that her eyes are glistening. She takes a savage gulp of the gin and then puts the glass back on the table before slapping her large hands flat before her. She wears a silver thumb ring that clacks against the wooden surface, loud as a gunshot in the quiet kitchen. We both flinch slightly at the sound and the baby jerks in his sleep, grunting a little before becoming still again.

Then I wait.

'Just my fuckwit of a boyfriend,' says Angel finally. '*Ex*, I mean.'

She lifts the glass again and drains the last of her drink. All her movements seem to have this jerky violence to them; she goes from perfect stillness to angry animation in a way that unsettles me.

But if I can get Angel to open up a little, surely it can only be a good thing?

'Have you been together long?' I ask gently and immediately regret it because Angel's eyes seem to jolt back to mine, her nostrils flaring. Then her face seems to soften. She rubs it, two-handed, with a loud sigh of weariness.

'Too fucking long,' she says. 'He's an idiot.' My gaze falls to her wrists, still hidden. Hard to imagine anyone intimidating Angel. But then she is still no match for a man's strength.

I find myself thinking of Ian, trying to imagine how this night would have played out had he really been here. But I can't. It's all too odd and unexpected. How would anyone deal with a situation like this? What is the right thing to do?

I decide to change tack.

'What about the restaurant? Think you'll go back?'

Angel snorts derisively. 'What, you mean when we all go back to our lives and carry on as though nothing has happened?' she says. Then, 'Look, I know what you're trying to do, Nina. Get me talking. Wear me down a bit.'

She pauses and scrapes her fingers into her hairline, pulling her hair away from her face so that for a moment she looks younger, exposed. Then, 'I've already said: this is nothing personal. I'm sorry it had to be you who got caught up in this because you seem like a nice woman, albeit it a little . . .' she frowns, casting about for the right word. I hold my breath as I wait for it to come.

'. . . beaten down.'

I look away, feeling something soft bruise inside me. It's unexpected, how much this verdict hurts, even from an unpleasant stranger such as Angel. Is that really the face that I present to the world? When I was in that restaurant earlier, in my new dress and sandals, did I exude the whiff of a reject? If so, no wonder the date got off to a bad start. I try to remember what I did with my face when Carl arrived. Whether I smiled as though I meant it. Because after all, I hadn't meant it.

A wave of pure anger at Ian, of all people, surges from nowhere. I've had one identity for so long: wife and mother.

86

I'm no longer a wife and it won't be that long until Sam doesn't need me any more. What will be left? Teaching Shakespeare to uninterested teens and then coming home to drink too much wine?

I try to quash the terrible sadness blossoming inside me.

'I'm not beaten down,' I say, ashamed of how much I want to cry. Then I can't stop myself from adding, 'After all, I'm not the one with bruises on my arms.'

I wait for the sweary storm to rain down on me. But Angel doesn't respond straight away. Then, to my great surprise, she shrugs and says, 'Fair enough,' before leaning back in her chair and looking around the kitchen. 'But it's not what you think.'

I keep the words 'They all say that' inside my head.

Emboldened a little, I lean forward, hands open before me in a gesture I hope looks friendly, lacking hostility.

'Look, Angel, what is it that you are intending to do with the baby?' I say. 'So many people will be looking for him. You must know that there is only one way this can end . . . with you getting into a lot of trouble.'

Angel has begun to shake her head slowly in response but I press on. 'If you want to just leave, right now, you and Lucas, I will wait for a bit before calling someone. I promise you. I'll let you both get away.'

When Angel turns her attention back towards me, her eyes have that strange blankness again. It's unnerving, like she has tuned into some other frequency. I know I've lost her again.

'Look, just leave it, alright?' she snaps. 'I've had enough of you yacking on. We'll do what we do when we do it, OK?' At this she pats her pocket, clearly indicating the gun, and I feel another flash of fear. Then she looks at Zach. When she speaks again her voice is even louder. 'Don't think for one minute that getting into a cosy little chat with me

means I won't do absolutely anything I have to do to protect
my brother. Do you understand?'

I nod, tightly.

I understand perfectly.

18

Lucas

There are a series of school photos on the mantelpiece, which, like a speeded-up film, show the ageing process of a boy with dark hair and glasses. He goes from cute and gap-toothed in a red polo shirt, to someone in a blazer and tie, with serious dark eyes and a guarded expression.

Lucas tries to imagine this boy's life, living here with his nice mum and dad (where is the husband anyway? Angel seems convinced no one else is coming) and the worst things in his life being issues like not being picked for the football A team, or . . . well, he doesn't even know. What kind of thing did worry kids like him?

Hard to imagine this lad knowing right away when to get the ice pack from the freezer or when a cup of tea and some paracetamol would be enough.

He thinks about a parents' evening when he was in, what, maybe Year Five?

His teacher, a rather beautiful woman with a cloud of black hair called Miss Christou, had stared at Marianne before reassembling her features in a welcoming smile. It wasn't the usual thing people did, reacting to her looks before seeing anything else about her. Not this time. It was the fact that Marianne had a long scarf all bunched around her neck, even though it was unseasonably warm for March. When she spoke, she only opened her mouth a tiny bit.

Miss Christou had wanted to talk to Marianne about Lucas's quietness in class and his lack of engagement with his peers. Marianne had told his teacher they'd had a little bit of bad news at home – not true – and that things were beginning to settle down again. Lucas had stared at some chewing gum under the desk and tried to stop his leg from jiggling up and down. He didn't want to meet his teacher's eyes because he knew the pointlessly sympathetic look he would see there. It wasn't as though she could do anything.

Before they left, Miss Christou had touched Marianne's wrist and whispered something Lucas didn't catch. Whatever it was had annoyed Marianne very much and she had stiffly thanked the teacher and then snapped at Lucas that it was time to go.

Now, he thinks Miss Christou said something like, 'Help is out there if you need it,' or given her the name of a shelter for battered women. He knows the humiliation of this would have almost trumped the pain in her neck and bruised jaw.

It would have been his last parents' evening at that school. After that he was at Hadley Hall in a whole new circle of hell. Lying in his dormitory, listening to sniffs and farts and whispers from the other boys, he would wonder who was getting the ice packs ready now.

19

Nina

Zach is crying again, a plaintive, unhappy cry. I wish I had the skill, or familiarity with him, to understand what it signifies. Hunger? For breast milk perhaps, but surely not for formula milk. Isn't that much more filling? Irritation pricks me and then I feel guilty. The poor little lamb. All he needs is his mum.

But I must be able to do something to help him.

I lift him and give his bottom a sniff but no, that isn't the problem either. Trying to make soothing sounds I rub gentle circles into his back, feeling the delicate wings of his shoulder blades through the sleepsuit. The baby twists his head into my shoulder, giving short creaky gasps, and I breathe in his milky-biscuit scent. He's so small but so dense and warm. He squidges his legs up high into his chest so I have to hold him a little tighter.

I'm exhausted.

A pale, violet-tinged light is filling the room now as the new day comes.

Angel has been silent for a few minutes, still engrossed in whatever was on her phone screen, but now she regards me and lights up a cigarette, smoke curling from the side of her mouth.

I can't stop myself.

'For God's sake, Angel,' I snap, 'you can't smoke a fag right next to a baby. Surely you know that?'

Angel swoops her eyes but gets up anyway and goes to the back door. She takes the key from her pocket and opens it, leaning half out. The air is cool now. Dawn can't be far away. I try to imagine myself scooping up Zach and making a run for it.

But I'm too unfit. What if I tripped and fell? The baby could be seriously injured. And what if Angel really was prepared to use that gun? The fact is, I have absolutely no idea what is going on inside the heads of either of them. They could be capable of anything.

If I could only get my phone and call for help.

I think about the private message I sent to Nick Quinn. Looking at Twitter is probably the last thing he feels like right now, with his wife murdered and his baby kidnapped. It was a stupid, pointless gesture.

I've been swaying gently on the spot while thinking and somehow this, combined with my palm circling the baby's back, has quietened him again.

'I think he might have a temperature,' I say at literally the moment the idea comes to me. I hadn't rehearsed the words. They just seemed to pop out of my mouth. 'He's a bit hot.'

Angel frowns and sucks on her cigarette before throwing it out the back door. She closes it again and locks it, carefully placing the key in her pocket again.

'Let me,' she says, coming closer. I recoil at the ashy smell of her so close to the baby. She places her bony hand over Zach's head, cupping his scalp, as though this were the correct way to take a baby's temperature.

'Feels OK to me,' she says with a shrug.

'No,' I say adamantly. 'I think he might have a bit of a fever.'

Angel sits back at the table and regards me.

'Haven't you got any of that stuff ... whatjacallit, Calpol?'

'No,' I say. 'My son doesn't have that any more. He has paracetamol.' It actually hurts to mention Sam. I want him separate from what's happening here. I don't even want to say his name aloud. 'And anyway,' I add, 'I don't think he's even old enough for Calpol yet.'

Angel thinks for a minute. 'What about crushing tablets up?' she says, looking pleased with her idea. 'Maybe you could put them in his milk?'

I feel my throat tighten. The potential for disaster, if these two were left in charge of the baby, is huge. I'm not even sure Angel actually means the things she says. But that makes her even more difficult, scarier, to deal with.

I take a breath, trying to stop myself from shouting at her. When I speak, my voice comes out clenched.

'You could kill him doing something like that.' My heart-beat starts to thud in my ears. 'You mustn't ever, ever give adult medicines to a baby.'

'God, keep your hair on,' says Angel, her expression mutinous. 'It was only a suggestion.' She pauses. 'Anyway, he's probably fine. We're all a bit too hot, aren't we?'

It's true, but the temperature is more comfortable than it has been for weeks now, in the early hours of the morning, after the freshening rain. I decide to leave this for now. Maybe I've planted a seed that could bloom later.

If I have the nerve to take it further.

I turn away to sit on the sofa with Zach.

'Well, I'm just giving you a heads-up, that's all,' I say. 'I know from experience that when babies get sick, it's very dynamic. They can go from right as rain to really poorly in no time.'

Angel eyes me as I position Zach in the crook of my elbow.

My eyes are gritty and sore from not having slept. My knees hurt from running earlier and my arms ache from the unaccustomed weight of the baby.

It seems Zach doesn't like this change of position, because he starts to flail his arms and legs. A piercing cry of misery fills the air again and his bottom lip trembles with its force. Oh God, I'd completely forgotten what hard work small babies are. How you only ever get the giggling, gurgling, holding-toes times on television and films. I hadn't remembered the grinding relentlessness of constant care for a defenceless human.

'Shh, shh,' I say, re-positioning him a little exasperatedly. 'It's OK, it's OK, Zach.'

I freeze the second the word leaves my mouth. I think I might have got away with it but now Angel's head is up and she turns, meerkat-like, towards me.

My face burns as I fuss with the baby and pretend I haven't seen her. Then she is right there next to me, and I gasp in shock. She glares down, arms by her sides, fists clenched and pressed against her thighs as though struggling to control them.

'What the fuck?' Angel's voice is shrill and loud over the baby's screaming. 'How do you know its name? I didn't tell you. I didn't even know its name.'

Fear and a strange anger wash over me all at once.

'He!' I say pointlessly. 'Stop saying "it". He's a *he*. A *person*.'

Angel blinks, apparently wrong-footed for a moment. 'I don't care about that!' she yells, making me instinctively pull the squirming baby boy closer. Zach seems to be shocked into silence by the shouting. I place him against my shoulder and whisper shh-ing sounds, feeling him pant quickly against my hand.

I make myself meet her hostile eyes with defiance.

'I heard someone talking about it in the garage,' I say, thinking quickly.

Angel holds my gaze for at least ten seconds before saying, 'I don't believe you.'

Lucas comes into the room now, rubbing red-rimmed eyes. His hair is tousled, and he looks very young for a moment. I think of Sam when he's all rumpled by sleep and yet again I wish I could keep my son out of my thoughts. Just for tonight. Just until this, whatever this is, is over.

'What's going on?' he says quietly.

'I think she's told someone,' says Angel and Lucas's eyes go wide.

'What?' he says, 'Shit! Oh shit!' He looks as though he might cry as he begins to cast his gaze around the room, like the answer to his predicament might be visible there.

My mind is whirring. If they bolt now, I might never have to see them again. I'd be free. But can I really let these two people leave, taking this helpless baby? No, not when they are so useless. Plus, Lucas might be a violent, dangerous man. Not to mention her.

'You must believe me,' I say, voice quivering a bit. 'I didn't speak to a soul. I overheard someone in the garage who—'

But I don't get to finish the sentence because Angel says, 'I left you alone in that bathroom, didn't I? Fuck!'

She almost runs out of the room and then I hear the thud of her feet on the landing above. Lucas is staring at me, then I realize it is Zach who has his attention. His expression is odd – soft, perhaps? I feel a flicker of something hopeful. Then, yet again, I remember with a rush that Lucas may have brutally murdered Zach's mother.

I try to suppress my disgust and fear when I appeal to him.

'Lucas,' I say quickly. 'This is all wrong, you know this. You know that you can't—'

'Got you,' says Angel, coming back into the room and holding up the iPad in triumph. 'Bet you thought you were very clever, didn't you?' Her accent seems to slip now and then and a certain RP clippedness seeps through. I realize her regular accent is more Mockney than genuine. Why is she pretending? She doesn't speak like her brother. It's as if she is trying to be someone entirely different.

Angel sits down at the table and places the iPad in front of her.

'PIN,' she demands sharply. 'Don't fuck me about either. I'm not in the mood.'

Resignedly, I tell her the number to unlock the iPad. I haven't the nerve for a standoff over it. Is there a way to recover a deleted tweet? What will they do when they find out I sent out a virtual distress beacon, albeit with not much chance of success?

Please don't have replied, I think.

Although if he has, it will mean help is on its way. Maybe Angel and Lucas have asked for a ransom. Maybe, if the police came bursting into the room right now, Zach would get hurt. I swallow down my dread; my mouth is dry and my tongue feels thick.

Angel taps away and glances up at me, suspiciously. I can only wait, while Zach mewls miserably in my arms.

A few minutes later she looks up, a sly expression on her face.

'Well?' says Lucas, voice sharp with panic.

'I don't think she emailed anyone,' says Angel. 'I checked her deleted messages. I've looked on Twitter and Facebook too.'

I try to hide the flush of relief I feel that the deleted private message wasn't visible. But I can't help thinking that she knows something, all the same.

'I told you,' I say, stiffly, hoping I have managed the right degree of righteous indignation. Zach snuffles and twists into my neck as though trying to burrow away from here. I know how he feels. 'I heard someone in the garage talking about it,' I say. 'That's all.'

'If you're lying . . .' It's perhaps the first time Lucas has spoken to me directly.

My cheeks flush treacherously but I make myself look into his toffee-coloured eyes.

'I'm not lying,' I say and quickly construct a scene in my mind. 'I heard a conversation, that's all. I just put two and two together.' The other two remain silent, glaring at me and I feel a dropping sensation in my stomach that forces more words out of my mouth. 'And anyway, there is no harm in me knowing that, is there? At least I know what to call the little mite now.'

I tip my chin defiantly, as they exchange glances.

'Angel, I think we should go,' says Lucas sharply. 'Right *now*.'

Hope leaps in my chest.

'Yes, why don't you do that,' I say hurriedly. 'Leave Zach here and go. Just get away.'

Angel is looking at me with an odd, half-amused expression.

'No,' she says. 'I don't think she did tell anyone. You wouldn't endanger *him*, would you?' she says, nodding towards Zach. 'Especially not when you're feeling so . . . broody.'

'What does *that* mean?' My breath huffs in noisy outrage for a few moments before I can continue. 'I wouldn't ever want a baby to be in danger. No decent human being would!' And then I can't stop myself from adding, 'And I'm certainly not broody.'

'No?' says Angel and her eyes are bright with malice now. 'But all this business with your ex is really getting to you, isn't it?'

This brings an almost physical thud in the pit of my stomach.

'What are you talking about?' I say, but I know.

Angel turns the iPad round and I see Messenger is open to my exchange with Carmen. My cheeks burn. This feels like a personal invasion too far. It's not that logical, but there it is. I've been threatened with a gun tonight, but having my weak places prodded and poked like this feels even worse.

'That's none of your damned business,' I say, fighting to keep my voice calm because, incredibly, Zach is beginning to drop off. He seems to be getting heavier by the minute, as though sleep is making his limbs sodden.

'Angel!' Lucas's voice, however, is a loud bark of frustration that makes me wince, although Zach remains still. 'What should we do? Should we go?'

Angel looks at her brother. 'No,' she says. 'Not yet . . .' and then, 'So tell us exactly what you heard. In the garage.'

She crosses her arms and leans back against the sink. 'And I mean word for word.'

I take a small quick sip of breath to steady myself. Both sets of eyes bore into me.

'Well, I can't remember it like a script,' I say, feigning indignation. 'But there was an elderly woman . . .' I cast around for details of the actual woman who had been in conversation at the till. Will this give the whole story the ring of truth required? 'And she was really chatty,' I continue. 'Going on about the weather and stuff. She kept talking to the man behind the till even though there was a queue and people were getting fed up. I had my eye on the clock because of,' I pause, 'because of what you said about a deadline. And I heard her say something like, "Have you heard about that little mite that's been kidnapped?"'

I sense Lucas stiffening and my own belly clenches in

turn. I force myself to continue, despite feeling like my dishonesty is emblazoned across my forehead in neon ink.

'And then,' I continue, 'I couldn't really hear the next bit but I caught the woman saying something about "Baby Zach".' I pause, cringing at how unreal this all sounds, and gaze down at the child in my arms to hide my eyes. Surely it is obvious that I'm making this up? I go on, 'I only caught that small snatch of their conversation. It was quite frustrating.'

A silence follows this short speech and my breath tightens in my chest. I maintain eye contact with Angel, even though it feels about as pleasant as placing my hand directly on a hotplate.

After a moment, Angel lets out a small huffing sound.

'I don't think she told anyone. I don't think she'd dare.' She lets her eyes wander over Zach now, very deliberately, and her implication is quite clear.

20

Angel

Angel goes through to the sitting room, claiming she needs some headspace. She takes Nina's iPad with her.

Slumping onto the comfortable sofa, she yawns expansively and rubs her sore eyes.

What a mess this is.

The first thing she does is check local news sites for anything she didn't already know. All this does is make her feel more anxious, so she closes down those tabs and opens Google Maps.

If she can work out where their grandfather's house had been in Inverness-shire, it would at least provide her with something to aim for. Trying to locate the house is pointless, she knows this. It would be long sold and it's not like there was any family there any more. No family anywhere, in fact. It's just her and Lucas.

But it's as good a plan as any, because Christ knows her brother doesn't seem to have one.

Angel stares down at the screen, frowning hard. It hadn't been too far from Nairn, the seaside town. She can remember being taken there by Marianne and Grandad one day. She had been promised that she might see seals. The seals never materialized and it rained.

She shifts her legs on the sofa and curls them beneath her. It's so comfy in here. She moves the iPad onto a cushion on her lap and gives a few desultory swipes at the map on the screen. But her concentration has slipped somewhere else.

She'd worked hard at putting her childhood behind her. Part of her is incensed with Lucas for allowing the past back in. Why couldn't he just leave it alone? What was it, revenge or something? Was that what made him do this?

Angel has spent her life covering those memories in a kind of mental plaster that obliterated all the finer detail, while all Lucas has done is chip, chip, chip away. And now everything has come crashing down around them.

She can't seem to stop the deluge of memories now.

She starts tapping her hand against her leg because now – *shit shit* – she's thinking about the bloody guinea pig.

Angel spins round so her feet are on the floor and scrunches her hand into her hair. Her foot bounces up and down as the whole thing plays out in her mind.

It was the phone call from school that started it. Her teacher – name long forgotten – ringing to say that Angel had been mean to another child in the class and made her cry. She was ashamed of having done it, but it seemed to ease the soreness she constantly carried in her tummy when she hissed mean things about this particular girl, Mallory Foster, who had braces and weird glasses.

Marianne had been quietly furious and was in the middle of reprimanding Angel when *he* had come in and demanded to know what was happening. Marianne had tried to play it down, but *he* had calmly walked across the kitchen to where they kept the guinea pig, Sasha.

It was Angel's pride and joy, that guinea pig, and she

would often lie on her stomach whispering her secrets as the little sniffly nose twitched and the beady eyes watched her.

She had barely dared to breathe as *he*, Daddy as they called him then, even though he wasn't, lifted the little fat body from the cage, quite gently.

Then with a sharp twist he had broken its neck and turned to her, calmly.

'If you can't be trusted not to behave like an animal at school, then you can hardly be trusted to take care of another animal, can you?' he'd said.

Even after all these years it makes nausea roil inside her and she reaches into her pocket with shaking hands for her cigarettes.

Lighting up, she breathes in deeply and tries to slow her thudding heart.

None of this is helping.

Angel squeezes her eyes shut and rubs them with the heels of her hands.

It's like all this has opened a gate and allowed sewage to gush in.

She's seeing her ninth birthday now in bright, vivid detail in her mind.

Marianne had baked her favourite chocolate cake, but something had gone wrong in the oven, and it had collapsed in the middle. Her mother was full of apologies and she had reassured her the cake was perfect anyway but, inside, disappointment was churning like a muddy soup because that wasn't the only thing that was wrong about her special day.

She had specifically asked for a Bop It but had been given some other thing that wasn't the same at all. But the worst thing was that she had begged for a party at the Teddy Bear House at Hamleys. She'd *cried* and almost made herself sick, she'd begged so hard. But Marianne was having one of her 'wobbly' times – that's how Angel thought of them

– and it just hadn't happened. She always got like this right after *he* came back and all the easy things of normal life seemed to go into a different mode, of watching and waiting.

Now, her mother had a bright, sharp voice, the volume turned just one notch higher than felt comfortable, and her hand shook as she put the candles into the gloopy chocolate icing on the surface of the cake. Lucas was all overexcited and trying to help but he wasn't putting them in a nice circle in the way Angel liked best. Their mother was laughing at his botched attempt and the sound made the angry monster that sometimes lived in Angel's stomach start to growl.

She grabbed the candles from Lucas, who began to cry, as usual. Then the whole kitchen was filled with noise and upset but there was a terrible roar, so loud and terrifying it instantly stilled the chaos, and they all turned to look at its source.

He didn't need to shout that often. A look was enough to send everyone scurrying to different rooms as a rule. Angel remembered squeezing her fists closed so her nails dug into the palms of her hands and thinking, 'But it's my birthday. Not on my *birthday*.'

A vein was pulsing in the side of his head. His hand was clasped around the crystal tumbler of whisky, gripping it tightly so the knuckles on his hands blanched white.

'Shall I tell you what it looks like,' he had said in a low, soft voice, 'when a child stands on a landmine?'

He swirled the golden whisky in the glass and then drank it down in one go, giving a small grimace. He lit a cigarette and sucked hard on it in the way he always did, drawing his cheekbones in. People would say he was handsome. One of her mother's friends used to get all giggly and silly around him but, to Angel, he could sometimes be the ugliest person in the world.

She'd wanted to cover her ears but she knew better after the last time, when she'd had a smack around the back of the head so hard it gave her a headache all the next day. So she forced herself to listen to all the horrible words spewing out of his mouth like sick, about legs lying in the road that still have a sock and trainer on them, and the blue of intestines when someone's guts were on the wrong side of their body.

Their mother had tried to intervene.

'Come on, darling . . . it's her birthday!' she'd said. 'Can't we just . . .' but he was on his feet, stubbing his cigarette in the middle of the cake then grabbing the back of Marianne's hair and yanking it backwards.

'The lot of you make me sick,' he'd said, hissing into her face. 'You are so ungrateful for the things you have.'

Angel grimaces and sucks hard on the cigarette. She wishes she had some weed but it probably wouldn't help when she needs to keep sharp.

If they can just get far away, her and Lucas, she is certain that things can still turn out alright.

If only he would trust her.

She must *focus*. Make a plan.

Angel runs through various possibilities in her mind.

1. Get on a train to Scotland.
2. Get Nina's car back – didn't she say it was at the garage? – and drive there. They'd have to try and disguise the number plate or something.
3. Get Nina to drive them to Scotland.

The two things that keep coming up, though, are that the bloody baby can't come with them.

And what are they going to do with Nina?

21

Nina

I try to get comfortable on the sofa; Zach curled like a little bug on my chest. I remember sitting in this exact spot with Sam, knowing it was a bad habit and that I should be sleep training him. But it was so easy to nap with him nestling on my chest, even though I got nothing else done for hours at a time.

My top is damp with sweat where the baby lies. He does feel a bit hot. But I can't remember whether this is normal for babies or not. All the knowledge of those early days feels locked away in an exhausted, milky past.

Maybe, if I'd had another child, it would be coming back to me more easily.

I hadn't specifically wanted more than one to start with, and nor had Ian. We were happy enough having Sam in our lives. But we hadn't worked hard at preventing another child from coming along, if it was meant to be. Then it appeared that it wasn't going to happen anyway. Turned out I had severe fibroids and was told my chances of conceiving again were almost non-existent. This had been surprisingly painful to know, as though there were an alternate universe where I'd been mother to a whole brood of offspring. But I always felt we were a good little unit of three and told myself that things were just perfect as they were.

Ian had been a good enough father to Sam. But he wasn't one of those men who relished fatherhood, if that makes sense. I mean, he didn't take Sam to cricket matches, or organize Dad and Son days. It was always me who went to the playground when Sam was small, or took him to the zoo or to see the Christmas lights on Oxford Street.

It always seemed as though there would be more time for things in the future.

But now Ian might have a whole second chance, while I watch my mothering years fade away. I don't even want another baby, damn it. I just don't relish having this phase of my life end forever. I may have expressed this very sentiment in an exchange online with Carmen too, thereby giving Angel further ammunition to use against me.

Beaten down . . .

I lean my head back on the sofa, so tired that my neck feels like a thin stem that can't support the heavy weight it must endure.

My eyes start to drag closed and a giddy exhaustion comes in nauseating swoops. I force my head up but my eyes are so sore.

I only need a minute to rest . . .

I'm on a beach. Sunlight sparkles off the water like dancing fireflies. Sam is turning cartwheels on the sand. Ian and I are on the kitchen sofa, which makes perfect sense, as we watch our son. He turns and turns. It's incredible how good he is and I say, excitedly, 'This is Sam's thing now. It's what he does. I can't seem to stop him.' My son is turning and turning, until he becomes a small speck on the horizon. But

106

hasn't he gone too far now? I wake up with a gasp and a sickening lurch in my stomach.

My heart is jackhammering in my chest and my mouth feels foul. I look around, disorientated. Zach has slipped a little on my chest but remains asleep. It takes me a few moments, though, to process the fact that I'm alone in the kitchen with the baby. I sit up straighter, feeling the sweaty weight of Zach shift, looking wildly around the kitchen. If I could get down the garden, maybe I could find somewhere to hide.

But how would I get out of here? Angel has the keys to both doors and the kitchen windows are far too small for me to crawl through, especially with a baby.

It's hopeless and a moot point anyway, now, because Lucas is in the kitchen again, moving silently across the tiles on his socked feet. He walks to the fridge, then turns and says, 'Is it alright if I get some more juice out?'

I almost laugh. He's like a polite little boy, despite the fact that he has most likely murdered a woman and kidnapped a baby. A sour nauseous feeling ripples in my stomach as I look at his slender hands, one shoved into the pocket of his – or rather Ian's – trackie bottoms, the other resting on the fridge while he awaits permission. What did those hands do tonight?

'Knock yourself out,' I say and then, as he opens the fridge and removes a new carton of orange juice, 'I don't know why you're asking permission. It's not like I have any say in anything, do I? Despite this being my house.'

He ignores this and walks to the sink to get one of the glasses that have been draining there for a couple of days. He pours a glass of juice and then drinks, eyes closed and his Adam's apple working in his pale throat as he swallows.

When he has drained the glass, he rinses it under the tap and places it exactly where it was. Bizarre.

'I can assure you,' he says, 'that however badly you think of me, of us, it's a drop in the ocean in comparison to what I think of myself.'

I pause and then sigh at this gnomic utterance. How am I meant to respond to that?

Lucas moves to the bookcase in the corner and picks up a picture of Sam. My body clenches. I want to slap it out of his hand. He studies the picture carefully, as though looking for something important.

It was taken on a day out to a city farm, when Sam was five. He had found the goats to be insanely funny for some reason. In one of those moments that can never be recreated, Ian had snapped a picture just as one was trying to nibble the cuff of Sam's sleeve. Sam was collapsing in giggles, his eyes shining and his mouth open, revealing the gap where his two front teeth had recently come out.

'This your boy?' he says after a few moments.

'Yes.'

'He looks like a lucky kid.'

There's a silence while he looks at the picture again. Can I see the merest suggestion of a smile tugging at the corner of his lips?

Hesitating for just a moment, I speak.

'What about your mother, Lucas?' He visibly stiffens. I can see a nerve jumping in his cheek, but I plough on. 'Is she in your life?'

He stands stock still. The merest wash of pale sunlight is beginning to spill into the kitchen from the window behind him.

'She's dead,' he says very quietly.

I pause.

'I'm sorry to hear that,' I say, then, 'When did that happen?'

Lucas takes a shuddery sort of breath and says, 'When I was ten.'

God. It's hard not to feel genuine sympathy for this. No wonder he, and Angel too for that matter, have taken such a wrong turn. Although nothing justifies murder and kidnap.

'That's very sad,' I say. Lucas doesn't reply, but looks down at the picture again.

My heart pitter-patters in my chest but I force myself to continue down this potentially perilous path.

'Lucas,' I say. I can tell his thoughts have been far away.

'Don't you think,' I pause, 'don't you *know* deep down, that your mother wouldn't have wanted you to do this? You know this situation is all wrong, I'm sure you do. Whatever happened to this little chap's mother, I'm sure it was an accident. That you didn't mean for her to be . . . um, hurt.'

I'm flailing. But I'm getting through to him because his chest is rising and falling quickly, his breath coming in fast spasms. I press on, 'I think your mum would want to know that you've done the right thing, however difficult the situation has—'

I don't manage to finish the sentence because the picture has slipped from his hands and smashed on the tiled floor. Oh no . . .

'Just stop talking!' Lucas's voice booms through the kitchen. He no longer looks like a delicate man-boy who reminds me of Sam. He looks like what he is, a grown man of wiry strength who may have stabbed a woman to death.

On cue, Zach begins a thin, plaintive wail. A sleepy-eyed, hair-mussed Angel pads into the room now. She has clearly been dozing but is quickly alert as she looks down at the broken glass on the floor and at her brother. He slides down against the surface of the breakfast bar until he is in a desolate knot, wrapped in on himself, arms around his body, rocking on his knees.

'What the fuck is going on in here?' spits Angel and as she goes to Lucas she almost skids on the broken glass and swears again.

'What did you say to him?' she says as she squats down by Lucas and tries to prise his chin up so she can meet his eyes.

I get up awkwardly, holding a now screeching Zach.

'I'm sorry, I . . .' I begin but trail off because Angel isn't really listening to me any more. I burn with anger and resentment at the smashed picture frame.

Zach thrusts his legs into my belly, making himself stiff with misery, and I'm overwhelmed with weariness. Right now, I'd do anything for someone else – someone competent – to take over.

But there is no one else.

Angel tries to coax Lucas to his feet, murmuring encouraging sounds. He gets up, shakily, blinking as though the light hurts his eyes. Angel turns to glare at me as I manoeuvre a rigid, screaming Zach into a different position, his small, cross face burrowing into my shoulder.

'Will you just get that kid to shut the fuck up!' screams Angel, slapping the countertop with an open hand.

My resentment and tiredness bubble over in a hot, frothing fury.

'No! I can't!' I yell back. 'He's not a machine! He needs his mother, for Christ's sake! Can't you get that through your thick skull? *I'm not enough!*'

Angel's face twists and she lurches towards me. I'm so sure of the blow to come that I hold Zach away to protect him. But Angel stops and thrusts out her arms.

'Give,' she says. 'I can't do a worse job than you. Give him here.'

All instinct, I pull the baby closer.

'No,' I say. 'I don't trust you with him.'

We glare in wordless standoff and even Zach briefly quietens.

Then I hear a familiar sound chirruping from somewhere about Angel.

It's a distinctive sci-fi tone Sam downloaded without my permission and which I hadn't got round to changing.

Someone is calling me.

22

Nina

Angel and Lucas exchange looks. He is slumped against the sink now, even paler than he was before.

Angel reaches into her pocket and removes the buzzing phone. She glances at the caller ID.

'Someone called Sam,' she says.

It's like someone has reached into my chest and yanked my heart sideways.

'That's my son,' I breathe the words out, barely able to speak. 'Please, he wouldn't be ringing if wasn't important. He gets quite anxious, he—'

The sound of the ringing phone is terrible. I can't bear it. Then it stops, abruptly, and the sudden silence is even worse. Angel begins to stuff the phone back into her pocket.

'Can't be that important,' she says in that same way, as if it's nothing.

'Please!' The word comes out as a half-sob. 'Please,' I whisper. I reach out my hand. I want to grab her, shake her, make her understand. I try to smile reassuringly but it is a panicky rictus, I know, because she draws back with a frown.

'Let me call him back,' I say. The effort to be controlled

makes this come out far too loud. But I press on. 'I promise I won't say anything.'

I'd get on my knees and beg if I could. I even contemplate it for a moment. Then I have an idea.

'Look,' I say carefully. 'How about I put it on speaker phone? That way you can cut me off the second you aren't happy. What do you think?'

Please, please . . .

Angel makes a doubtful face. 'Hmm, not sure that will work. You might just blurt something out.'

'For God's sake!' I can't control myself any longer. 'You really think I'd frighten my own child by telling him I'm being held *hostage*! Can't you understand that he is the only person in the world I wouldn't tell?' I let out a groan of pure exasperation. 'You're not a mother so you don't understand this. But I would never want to scare him with . . . *this*!'

Angel studies me. 'What if your ex answers the phone?' she says doubtfully. 'Or the new bird?'

Wincing, despite myself, I shake my head. 'Sam will have his phone next to the bed. I'm sure his father doesn't even know he's calling. He wouldn't like it,' I finish, lamely.

Angel sighs heavily and turns to her brother.

'Lu, you need to take the baby out of the room. I have to watch her. We can't have her kid turning up here.'

Lucas starts to protest but Angel shushes him irritably.

I feel a quickening of hope. 'No,' I say. 'And if something's wrong and he can't get through to me, his dad might bring him back here.'

There's a pause and then she groans.

'Jesus,' says Angel. 'Let's get on with it then. But I swear Nina, if you even so much as . . .'

'I *won't*,' I say firmly. 'I just want to talk to my son, that's all.' Then I add, 'Thank you, Angel. I mean it.'

I'm aware, as I say it, that this is another strange echo of how this nightmare began.

When Lucas has left the room with the baby, his head and shoulders rigid, Angel demands the PIN for the phone and taps it in, then quickly starts scanning my recent activity with nimble finger strokes. She stands close, close enough for me to smell her musky perfume mixed with sweat and a slight cooking odour. Left over from the restaurant, no doubt. The phone is on speaker, held in her palm, her thumb hovering over the screen in readiness to cut the call. My heart is beating so hard I feel like we can both hear it.

'Mum?' Sam's sweet voice, always so much younger on the telephone, soaks me with love. I squeeze my lips together and breathe shallowly, trying to stop an eruption of tears.

'What's up, mate?' I try to be brisk, to counteract the bruising inside my chest. 'Can't sleep?'

'Not really,' he says. 'And I've got a stomach ache. I don't think I'm going to be able to go to France tomorrow.' The formality of this sentence reveals that it has been rehearsed.

I swallow.

'Look, we talked about all this, didn't we?' I say carefully. 'About what a brilliant time you're going to have? Remember the dog? And the horses that Laura said were in the field next to the cottage? And how you were planning to take them carrots?'

'I'm not that fussed about horses,' says Sam. The attempt at sounding breezily grown-up tears my heart with clawed talons. 'And Dad says the dog is really old anyway so might not want to play that much.'

Then there is a muffled sniff and, 'I want to come home, Mum.' I realize he is fighting tears as he continues in a breathy whisper, 'Laura always cooks weird things. She says it's OK if I don't eat everything, but I can tell she's annoyed. I heard Dad saying that she would find out that children don't just do what you want them to do.'

I breathe deeply and finding myself meeting Angel's eyes. She makes a face, which is hard to interpret.

'Mum?'

'Yes, darling,' I say. 'I'm here. But Sam,' I pause, 'Dad will be so disappointed if you don't go to France. He's been looking forward to it for ages. You really will have a brilliant time, you know. Much better than kicking about at home all summer with nothing to do.'

'But *we* can do things!' Sam's voice shines with childish hope now. 'I was thinking that we could . . .' he casts about, 'go swimming a bit, or I would even go into a club or something if you wanted me to.'

I squeeze my eyes tightly closed, trying to pull together the unravelling feeling inside me. Sam has never enjoyed clubs. His pretend eagerness is almost more than I can bear.

'Samster,' I say, gently. 'Honey, you have to go to France tomorrow. It's going to be brilliant, I promise.'

'But why?' Sam is starting to cry now, his voice shrill. 'It's not going to be brilliant, it's going to be rubbish! I'm telling Dad in the morning to bring me home. Nobody can make me go to fucking France!'

'Sam!' I've never heard him swear like that before. 'Just calm down!'

Angel hands me the phone and I take it gratefully, switching it off speaker function.

'I want to come home!' He's crying properly now, a heart-breaking sound magnified by the phone's speaker. It seems to echo throughout my skull. 'I'm coming home and there's nothing you can bloody well do about it!'

'You can't!' I cry out in desperation. 'You just can't. *Please* Sam.'

At that moment Angel bangs against the table and knocks a knife onto the floor, where it clangs to a spinning stop.

She freezes and turns to me; a warning look on her face.

'What was that?' says Sam suspiciously. 'What was that noise?'

'I just . . . dropped something, that's all,' I say, glaring at Angel. 'It's nothing.'

'Is someone there with you?' says Sam, suspicious now. 'Is that why you won't let me come home?' There is a long, terrible pause and then, 'Have you got a *boyfriend*?' This last word is said in a tone of incredulity mixed with disgust.

I swallow back the tears clogging my throat. The thought of my son entering this kitchen where there is a gun, and these two unstable people, is appalling. No, no, no. It can't happen. It just can't. Sam *must not come home*. Even if it hurts his feelings, I must keep him physically safe. It's my most important job. The only one that really counts.

'Yes,' I say so fast it comes out as a gasp. 'I've got a . . . guest. It wouldn't be the right time for you to come here. I'm sorry.'

I can hardly breathe. I want to gasp for air. This is unbearable.

There's silence on the other end of the phone.

'Sam?' I manage to say.

But he has hung up.

Winded, wracked with actual, physical pain, I slump forward, head on my arms outstretched on the kitchen table.

My misery is absolute, worse than the very darkest days since Ian left.

I picture my sensitive little boy, curled in the dark in an unfamiliar house, dreading his holiday and knowing that he *isn't allowed* to come home. All the times I've said I will always be there for him have come to nothing.

It's intolerable. I can't stand it. I have failed him in the very worst way.

Then my sorrow hardens into a bitter fury at Angel and Lucas for coming into my house and bringing this nightmare with them.

The reasonable part of my brain is trying to intervene, to say I'd never have been able to let him home anyway. That it would have caused irreparable damage to the relationship with Ian. But the fact remains that it wasn't an option. I couldn't allow my own son to come home, to this place of danger, even if I had wanted to.

I hate these two cuckoos in my nest. I *hate them*.

'The other woman sounds like a bitch,' says Angel.

'I don't care what you think,' I snap. 'Just make up your mind about what you want from me then get the hell out of my life.'

Angel smiles thinly, as though this pleases her in some way. 'Well, I'm hoping to do just that,' she says. 'But I want to know when you can get your car back.'

I glare at her, then rub my face hard with a shaking hand and look away. I must get through this. Then I can find a way, when Sam comes home, to make it right again. One day it will just be a strange story. It has to be.

'The garage said they'd bring it back first thing this morning,' I say flatly. 'I don't know exactly what time.'

I've been a customer for years and, for the last few, they have returned the car to me after servicing. I'm thankful more than ever for this now.

We both look at the clock on the wall. It's just after six. Sunlight is blazing into the kitchen now, sharpening my queasy headache and highlighting the shadows on Angel's face. She is all hollows.

Lucas comes into the kitchen now, yawning, Zach held over one shoulder, a thin, pale hand starfished across the small back. The baby is awakening; fussing. I find myself getting up and taking him from Lucas without asking or considering the move for a moment. Lucas hands him over, throwing a worried look at his sister, who shrugs and then yawns expressively.

'So what time does the garage open then?' she says in the strangled throes of the yawn.

'Early, I think about seven thirty,' I reply. 'Look, I'll ring and ask if they are able to bring it straight away and then it's yours, OK? Take it wherever you want.'

Even as I am saying it, I'm thinking, *But what about me? And Zach? What will you do with us?*

'We're probably going to have to tie you up or something,' says Angel, as if reading my thoughts. 'Just until we've got a decent distance away.'

I stare back at her. Panic begins to stir up inside me again. How long would it be before someone came to my rescue? I try to work it out. Ian will be on his way to France. Carmen would probably try and ring, rather than coming around. We have no cleaner, or anyone else who might have a key and who could enter the house.

I might be tied up here for days.

'Ring the garage,' says Angel reasonably. 'Leave a message. Tell them it's urgent.' She holds out my phone. It is unlocked. I picture myself hurriedly thumbing 999 before she notices but she stands close.

I find the number in my contacts. One of the mechanics there, a smiley man called Loz, flirts gently with me every time I see him. But whether they will be prepared to return the car straight away is another matter.

A few minutes later, the message has been left. Flailing for a justification, I'd claimed I urgently need the car to see a sick relative.

Angel gives a satisfied nod and takes the phone away again, turning it off and then sliding it into her pocket.

'What about Zach?' I say. 'What are you going to do with him? Is he going with you?'

Angel looks at her brother now and he meets her gaze and then drops his eyes.

'That's still to be decided,' says Angel quietly.

23

Lucas

Lucas had many years in which his stepfather ceased to exist, beyond his nightmares.

It was surprisingly easy, if you had no television and didn't watch the news.

People would ask Lucas why he was unaware of *Game of Thrones*, or any of the reality programmes that others seemed obsessed with, and he'd shrug and say he just didn't have the TV habit. It was because he was a bit of a hippie. All part of the persona he'd cultivated.

The other gardeners on the council team laughed at him. He didn't like football and he didn't watch telly?

Then there was the slightly posh voice.

When they talked about their school days, whether it was the UK or Eastern Europe, he'd smiled and kept quiet. He still remembered what it was like to walk home at the end of the day with a bag of chips in his hand, breath misting in the winter air, thinking about doing homework in front of *EastEnders*. But so much came after that, it felt like another life.

*   *   *

One evening just over a year ago, Lucas was slobbed out on the comfy old sofa in Simon's sitting room. Alone. Simon was working a late one in the restaurant.

Simon, with his broad back and gentle Geordie voice, was starting to feel like home. When Lucas went into himself he didn't pass judgement, or complain. He'd rub his back and simply wait.

Lucas had had a curry and a few cans of cider. He was stretched out, his mind free and easy, body pleasantly exhausted after a long day planting in Regent's Park with the ground crew. He liked this job. Relished the feeling of starting something new, something that was waiting to happen and would bring pleasure to people.

As he had flicked around the channels he'd come across *The Graham Norton Show*.

An elderly actress he'd never heard of was being asked about a new Harold Pinter play. She was telling an anecdote that involved standing on the sofa and lifting her skirt over her knees, to raucous laughter.

Distracted, Lucas glanced down at his phone, looking at a WhatsApp message from his sister. She was asking him if he wanted to meet for a drink over the weekend. He guiltily noted the number of white bubbles from her on the app, and the lack of green ones.

The truth was that he didn't like Leon, her boyfriend. He was the kind of musclebound man who made Lucas uncomfortable, even though he was friendly enough to Lucas.

He and Angel seemed to enjoy winding each other up and the physicality of their relationship made Lucas squirm. Angel would pinch him, playful but hard, as she sat next to him on the sofa. Leon would reply with a roar of outrage and pull her over his lap, slapping her on the bum hard enough to be audible. They both laughed uproariously while

Lucas pretended he had an urgent message on his phone. Simon had described Leon as 'pretty but thick as a plank' and had no interest in going out as a foursome.

Lucas wasn't really paying attention to the television so when certain words drifted into his consciousness it took a moment for them to stick. Then his head snapped up to look at the screen.

And there he was.

That rich, smooth voice sounded exactly the same.

Electricity seemed to zap painfully from Lucas's fingertips up his back to his scalp. Breath coming sharp and fast. Sweat breaking out under his arms and in his clenched fists.

The blond hair, silvery now, was still thick and wavy, the creased, handsome face not as tanned as it once was. More lined. But those ice-cold eyes looked just the same. Lucas couldn't stop staring at the hands, resting comfortably on the legs of his black trousers.

He didn't make it to the bathroom in time to be sick, the lamb curry and ciders splashing over the carpet in the hallway and up the wall.

When Simon came home, tired from a long shift in the kitchen, and found the sick-covered hallway, and the hole punched in the partition wall, they had fought.

Lucas didn't say anything about what had made him do it. No one would understand.

But it was the beginning of the end for him and Simon.

The baby makes a sharp noise of distress and Lucas is torn from his thoughts. Nina is trying to settle him but he's squirmy and unhappy.

Lucas hasn't been able to bring himself to properly look at Zach. He's too scared he might see the mother's eyes looking back at him. And this, he thinks, might unravel what little of him is still holding together.

24

Nina

Zach is fussy again. As he stutters out a cry and draws in his knees, I pat his back and try to rearrange the wriggling shape of him. But nothing really seems to settle this fretful baby. Maybe he really is sick?

At that moment, I glance at Lucas and his expression makes the hairs on the back of my neck rise. What am I seeing? It's not indifference, that's certain. It's not the expression his sister holds whenever she comes near the baby. There's definitely something softer there. Can I risk that he wouldn't hurt this child?

An idea forms in my mind. I lower my eyes to the baby's downy red hair while I try to think it through.

'Lucas?' I try to sound matter-of-fact even though my stomach is twisting with anxiety.

He jerks his head at me in response. I get up and approach him before he has time to stop me and calmly hold Zach towards him.

'Take Zach for a minute? I need a glass of water.' I don't meet his eye and after a moment's hesitation he takes the writhing bundle of baby. I force myself not to say anything about holding the head, terrified I'm endangering Zach for nothing, but out of the corner of my eye, I see Lucas rest the baby against his shoulder, one hand expertly against the small head. He makes a gentle shh-ing sound and his face is soft. He sees me watching and I have to turn away to the sink to hide my delight.

He cares about that child. He's not going to hurt him, I'm sure of it. I wonder again if Zach is actually his flesh and blood.

Angel is another matter. But it would take a special kind of sadist to be able to actively hurt a tiny baby.

So it's only really me they might be prepared to hurt . . .

There must be something I can do. I just need to *think*.

After I have drunk a glass of water at the sink, I go back to Lucas and take Zach without meeting his eye.

Back at the table, I search the room with my eyes.

My back aches and when I stretch my legs out, my foot knocks something under the table. Glancing down, I spy one of Sam's felt-tip pens under the table; a dark red one.

As Zach squidges his hot, cross little face into my shoulder a thought blossoms in my mind. My heart races. Is it a laughable idea? Or might it work? I glance at Angel. Her long body is curled over her phone, attention completely taken up by the screen. Lucas is lying on the sofa, hands between his knees, staring down at the floor.

Lucas wouldn't do anything to actively harm this child, I'm sure of it now. Angel has been playing up the threat to Zach because it is the way of controlling *me*. But would Lucas really allow her to hurt the baby?

Sam comes into my head again and I squeeze my eyes shut against the wash of pain, remembering that small voice on the other end of the phone. He's almost taller than me now, filling out in all the ways he should. But he's still my little boy. He'll always be that.

Being forced to deny him access to his home – to what

should always be his sanctuary – is so terrible I can't think how I will ever be able to bear it. Some time I will be able to explain that this is entirely about his own safety. But that doesn't matter now, it won't erase the lonely sense of abandonment he must be feeling *right this minute.*

The anger smouldering at the edges of my misery takes light. I have to do something.

I reach with my toes for the marker pen, then deliberately knock the kitchen roll I'd been using to wipe away Zach's milky spit-up onto the floor. Angel grazes me with the barest glance as I reach down, sliding the marker pen inside my sleeve.

Zach has quietened, unhelpfully. His eyes are glassy with fatigue and his lips twist and pucker. There's a tiny milk blister on his bottom lip. His cheeks are flushed, which is helpful.

I murmur something deliberately, making Angel look up. 'What?' she says.

I scrunch my face into a deep frown. 'I just heard some kind of explosion in his nappy,' I say, then lift Zach to smell his bottom and grimacing dramatically. 'I think this is going to be a really bad one.'

Angel stands up.

'I can live without this,' she says, just as I hoped she would. 'I'm going for some me time. Lu, keep an eye?'

Her brother acknowledges her with a nod and Angel walks out of the room. Lucas pays scant attention as I get up. I stand and angle my back to block the view of what I'm up to.

Must act quickly. I mutter in a stage whisper, 'Going to need some hot water for this one,' and, with Zach over my shoulder, I run the hot water and push a hand towel under the stream until it is drenched.

Back at the table, I slide the marker pen out from my

sleeve and begin to undress Zach. He whimpers and complains but is more compliant than I could have hoped. He's exhausted too, no doubt. This whole experience must be so unsettling for him. At this age, he doesn't even understand that he is a separate person from his mother.

Come on, little fella, I think, *try and be a bit floppy. Play the part.*

The nappy is completely clean and dry, which is no surprise, but I whip it off and tie it into a tight ball. As I lay the new nappy under the wrinkled little bottom, I glance at Lucas to check he is not watching. But he appears to be somewhere else entirely, his shoulders hunched inwards and his eyes clouded and distant.

My breath comes faster as I un-cap the marker pen. Hesitating for a second, I mouth a silent apology and begin to dot it across the baby's belly and chest. Zach responds with a howl of outrage. I'm doing it so softly, but his skin is so fragile I'm scared of hurting him. I look anxiously at Lucas again, who responds to the noise by turning his body the other way on the sofa and covering his head with his arms.

I work as fast as I can with clumsy, shaking hands. Dab, dab, dab goes the pen, speckling the baby's fragile skin, and my heart sinks because it looks so fake. I can only pray that an untried eye will not be able to tell the difference between this and the real thing.

Then, whispering another apology to Zach in my mind, I test that the wet towel is hot but not scalding, and lay it across his brow. Zach's screams intensify. I try to stop the swell of panic about the discovery of my plan. What if I'm hurting him?

I'm so sorry, baby, I say silently. *But this is our only hope.*

I can hear Angel moving in the hallway and so I quickly stuff the pen inside my sleeve again, but it slips out and rolls under the table with a slight *ting*. Seconds before Angel enters the kitchen, I stuff the wet towel under the table.

'Angel, come here, quickly,' I say, holding Zach up. I'm trying to keep his body away from my clothes, which might smudge the ink.

Angel moves to the table in her languid way and sighs. 'What now?' she says, looking at me, rather than Zach.

'I think the baby is sick,' I say. 'Feel his forehead. He's burning up!'

Angel lays her bony hand on the baby's face and turns her mouth down.

'Aren't babies always a bit warmer though?' she says but I hear the doubt creeping into her voice.

'Not like this,' I say. 'What's really worrying me is the rash.' Barely able to breathe, I pull Zach away, so Angel can see the red spots covering his belly and chest.

Angel pulls sharply away with a loud, 'Fuck, what is that?' turning her head away. I'd suspected she was squeamish about illness from her overreaction about nappy changing and say a small silent prayer of thanks.

'It could be a number of things,' I say in an urgent tone, 'but I'm really worried that it might be . . . well, it could be meningitis.'

'What?' Lucas is sitting bolt upright now, his eyes wide and his skin ashen. 'Did you say you think the baby has menin-fucking-*gitis*? Shit!' He's on his feet, ruffling his fingers through his curls, expression stricken. 'Let me see!'

He crosses the room at speed and looks down on Zach. When he places his pale hand on the baby's quickly rising and falling tummy, *right where I've daubed the ink*, I almost break down on the spot. But he is looking up at me, apparently fooled.

'That can be really fucking serious, can't it?' he says. 'Kids die of that, don't they?'

'Yes, I'm afraid they do,' I say. 'It can be very bad indeed.'

Lucas gives a moan of distress and walks across the kitchen, hands buried in his curls as he paces.

'Let's just calm the fuck down, shall we!' snaps Angel. 'It might not be anything like that! She's not a doctor, is she? What does she even know?'

'No,' I say, reasonably, aware that my over-jiggling is making Zach even crosser and louder. But I have to do it. Have to make him uncomfortable for his own good. 'But I *am* a mother and I know what a sick baby looks like. Even if it isn't meningitis,' I have to raise my voice over Zach's rising screams, 'just having an untreated fever can make a baby have febrile convulsions. *Fits*. Did you know that?' I pause for effect. 'They can die from these too.' I don't even know if that part is strictly true but it seems to work.

Lucas emits a distressed sound and brings his hands to his face, gazing wildly at his sister, who tells him to 'Get a grip' and turns back to gaze doubtfully at Zach.

When she turns her basilisk-stare on me, I attempt a shrug. 'You guys are in charge here. What do you want to do?'

Turning my face away I quickly began to re-dress Zach in his vest, clipping the poppers between his bicycling legs gratefully and hiding the evidence of my work. I hope the marker pen won't seep through the soft cotton fabric of the vest. No one questions whether it is wise to put more clothes on a feverish baby, to my relief. It feels like the power has shifted in the room. They are relying on me knowing the things they don't know.

There's a pause when everything seems to hang and then:

'Shit!' Angel pounds her fist onto the table and we all flinch, including the baby, who is shocked into a series of miserable hiccups. 'I don't know what to do.'

'I do,' says Lucas. 'We're letting her go, Ange.' He sounds

more assertive in tone than I've heard to date. 'I'm not having Zach on my conscience. Not him too.'

The words 'Not him too' chill me but I say nothing as some unspoken dynamic plays out between the siblings.

'Oh, for fuck's sake,' says Angel, bitterly, after a few moments. 'This is all such a fucking mess!'

She starts to say something else, but her words are drowned out then by the sharp trill of the front doorbell.

It feels like there is a collective intake of breath and we all look at each other wildly.

Angel seems to relax. 'It'll be the car, won't it? Go on, Nina. Give me the baby. I'm going to have this,' she pulls the gun from her pocket and waves it around, 'trained on the back of your head the whole time.'

They have lost the bargaining chip of harming Zach. Any threat will now rest solely on hurting me. This is a funny sort of consolation prize to contemplate.

Reluctantly I hand Zach to Angel, glancing anxiously at his belly. But the pen hasn't leaked through yet, thank God.

I try to pat down my hair, which is springing from my head in an unruly way, and wipe away the smudged make-up under my eyes.

At the front door, I pause and then open it. My breath seems to die in my throat and I am just able to force out the word.

'*Ian?*'

25

Angel

It is obvious from the way Nina's entire body has gone rigid that this is not the mechanic, returning her car, but someone else entirely.

Angel gestures wildly at Lucas to take the baby as far away as he can go and, wide-eyed, her brother obeys, taking Zach and fumbling so he almost drops him. He closes the kitchen door with a gentle click.

'What are you doing here?' Nina's voice is strangulated, like someone has their hands around her throat. Standing as she is at the doorway to the kitchen, out of sight of the front door, Angel can see that Nina has started to shake, quite obviously.

Shit. Keep it together for fuck's sake, she thinks. She couldn't make it more obvious that something is wrong if she came right out and said she was being held hostage.

'Sam's passport,' says the person at the door, in a slightly pompous male voice. 'I thought you'd packed it? I've been ringing you but your phone's going straight to voicemail.'

'Oh, I, er . . .' Nina flails. Angel lets out a slow hiss of breath. 'I really meant to,' Nina continues. 'I was sure I had.'

'Well, you didn't,' says the man.

It's obviously the errant shagger of a husband. Even his voice is annoying to Angel's ear. She'd quite like to get a look at him, give him a piece of her mind about trading in his wife for a younger model. *Typical man*, she thinks.

He's still talking.

'Look, I didn't use my key out of . . .' He pauses and the weird atmosphere between these two thickens so much, Angel swears if she thrust her hand into it, it would have a texture. He continues, 'Out of courtesy.'

'What does that mean?' says Nina sharply. Even her hair appears to be bristling.

'Sam told me,' says Ian, 'about your . . . guest.' There's a pause before he goes on. 'Only we leave for the airport in an hour and I have to have the passport.'

'Oh God.' Nina's distress is so obvious now that Angel's hand tightens around the gun. She's going to blow the whole thing, right here on the doorstep.

Angel's heartbeat is thudding in her head and a series of panicky images are crowding into her mind but Nina is speaking again, sounding calmer.

'Well, I'm sorry,' says Nina. 'I hope he's alright. He seems really anxious about this holiday.'

The irritated sigh that puffs from Ian is loud enough for Angel to hear three feet away.

'We've been through this, Nina,' he says. 'He's going to have a wonderful time. If you hadn't poisoned his mind about the whole—'

'Poisoned his mind! I did no such thing!' Nina is yelling now. 'I've done everything I can to calm his fears! How dare you? How *bloody dare you*, Ian!'

'Neen, look, I'm sorry, I shouldn't have said that. But can I come in? Or can you at least go get the passport?'

'*You* can wait here,' says Nina, 'I'll get it.' She slams the

131

front door so hard Angel feels the vibrations through the soles of her feet. Nina doesn't meet Angel's anxious gaze as she runs upstairs. Angel can hear the sound of drawers being yanked open and closed again and then she is charging back down the stairs.

She opens the front door again.

'Here, take it,' she says, 'and please promise me that you'll remember that Sam can be anxious about journeys like this.'

'I do know that,' says Ian quietly. 'He is my son. It's not like he's going away with some strangers. You really ought to give me a bit of bloody credit for knowing how to look after him.'

There's another pause and Nina blurts out, 'He thinks Laura's parents are going to make him eat frogs' legs.'

There's a moment of silence that makes Angel stiffen and edge closer. Is Nina mouthing something to Ian about getting help? Then she realizes that Nina is actually *laughing*.

She can hear Ian laughing gently too, indicating this is clearly some kind of shared parenting moment. Angel wouldn't know about that.

'Oh, bless him,' he says in a softer voice now. 'He wouldn't tell me what it was.'

'Well, now you know,' says Nina. Already, the warmth has begun to drain away again from her voice. 'Just please tell him I love him very much, OK?' The end of her sentence skids away from her and Angel thinks, *Come on, don't mess this up now.* 'And that he can ring me any time of the day or night for a chat?'

'Course I will,' says her ex.

Nina starts to close the door without another word and then Ian must say something.

'What?' she says.

'I hope he's a good bloke,' says Ian. 'You deserve that.'

Nina emits a sharp laugh of pure bitterness now.

'Yeah, well I thought I already had one of those,' she says. Then, 'Bon voyage, Ian.'

She closes the door and slides onto the bottom stair, resting her head in her hands so her face is hidden.

Angel watches, wondering if she is distressed. Her shoulders shake, and she thinks Nina is crying. But the other woman looks up and Angel can see a bitter sort of amusement on her face. She has a weird sense of humour.

'What's funny?' Angel hates the feeling that she is a heartbeat off what is happening around her. 'Didn't seem all that funny to me.'

Nina lets out a huge sigh.

'No,' she says, 'you're right. None of it is funny.' She pauses. 'It's just . . . this imaginary boyfriend of mine. I wish I was having the fun people *think* I'm having right now.'

Angel doesn't know how to respond so she says nothing.

The kitchen door opens and Lucas peers out. He is evidently Zach-less.

'Where is the baby?' says Nina, hurrying towards him.

'It's OK, he's sleeping,' says Lucas, a bit sulkily.

There's a noise then and they all turn to look at the front door. Car keys have been pushed through the letterbox and sit on the mat.

'Thank God for that,' says Angel. 'We can get the fuck out of this place.'

26

Lucas

At first, it had been easy enough to avoid the stuff about the new book.

Lucas has never been much of a reader. Once he was at boarding school, his poor performance in any subject beyond art became one of the things that defined him. Well, that and the bed-wetting, which had continued until he was thirteen and resulted in him gaining the nickname of Pissant for the entirety of his time there.

Lessons had been a nightmare and Lucas could still recall the biting shame when the words on the page would wriggle and jump away from him. There was one teacher he still remembered, and he hoped there was a special circle of hell just for him, who would belittle Lucas's poor reading in front of the rest of the class.

It was only when he had left and the kindly sister of a boyfriend said Lucas was 'obviously dyslexic' that it had made sense. He wasn't thick, or lazy, or a 'philistine' for not reading books (as a particularly nasty little shit called James Burrowes had said in Year Eleven), just wired a bit differently to most people when it came to reading.

But avoiding papers and magazines wasn't enough. There

was a poster for the book at his local train station, for a start.

It had caught him short one evening, causing the woman walking behind him to crash into his back. He had barely heard her berating him as he stood there, staring, fists clenched so hard his nails bit into his palms.

Looking at the oversized face, craggy and weathered, before him, he'd been overcome with a desire to smash that billboard to pieces. He wanted to tear the face up, gouge out the eyes. Stamp on the head. Do all the things he had fantasized about since he was ten years old.

On another occasion, he'd caught a snatch of Radio 4, which one of the groundsmen – Ted – liked to listen to in the truck. An interview. Lucas had buried his earbuds deep into his ears and drowned it out with some grime turned up loud.

But turning off radios and averting his eyes from newspapers and posters wasn't enough. It was too late.

The face was always there; sneery lip and the cold blue eyes. He'd started having nightmares again and he hadn't wanted to see his sister. He knew what she would say.

'Why the fuck can't you let him go, Lu?'

But he couldn't. Because every time he heard the name or saw his face, the same terrible picture came into his mind . . .

Marianne's pale skin. The curled hand resting on the side of the bath. The shock of seeing his mother's breasts and pubic hair for the first time. The filmed-over eyes staring up. And the empty pill bottle.

Easy for Angel to talk about letting it go. She hadn't been the one who came into the house and immediately knew that the air felt different. Like the house was holding its breath, waiting for him. She hadn't had to climb the stairs, which had suddenly loomed above him, bigger and taller than usual. Or walked into that bathroom with all its familiar things. Known what it felt like to stand there for a surprising number of seconds before his brain dropped the trapdoor and allowed what he was really seeing to rush in.

No, Angel had her own ways of dealing with things. She got drunk, got stoned, shagged unsuitable men. If that was her way of keeping the noise at bay, then fair enough. But Lucas was made differently.

One night when the darkness felt like it would consume him, Lucas decided trying to hide away wasn't working. He would look for information, rather than shying away from it.

The book – *A Bitter Cosmic Joke: Stories from the Frontline* – was a bestseller. It was from a Martha Gellhorn quote, apparently.

The stories would get trotted out – the more gruesome and distressing the better – whenever it was thought that the children weren't showing sufficient gratitude for what they had. Lucas had felt sorry for these blown-apart children in far-off places, but couldn't really connect it with why he had been slapped so hard his ear buzzed all evening. It felt like a conundrum he was too stupid to work out at the time.

So, no, he wouldn't be reading this book.

Instead he trawled the internet, looking for interviews and mentions. It was like picking at a scab until it drew blood.

A couple mentioned the wife, Marianne, who had tragically taken her own life in 2004.

But something kept him alert for each new interview, as though it were all leading to this.

And that's how he found Alice.

27

Nina

I'm dozy with the effects of fatigue and shock from this strange, awful night.

Sam is safe, I say to myself, like a mantra. *Sam is safe, Sam is safe.*

That's the most important thing of all. Even if he hates me right now, he hasn't come anywhere near this mess. If I can just get baby Zach away now, I'll be free. They can do what they want with the car, I don't really care. I just want distance between myself and the two damaged people in my house.

I go to the baby, who is lying on the sofa, splayed like a little frog, chest rising and falling quickly. He is on his back and I quickly lift him and place him lengthways on my arm, fretting about whether the ink has bled through his thin vest from the heat of his body.

But Angel and Lucas's heads are together and they are in murmured discussion, which I can just about make out.

'What about ANPR?' says Angel. Then, when Lucas looks blank, 'Automatic number plate recognition.' She goes on. 'Once they have the details of the car, we won't get as far as Luton, let alone Scotland.'

They think about this silently for a moment or two then Lucas speaks again.

'Let's obscure it then. With mud or something. I saw it on a film once. We might risk getting pulled over if it's completely hidden, but if it just makes it difficult to get the whole number it might do the trick.'

'OK, good idea,' says Angel.

But then Lucas leans in close and whispers something that makes Angel flare, seizing his arm in fury.

'Just look at yourself,' she hisses, loud now. 'Can you imagine what prison would be like for someone like you? I've read about this, Lucas. It's not a joke. Do you really want to be raped? I mean, *look* at you!'

Lucas flinches and I can't help but wince, thinking about the *Panorama* programme I saw on sexual abuse in male prisons.

Lucas drops his head, defeatedly, and then nods.

'I'll sort out the car,' he mumbles. 'But it's been too dry for mud, even with that rain. It'll have just run off the top.' He thinks for a moment and then goes to the sink where he fills the plastic washing-up bowl with water. 'I'll improvise,' he adds.

Before he goes he glances at the baby, his face creased with worry.

'It won't be long now,' he says gruffly. 'Then he'll be OK. Can get the help he needs.'

Then he leaves the room. I hear the front door open and close. Maybe they plan to tie me up and then drive Zach to a hospital. I picture Angel thrusting the baby into the arms of the nearest nurse and then fleeing.

My guts turn over at the thought of being tied up here and left alone for days.

'Right,' says Angel wearily. 'This is the plan. We're letting you go. You'll have to walk. Obviously.'

My heart skips in my chest. 'What about Zach?'

Angel waves her hand. 'I meant that you take him. Take him to hospital, or wherever the fuck you want. We're leaving first. And I'm not leaving you a phone or anything, sorry. We need time.'

She emits this series of staccato sentences like a burst of machine gun fire. Rat-a-tat-tat. Then she looks around the kitchen and goes to pick up her bag.

'My clothes,' she says. 'The ones I came in. Where are they?'

'I'll get them for you,' I say but Angel shakes her head.

'No,' she says. 'When Lucas comes back in, I'll get them myself.'

Zach has begun to mewl again and I realize he is bound to be hungry. He's only had one feed in how many hours? It's almost eight now and they arrived at three am. I have no way of knowing when he had been fed before this. He starts to cry harder again.

My head aches with the responsibility and juggling all these complex balls.

But I can't feed him. It works for me that he sounds miserable. *Just wait, Zach*, I think. *Not long now, poppet. Not long now.*

A few minutes later, Lucas bursts into the room. For the first time, he has a little colour in his cheeks.

'Done the best I can,' he says, and wipes his hands down his jeans. 'Too much and we might get pulled over, but that should be enough to buy a little time.'

'Right, let's go!' says Angel. She sounds excited now and evidently intends to leave without another word.

But Lucas is staring at a fussy Zach. His eyes seem to brim with pain. I can't work him out at all. Is it his baby after all? He's far more concerned about Zach than his stone-hearted sister appears to be, anyway.

'Goodbye, little man,' he says, quietly, and then, his voice, cracking, 'I'm so sorry.'

They lock the back door and go out the front way. Without another word those two awful people – who muscled their way into my home and caused the worst night of my life – are gone.

Moments later I hear the car start up outside and relief comes over me as pure, sweet warmth.

'Oh, thank God,' I say. 'We're OK, Zach! We're OK!'

I hurry from the room, Zach bobbing in my arms, to check for phones but the two landlines in the house have been removed. There is no sign of my mobile.

'Shit!' I say but without much feeling. I never really expected Angel to make things easy. I'm just going to have to walk.

Zach complains at being jiggled about and I make impatient shushing sounds. How can someone so tiny feel so very heavy? My arms and shoulders ache. I feel sick with tiredness and my head throbs.

But I'm *free*.

Briefly, I wonder if I ought to feed Zach first, but my impatience to get out of this overnight prison is too strong. Grabbing the dirty bottle and the remaining carton of milk, I find my handbag in the hallway. No keys, of course. The door will lock behind me so once I'm outside I won't be able to get back in again.

I have to tell the police what has happened. That's the priority.

They can break in if necessary.

Murmuring quietly to the little boy in my arms, I hurry out of the house and hear the door click behind me.

As I move away from the front door the thought comes to me I may never be able to see this place as home in the same way again.

Last night's rain has done little to cool things down, it seems, and it is already a warm morning. The traffic on the main road is rush-hour thick now, the familiar roaring of cars fuzzy with the rising heat of the morning.

But the relief of being free, of being away from those people, is immense. I turn my face up and allow myself a second of pure, uncomplicated pleasure at the feel of sunshine on my skin.

I have to move though. This little boy needs to be back with people who love him.

Perhaps for the first time ever, I truly curse living so far out of town. I think about climbing the bank and trying to flag down a car for help. Anyone would stop for a waving woman with a baby, wouldn't they?

But it would be so dangerous. It's a fifty mph zone along here but most people seem to drive much faster.

No, it's too risky. I'll have to make my way towards town. I'll knock on a random door if needs be.

Arms aching with the effort of holding the baby for so many hours, and sweat already beginning to prickle under my arms, I start to walk up the hill.

28

Angel

The journey hadn't started well.

Angel hasn't driven for ages and, at first, she keeps stalling the car.

When she goes to start it again, Lucas holds her wrist and says, 'Careful. You might flood the engine.'

'Thanks, Jeremy Fucking Clarkson,' says Angel, 'but I know what I'm doing. Or would you rather take over?'

Her brother shoots her a wounded look then shrugs and turns in on himself.

When they get to the end of the road, Angel hesitates, then goes around the roundabout, heading in the direction of the motorway.

They are silent for a couple of minutes and then Lucas gives a small cry.

'What is that?' he says, his voice panicked. He's staring at his hands, which are blotchy and red.

Angel glances at him and says, instantly, 'Looks like red ink to me. What did you touch?'

As she says the words, something in the back of her mind pricks uncomfortably but Lucas is evidently already ahead of her.

'Fuck!' he says and smashes his hand against the dash-board, making Angel jump.

'What is it?' she cries, trying to concentrate on the traffic, which is heavy on this road. Her head aches too and so she pulls down the sun visor, which helps a little.

'She fooled us!'

Lucas is yelling now, ridiculously upset. Angel glances wildly at him, making the car wobble.

'What is it?' she says. 'What are you on about?'

'*Oh, meningitis can be really serious,*' he says now, in a mocking facsimile of Nina's voice. '*I'm a mother, I know about these things!*'

'What are you talking about Lucas? For God's sake!'

'It's ink!' he screams, thrusting his hand in front of her face. 'She painted those spots on Zach! There was no reason to let him go!'

Angel is silent for a moment and then can't stop herself from giving a small laugh. 'Well well well,' she says. 'I didn't think she had it in her.'

Lucas is breathing heavily, like he is going to have an asthma attack.

'What does it matter?' she says. 'We couldn't really take him. You did understand that, didn't you? And have you got your inhaler?'

'Don't need my inhaler any more,' snaps Lucas. 'And you know why I took him. I made a promise. I . . .'

Angel looks sharply at her brother and watches his face crumple and fall. He starts to sob, his shoulders heaving.

'You did everything you could!' she cries, desperately trying to keep her eyes on the road. 'What more could you have done?'

'You don't understand,' says Lucas, his voice thick. He is hunched over in the seat, hands scrunched tightly into his hair and face lowered. 'Oh God,' he says, 'I can't stand it, I can't . . .' Then, 'We're going back,' he says.

'Are you insane?' Angel is shouting now. 'No we're not! We've only just got away! Why would we even think of doing that?'

'I want to take Zach with us,' yells Lucas. 'If he's not sick there is no reason to leave him. We're *going back*.'

'No we aren't!' yells Angel and then Lucas is wresting open the car door and Angel shrieks and swerves, causing a blaze of tooting from other cars. 'Stop it! Stop it! You'll get us killed!'

'Well pull over then!' bellows Lucas. Angel looks at him in exasperation. She can't believe this is happening.

'I mean it!'

If only to stop her nutjob of a brother from killing them both, Angel pulls over to the side of the road.

They sit there with the engine ticking, and the morning sun blazing through the window.

29

Nina

Zach is revving quietly like a small angry motor, evidently unhappy at being walked like this, and I long for a sling or something to carry him in. But I gave our BabyBjörn away years ago, when it became apparent that there would be no more infants in this household.

The bright colours of the day assault my eyes and I squint against the sunlight, hand shading my face. I can finally see the end of my road and the roundabout. Then I realize there is a car coming towards me from the opposite direction and cry out with the relief. Help at last! I'll wave the car down and they can take me to a police station.

But something feels wrong.

It's coming far too fast. As Zach squirms awkwardly in my arms, I let out a small moan of dismay when I recognize my own red Fiat Uno coming towards me, a furious-looking Angel clenched over the steering wheel like a malevolent crow.

'Oh shit,' I wail. 'No!'

The car slows and goes past me, then I can hear it turning in the layby.

I start to run, Zach an awkward bundle bouncing in my

arms. Wildly, I peer at the thick hedge lining the road. Could I climb through into the farmer's field beyond? But no, there are no gaps wide enough for me to squeeze through, not without possibly hurting the baby.

Shit.

I can hear the familiar purr of my own car's engine behind me and I let out a sob of frustration. I'm sweating and so exhausted now I can't run any further. I whisper a tiny apology to the baby at my abject failure to get away and kiss his downy head, which feels damp and seems to radiate heat. Incredibly, he has been quiet during all this but, now I've stopped, he begins to crank up a series of creaky little complaints again.

The car is beside me now. The passenger window lowers and Angel leans across her brother, who is staring straight ahead, white-faced.

'Get in,' she says, deadpan.

'No!' I say, trying to sound tough but it's no good because my voice wobbles as I continue. 'Can't you just leave us alone?'

'Get in,' says Angel again, her jaw set. 'I'm not messing around. Don't make me get out of this car.'

'But what about Zach?' I cry. 'I have to get him to hospital, he's—'

'Oh, cut the crap, Nina,' says Angel. 'You think you've been very clever, don't you? With your little red marker pen. But I'm afraid you've been rumbled.'

Of course they'd come back for him, I think now. He's worth something to them, isn't he? No ransom for them if he's in hospital.

I cast my gaze around me, wildly. To have almost got away and then to be yanked back into this nightmare feels like something I won't be able to bear. I want to scream, cry, cause violence to these people. For a moment, I bitterly resent the small boy in my arms. For several shameful seconds, I contemplate thrusting Zach into Angel's arms and trying to run on my own.

'Just get in, Nina,' says Angel. Her voice is weary now.

I hesitate for a few futile moments more. I have no way of escaping right now. I suppose if I am around at least I know this baby will be moderately safe. I tell myself this in an attempt to make up for the previous, shameful feelings about fleeing alone.

Sick with resentment, I open the rear passenger door and climb in, then pull it shut with such savage force it hurts my shoulder. On cue, Zach starts to cry again.

The journey back takes less than two minutes and never have I been so unhappy to see my own house. No one speaks as we get out of the car and close the doors.

Angel looks at me expectantly and for a moment I'm baffled before realization sinks in.

'I haven't got the fucking key, have I?' I say. I'm not the biggest swearer. Ian used to tease me about it a bit. Maybe it's hanging around these two people all night, or maybe it is just this intolerable situation, but I want to use all the swear words I can think of now. The filthier the better.

'Oh right, course.' Angel rifles in her handbag and produces my keyring. It feels so surreal. Even after all these hours, I still can't quite believe this is happening to me.

Inside, I'm mocked by the usually comforting smell of the house. I can't name what makes it, but it is the unique scent of home and it makes my eyes sting with emotion. Looking at my watch I see that, incredibly, it is still only nine am. I picture Sam in the car on the way to the airport, looking anxiously out of the window as he contemplates the worries to come.

Lucas, I belatedly realize, is crying softly. He climbs the

stairs, two at a time, and then the bathroom door slams shut.

'What's going on?' I say. 'I don't understand. What's wrong with him?'

Angel regards me for a moment and then shakes her head. 'It doesn't matter,' she says. 'But we're going to have to enjoy your hospitality for a little while longer.'

'Great,' I mutter as we go into the kitchen. 'That's just great. Come right in, make yourself at bloody home!'

'Look, don't get bitchy with me!' snaps Angel. 'I've got a lot on my mind, OK!'

'I expect you have!' I almost shout. 'What with holding people hostage! You're quite the busy bee!'

Angel mutters something and goes to the sink to fill the kettle again.

When she speaks, I don't catch it at first.

'What?'

'I said, *do you want some coffee?*'

I sigh heavily. 'Yes,' I say. 'I want all the coffee in the world.' Then, 'It's in the cupboard above the sink.'

Angel reaches for the cafetiere that is drying on the draining board.

She looks beaten; shoulders hunched over, face drawn. Whatever happened in that car, Angel seems to have been weakened by it. All the spikiness and energy that has been there all night long has been replaced with a flat kind of tiredness.

She doesn't want to be here either, is what I'm thinking.

That's when I notice that Angel has left her large black handbag on one of the kitchen chairs, about a foot away from me, the top of it sagged and folded over. My senses prick up. Is the gun in there?

Heart thudding so hard it pulses in my throat, I carefully edge a little bit closer and then say, 'I'm going to lay Zach on the bed upstairs. Is that alright? I can't hold him any more and it might give us all some peace if we can just get him to have a proper sleep.'

'Yeah, good idea,' says Angel distractedly, yawning. As she pours the boiling water in the cafetiere, some splashes onto her hand, making her cry out.

'You alright?' I say, getting to my feet. 'Run it under the tap.' Better if I look like I care right now.

Angel murmurs something in response. She looks as though she might, in fact, be close to tears. But she obeys the command and turns on the tap, plunging her hand into the cold water with a wince.

'Keep it there for a while.' My knees are knocking together with my own audacity and just as Angel squints down at her wrist, frowning, I scoop the handbag over my arm and hurry out of the kitchen, my body pulsing as one giant heartbeat. It weighs a ton.

Forcing myself not to run, I climb the stairs, but I can't stop myself from hurrying up the last two at the top, Zach heavy in my arms. Breathing hard, I see that Lucas has closed the door of Sam's bedroom, so I go into mine. There is no lock on the door but I quietly close it, wincing at the rasp of wood on wool carpet, which is absurdly loud to my ears.

I lay Zach down on the bed and, evidently surprised by this change of scene, he looks around benignly, sucking on one of his fists.

Shaking so hard I seem to have lost all fine motor function, I tip the handbag out onto the bed, as quietly as I can.

Cigarettes, a lighter. A purse, a packet of tampons. Gum, tissues, a pair of knickers. A grubby flowered make-up bag and a hairbrush thick with black hairs.

No gun. No phone.

Bugger. With frantic hands, I go to the zippered compartment inside the bag. Fingers scrabbling in there, I touch cool metal straight away and, with a gasp of relief, pull out the small handgun. I stare down at it, terrified I might accidentally fire it at Zach, too scared to grasp it properly. It's so much lighter than I always imagined a gun would be. It weighs hardly anything. Ridiculous that something so insubstantial can be so deadly. I don't even know what to do with it. But it's something.

The slow handclap sound from the bedroom door almost makes me drop the gun in shock.

Angel. Standing in the doorway, arms folded, expression unreadable once again.

Rising slowly to my feet, I force myself to point the gun at her, gently hooking my finger so it is over, but not touching, the trigger. I suspect there is some magical way I'm supposed to do to release it. But the important thing is that I have the gun *in my hands*.

I'm the one in control. Finally.

Angel is not looking worried though, or even angry. Instead, jewel-like tears are brimming over in her large eyes. This isn't what I expected. I expected fury; a torrent of swearing and bitterness. Angel sniffs loudly and runs a finger under her nose, appearing to gather herself.

'I suppose you think you're clever now,' she says thickly.

I stiffen my back and force myself to sound calm.

'I just want you to go,' I say, 'you and Lucas. Leave here and let me get this baby back where he belongs.'

There is a long, long pause.

I can hear my heartbeat, snuffles coming from Zach on the bed and the all-familiar low hum of traffic from the main road.

Angel is perfectly still. Then her shoulders rise and fall with an exaggerated sigh.

'Oh, Nina,' she says quietly. 'You don't know anything, do you?'

My anger begins to rise again. It's an intoxicating feeling, knowing I have a gun in my hand. I could shoot this home invader right now. No one would blame me. The thought then seems to curdle in my stomach. How could I even think something like that? What have these people done to me?

But I must pretend.

'I don't?' I say, raising the gun a little higher, so it is trained directly on her forehead. Then I cry out, 'Stay still! What are you doing?'

Angel is calmly walking towards me, hand outstretched for the gun.

'Oh, for God's sake,' she says. 'It isn't even a real gun.'

30

Lucas

The wedding announcement was in *Hello!* magazine, online, courtesy of a Google Alert for the name Nick Quinn. Now the book was no longer number one in the bestseller charts, the prompts came with a lower flow.

The piece said: *The renowned war reporter Nick Quinn married dancer Alice Sommerton at the bride's family's local church in Chester on Saturday.*

Quinn, the author of the bestselling book A Bitter Cosmic Joke: Stories from the Frontline, *has been reporting from war zones for over twenty-five years for the BBC. Alice Sommerton is a rising star at the English National Ballet but an ankle injury has meant she has temporarily stopped dancing. The couple met at a garden party in Henley-on-Thames held by the theatre director Anthony Lowly and had what they call a 'whirlwind romance' before the small ceremony with family and a select number of friends.*

Alice Sommerton beamed out at Lucas, her face a picture of innocent happiness. He had enlarged the picture and looked more closely. Large, blue eyes, dark hair coiled into an elegant bun and a wide, red-lipped smile.

Lucas had looked at her slim, pale neck and her delicate

wrists and all he could imagine was what they would look like bent and blued with bruises.

It wasn't very difficult to find out where they lived.

Hello! magazine helpfully ran a spread of the couple's new home 'in a charming Hertfordshire village' and then Lucas had studied Alice's Twitter feed for clues about where she lived. He narrowed it down finally to a village called Mirestone and then all he'd had to do was hang around, watch and wait.

The house wasn't as big as Lucas had imagined it. But it had still gone for over a million and a half pounds, according to the property website he'd researched.

It was red brick and three storeys high, fronted by a driveway and with a large garden at the back.

On the other side of the road from the house there was a little-used alley linking this road with the one parallel to it. It was a good spot to stand and watch the comings and goings across the way.

At first, the house was a constant hub of activity, with delivery vans from upmarket furniture shops and builders coming to and fro. Lucas noticed a woman who looked Middle Eastern who came in two or three times a week. She wore her dark brown hair in a tight ponytail and had nervous eyes. She would scurry into the house carrying a large bag over her shoulder and then emerge some time later. A cleaner, he realized after this pattern repeated a few times.

There was also a gardener, who came in a van a couple of times a week. Lucas managed to catch him one day as he was coming out of the house and asked if he had any work. The man, who was in his late fifties and called Bob, said he might need a bit of help. Lucas swiftly gave up his council job and found a bedsit in Redholt. And so it was that he found himself part of the household.

His careful watching had made him familiar with the rhythms of the house and he was easily able to avoid being there at the same time as Quinn. He always wore a blue beanie, pulled low over his distinctive black curls, just in case.

He got to know Nooria, the cleaner, who was almost monosyllabic. Not because her English was poor. If anything, it was rather good. But she was a shy person with a mousey demeanour who avoided eye contact when she brought out cold drinks to the garden as the days started to get warmer. Sometimes she brought her daughter to work, a happy little girl of about six.

Then Bob, a taciturn man, had a bereavement of some non-specified sort and Lucas was left in charge of the general gardening duties.

This was when he took to watching Alice as she practised in the upstairs room with the big window.

Watching, and waiting.

31

Nina

For a moment, it is hard to breathe.

Helplessly, I let her take it from my hand. Somehow, I know she's telling the truth. She waves the gun about, a sneery look on her face.

'It's a replica. Not even a good one,' she says. 'I can't really believe you even fell for it.'

I feel pure, hot rage now. It is all I can do to stop myself from slapping Angel across the face. But I'm better than her. Than them.

Instead, I sink back onto the bed and place a hand carefully on Zach's tummy, grounding myself in something pure and good. Incredibly, he is asleep.

Struggling to control my voice, I say, 'So you made me believe for all these hours that I was a prisoner? That you would *shoot* me? Just what exactly is wrong with you, Angel?'

Angel flinches, as though genuinely hurt by this comment.

'I'm sorry,' she says. 'I didn't know what the fuck to do, earlier! Lucas needed me and I just panicked. This belongs to my boyf . . . my ex-boyfriend, and I thought it might be useful. It was a joke thing a mate gave him. I was never really going to hurt you.'

When I stand up again she says, 'Wait, what, what are you going to do?'

I scoop the sleeping baby up, wincing at his immediate whinny of protest. But this must be done. I'm not leaving him anywhere near her now.

'I'm going downstairs and you're going to give me my phone,' I say in a confident, clear voice. 'Then I'm going to ring the police. I know that you won't deliberately hurt Zach now, and you have no gun. So how do you plan to keep me here?'

Angel reaches a hand towards me and I gaze down at it as though it is radioactive. She withdraws it again. Then she bursts into tears. The way people usually use that expression doesn't do justice to how Angel cries. It's like a storm. She seems to go from 0–60 in seconds; dry-eyed to tears literally dripping off her chin. It's not an act, I'm sure of it.

'Please,' she begs. 'Please just give me five minutes to explain. Then we'll leave. Please Nina!' When she sees the derisive expression on my face her voice skids into total panic. 'I'm literally begging you!'

I look at her, this messed-up wreck of a girl, and feel nothing but disgust. I owe her nothing. But I find myself saying, 'Five minutes. Then I'm ringing the police.'

On the landing, Angel peeks her head into Sam's bedroom – *Sam's bedroom* – where Lucas is, presumably, sleeping, then gently pulls the door over. I want to go in and shake the mattress until he falls off it. But something tells me this conversation might be easier without his presence. Not that I'm scared of him now. I'm not scared of either of them any more.

Downstairs, I walk decisively into the sitting room, finally in charge in my own home. Angel follows, somewhat meekly. The kitchen, once a place where I loved to spend time, feels unappealing. Maybe it's been spoiled forever. All the happy family meals, the peaceful cups of coffee with a newspaper in the morning sunshine, all feel wiped out by this strange, horrible night.

In truth, I've mainly been crying and drinking there lately anyway. But I dismiss this unwelcome thought and lay Zach on the sofa, before sitting down. He has dropped off again. Thank God.

Angel takes the armchair opposite, sniffing and snuffling into her arm. Her hands are around her bony knees and she looks like a little girl who has been sent to the head-teacher for a telling-off.

'So, come on,' I say and even to my own ears I sound exhausted. 'Let's hear your explanation.' I deliberately drag the last two words out, sarcastically.

I mean, how could she ever begin to justify what they have done tonight?

32

Angel

A photograph on the mantelpiece is all she remembers of their father. A man with light brown eyes and raven-black hair that flopped disobediently over his face, sitting in some dusty, hot backdrop. A wide, slightly goofy smile. But even the picture is hazy now, because it disappeared, and they never saw it again. He was a cameraman, killed by a road-side bomb in Lebanon.

That was how Nick Quinn came into their lives. They were dear friends, so he said, when he came to visit Marianne, Angel and Lucas's mother, a couple of years later.

The time Before was cuddling up on the sofa under duvets, watching movies and eating jam directly from the jar. It was having cartwheel competitions, their mother's slim, strong legs chopping into the blue sky and her funny, high-pitched laugh. It was also, sometimes, days when she was there but not there, when they foraged for cornflakes directly from the box, or took money from her purse for fish and chips. Those days were far fewer than the happy ones though.

Everything changed when *he* entered their lives. Mealtimes became regular again and there was no more wandering about the garden without shoes, or staying in your pyjamas all day if you felt like it. There were good things too, at first. Gifts started to magically appear in the house: the new television, the Tamagotchis, the MiniDisc players. It felt like Christmas every day for a while. Quinn didn't speak to her and Lucas directly that much, but would stand there with a slight smile on his face while they fell upon the presents with glee.

Then she and Lucas were sent off to Scotland to holiday with Granny and Grandad and, when they came back, they were told their mother was now called Mrs Nick Quinn. Marianne had shyly shown off the gold wedding ring and Lucas had squealed and been all stupid about it. But Angel remembers how cheated she felt, robbed of the chance to wear a pretty bridesmaid dress and lord it over her friends at school. She was so cross she hadn't spoken to her mother for a whole day afterwards. Quinn seemed to think her hot, fierce will was funny.

But not for long.

Angel had always been aware that Marianne wasn't like other mothers. It wasn't just that they could call her by her name, but something about the way others reacted to her. She didn't *blend*.

The way she thought of it was like this: Lucas had one of those Mega Magnet toys when he was tiny. He'd scoop up paperclips from a table until the whole thing bristled like a metallic hedgehog. Angel thought, when they had parents' evenings at school, or they were occasionally invited to a local party, that people's *gazes* did that with her mother. Stuck to her and couldn't be shaken free. There was something hungry about it that she didn't like. She sometimes used to imagine a wolf coming along and eating her up when she was little.

In a way, isn't that what happened?

That hungry look was magnified twenty times in Quinn, who, at first, they called Nick. Angel used to look at how he watched Marianne moving through the room, eyes greedy, and it made her feel funny inside. One day, early on, he had grasped Marianne by the leg as she walked past the chair where he was sitting and had slid his hand right up under her skirt. Just like that. Angel's face had burned furiously. She wanted to hit both of them for it; but her mother only laughed in that too-bright, sharp way she had sometimes and gently moved away.

She had changed, after they came back from their wedding. There was something brittle about her now. All her softness that made cuddling into her so good was disappearing into angles and planes. She'd heard Quinn say she was fat and now she didn't seem to like eating crisps or cake any more. There were no more multipacks of Monster Munch in the house. No more Coco Pops.

The first time they saw Quinn hit her, Angel had been too shocked to react. They had been eating dinner. It was Angel who started it. (It was always Angel who started it.) She had been complaining about her meal – just low-level whining after a tiring day – and Quinn shouted, telling her she was a little brat who needed discipline. Marianne had begun to defend her, saying it was no big deal and she could leave the broccoli, or peas, or whatever it was on her plate. His hand had moved so quickly that for a moment Angel wasn't sure it had happened. Then Lucas began to wail as the red mark flowered on Marianne's cheek and she knew it was all real.

The next time, Angel was quicker to react. She was just coming into the kitchen when she saw Quinn wrenching her mother's arm up high behind her back, so she cried out. Angel threw herself at him like a little monkey and he had

160

shaken her off so hard that she crashed into the kitchen cabinets and her ear went all buzzy. Her mother had spoken to her very quietly that night in her bed, about how they were all learning to get along with each other and that Angel must leave the grown-ups to decide things.

He went away quite a lot, which made it more bearable, and during those times they would slip into something resembling what they had before. But it never lasted long.

When he murdered the guinea pig, she thought that surely that would be the end of him in their lives. It seemed to Angel that something so huge, something so terrible, would warrant a response as explosive. She even attempted to call the police before Marianne intercepted and stopped her, holding her tightly and apologizing, saying she was the one to blame. She always did that. Said it was her fault.

One night, Marianne came into her bedroom and woke her up. Her voice was all funny, like her jaw didn't work properly, and she was using only one of her arms as she helped Angel stuff clothes into a bag. Lucas was too sleepy to understand that they needed to be silent and Marianne was forced to slap his legs to shock him into submission, which made her cry more than it did him. Angel had hated seeing that. Her mother said, 'He's right . . . I *am* a terrible, useless mother,' and however much Angel tried to argue she just shook her head and wept silently.

She doesn't remember the long journey to Scotland much but that was when they had an extended stay with Grandad, who had been alone since Granny died the year before.

Their mother was 'sorting things out' according to Grandad, whose face went all tight when they asked him where she was. They managed to be happy, during that time, in the way that children can. It seemed impossible that things could ever go back to how they were before, not this time.

But then the terrible night came when Grandad had a

heart attack, and everything changed again. They couldn't stay there. Marianne arrived, looking hollow-eyed and pale, and told them they were going home but things would be 'different'.

It wasn't long before they were told they would be going to boarding school.

Angel was thirteen and Lucas was ten.

It was during the Christmas holiday after their first, terrible terms that Marianne took her own life.

33

Nina

I watch the young woman opposite. Her eyes have been cast downwards the whole time she has been speaking. With her crossed legs, foot hooked around the other ankle, and her hunched shoulders, she looks oddly twisted, as though she is literally trying to hold herself together. She seems as though she has told this story many times before; it is recounted in such a logical and clear way.

'That's terrible,' I say and I mean it. I don't know what else to say. I wanted to throw up when Angel told me about the guinea pig. God, what sort of monster would do a thing like that?

My eyes burn with fatigue. It's hard to focus and my mind is skittering about all over the place, bouncing between horror at what I have just heard, relief that I am no longer in danger, and uncertainty about what the hell I am supposed to do next.

There is a small part of me, too, wondering whether this appalling story can possibly be true. I mean, does Angel seem like a reliable historian? Then again, everyone knows about violent men who appear charming on the outside. But can Nick Quinn, a well-known public figure for the last twenty years, really have kept this dark side hidden? *Jimmy Savile, Harvey Weinstein and others got away with so much in plain sight*, says a quiet voice in my ear.

I sit forward and place my hands on the cool wood of the kitchen table.

'Angel,' I say gently. 'I understand that you had a horrific childhood . . . one I can't even begin to comprehend. But I still don't understand what this has to do with the here and now. With what happened last night. Did Lucas murder that woman?'

Angel looks at me, finally. Her eyes are luminous and moist. She reaches for a cigarette and, with shaking hands, lights it. I decide to let it go this time.

When she speaks again, her voice is husky.

'No, of course not. Please, let me just tell you the rest. It was Lucas, you see. He found Marianne, in the bath. Dead.'

'Oh no.' I cover my mouth with my hand. Angel begins to speak quickly, the words almost tumbling over each other.

'I was out, seeing one of my friends from my old school,' she says. 'Lucas didn't have any friends around there any more. And we didn't like leaving her alone too long, then. It was like she was being eaten up from the inside with, I don't know, cancer or something. Except it was her sense of who she was, that she was our mother, which was being eaten instead of her cells. She was always going on about failing us, about not being the mum we deserved.' She pauses. 'That's what he did to her,' she says with heat, mouth twisted. 'Destroyed her and made her believe we would be better off with her gone.'

I don't say anything. I can't think of anything that would feel remotely adequate right now.

Angel swipes a hand under her noise, sniffing wetly.

164

'Lucas has always blamed himself for it,' she says, 'which is obviously fucking *nuts*, but there you are.'

'What happened after then?' I say gently.

Angel sucks hard on her cigarette. The smell nauseates me, but I say nothing. It won't harm Zach if it is just one, surely? My mother smoked like a chimney around me and my brother when we were small and we seem to have turned out OK, depending on how you look at it.

'We were packed off to school, with Quinn as our guardian,' she says flatly. 'We stayed away during holidays, or went to stay with his mother, who had a constant stick up her arse and hated the very sight of us.' She gives a small, bitter laugh. 'God, I hope that bitch is rotting in hell now, although she is probably one of these scaly old pterodactyl women who go on forever.'

'Go on.' I'm impatient to hear the rest.

Angel looks at the half-smoked cigarette in her hand now, almost as though she is realizing it is there, and then she violently stubs it out on the plate she has been using as an ashtray.

'Shit, I shouldn't do that with *him* about. I forgot.'

I gawp at her; she seems to veer between good and bad so easily. Saving my life one minute; threatening it the next.

Or is it that she just tries to be good in a very bad way? She is an enigma.

She continues. 'And as soon as we were eighteen he stopped paying for school and that was it. We got out of his life and never looked back. At least,' she pauses, 'that's what I thought we were doing. But then Nick *Fuckface* Quinn got married again and my little brother took it upon himself to look after her, after Alice.' She makes quote marks with her fingers when she says, 'look after her'.

I feel the hair begin to prickle on the back of my neck. 'Are you sure he didn't . . . hurt her?'

Angel does one of her looks. Swooping her eyes like a super-charged teenager. It simultaneously makes her look young and old again.

'My brother wouldn't hurt the teeniest bloody fly,' she says. 'Christ, he once rescued a frigging spider the size of your arse, even though I was screaming my head off about it.'

A great rolling wave of exhaustion passes over me now. I rub my face with both hands.

'Why in God's name didn't you say that before?' But I know the answer really. They wanted to control me. It was easier to do that through the threat of violence. 'OK,' I say, 'but I still don't understand what happened last night.'

Angel's expression darkens now. She becomes shifty, her eyes downcast as she starts to twiddle with the silver ring on her thumb.

'Well, I don't exactly know because he's being all secretive about it,' she says. 'But from what I can gather, our one-time stepfather is up to his old tricks again and getting handy with his fists. Lucas found Alice hurt, really hurt, and he panicked. Acted on instinct or something. He promised her he'd look after the baby, I don't fucking know. I told him it was insane to take that baby away. But he won't listen.'

I let out a long sigh and sit back in my seat.

'But why not stay and help her?' I ask. 'Surely he could have done *something*?'

'Well, maybe,' says Angel, her mouth a tight line. 'But if I know my brother at all, he would have tried everything he could for her. He'd have done anything to help Alice. Anything at all. You don't know him like I do.'

34

Lucas

Lucas had been about to come into the room when he heard the women talking. Had understood, with a sharp adrenaline spike, that everything had changed. Something had happened to the dynamic in this house.

At first, he had wanted to rush in and find out what it was. But then he had heard Angel talking about the things she never talked about. Not with him anyway.

He had listened at the door.

'He'd have done anything to help Alice. Anything at all. You don't know him like I do.'

Hand over mouth, he gasps and feels his knees start to buckle.

He has one person in the world. Just one. And if she knew what had happened, which she will, at some point she will, then he won't have her either.

It's too much. The weight of this pain and guilt is too much to bear and Lucas wishes he could tear his own skin off. He cannot bear to be inside himself for a second longer and he takes off his shoes and socks so he can walk on silent feet to the front door. He has the key in his pocket and he opens the door before slipping out, stumbling from the house in a daze.

The sun drills into his eyes like hot spears and the pain in his head sharpens but he welcomes it. Physical pain is a distraction from the thoughts flooding him with their poison.

The traffic is thick now. He feels himself drawn towards it. He walks out of the gate and stares up at the bypass. He can't seem to stop seeing it all in his mind. He will never be able to un-see it. Never be able to stop feeling it.

Lucas is crying now, remembering the numbness that began to spread through him as he had gone to Zach, who was still crying. He had only been able to think one thing.

I have to get him away.

He wishes the numbness would come back.

He can't stand to be himself for a moment longer.

Lucas begins to climb over the wooden fence separating the bank up to the bypass from the road. His bare feet are on fire with nettle stings but he doesn't care.

He just wants it to end.

35

Nina

I still don't know what to do.

I wouldn't trust Angel to mind my seat, let alone a child. I've seen her apparent lack of compassion for a helpless baby and been terrorized in my own home by her.

And yet . . . I believe her.

I do. I believe all of it.

She has gone to the toilet, leaving me alone here. I could go right now. But I don't move.

'Nina!' Her piercing shriek from upstairs jolts me in my seat and I get up, hurrying to the bottom of the stairs. She stands at the top, eyes wild and hair all falling around her face like a real-life Medusa. Angel is more terrified than I have seen her to date.

'What is it?' I say.

'Lucas,' she says, or rather shouts. 'He's gone! Where is he?'

I let out a long breath.

'Come on,' I say, 'let's go look. I didn't hear the car so he's on foot.'

Glancing at a sleeping Zach, I lay cushions along the floor next to him, for the unlikely possibility that he learns to roll several months early. I think he will be OK for just a few minutes.

The front door is unlocked, and we hurry outside. Angel is breathing heavily next to me as we come out of the gate and look down Four Hays in both directions. No sign of him.

And then the frantic sound of car horns makes me look up.

'Lucas!' I yell, 'Get back from there! You'll get yourself killed!'

He is standing at the edge of the dual carriageway, looking every bit as if he is about to walk into the thundering traffic.

All I can think of is Sam. What if it were my Sam standing there? His precious body that was about to be mashed into hot tarmac?

It's as if I am moving independently of any conscious thought now. I don't make a decision to do this. But somehow, I am scrambling over the fence and climbing up the bank. I can feel Angel at my heels, but she doesn't know how deep the ditch is under all the long grass and I hear a yelp as she staggers into it.

Lucas seems to tense and is about to step in front of a lorry that is bearing down on us when I grab his sleeve and I yank with all my might.

We tumble together down the bank, hitting the wooden fence. Nettles bite me and thistles claw at my bare legs and arms. Lucas lies trembling in a heap next to me and I find I'm saying, 'It's OK, it's OK now,' and reaching out to him.

As we make our ungainly way back over the fence and onto the road, Angel starts to pound her fists on her brother's chest, crying and shouting, 'What were you doing, you stupid fucking fuckwit?' before she pulls him into a fierce hug, body shaking with sobs.

My legs are jelly-like from shock as we make our way back into the house. New nettle stings make themselves known, and I wince. I long to be in clean, cool sheets that I can pull over my head until all this goes away.

Back inside the kitchen, I make tea and slop in generous shots of an old half bottle of whisky lurking at the back of a cupboard.

Angel stares at her brother, who sits with his head bowed, looking utterly defeated, unable to meet her gaze.

'Why, Lu?' Angel says at last, her voice husky. 'Don't we always look out for each other? How could you do that crazy shit just now?'

Lucas just shakes his head and says nothing. I put the cup next to him and say, 'Drink!' with such sharp authority that he lifts it to his mouth and takes some.

When I put Angel's cup down next to her, she surprises me by grasping my wrist. I meet her eyes and she mouths, 'Thank you,' her eyes wide and damp. I nod and go to check on the baby, who is sleeping soundly on the sofa. I decide to leave him there for now and move to the table to sit, groaning with weariness.

We drink the tea in the awkward silence. I've never seen anyone in the state Lucas is in before. He looks broken. As though his skeleton won't be firm enough for him to get to his feet.

Angel is silent, staring down at her cup.

'Hey,' I say, 'drink that. We can all calm down and decide what we're going to do.'

She blinks hard, twice. Her eyes gleam as she says, 'We?'

I sigh. 'Let's just go through the options, OK?'

This situation has become so much more complicated.

I take another sip of the nasty tea – I've always hated whisky – and try to calm my jangling mind.

And then something happens that feels like ten thousand volts of electricity passing over my skin and under all our feet.

'THIS IS THE POLICE. STAY WHERE YOU ARE AND STAY CALM. NOBODY IS GOING TO BE HURT.'

We rise as one.

'Oh shit, oh fuck, oh no,' says Angel, standing so abruptly that she knocks the chair over and bursting into hysterical tears. Lucas is up and pacing around the room, hands buried in his black curls, his face grey-white.

'We want everyone to be safe,' says the amplified male voice. 'This must come to an end now. But everyone is going to be OK if we all just listen to instructions and remain calm.'

'It's me they want, I'm going out there,' says Lucas and starts to head towards the door but Angel screams, 'No! Stop, stop!' in the most desperate, agonized way.

Later, I'll learn that the police thought it was me screaming. That they believed I, or the baby, was in immediate danger and the only option was to batter the door down.

But for now, there is no logic or thought.

Just an explosion of sound.

My front door smashing open.

The air filling with the thunder of steel-toe-capped boots. Bulky black vests and so many bodies suddenly, after this night of it being just four.

172

Voices shouting, 'POLICE! STAY WHERE YOU ARE! STAY WHERE YOU ARE!'

Angel's plaintive screaming.

Lucas crying out in pain as he is Tasered and falls, jerking to the stone floor.

36

Angel

'*You bastards!*'

Angel lunges towards the now-inert form of her brother but a chubby ginger policewoman is faster than her. Before she even gets the chance to breathe out, she is slammed over the kitchen table, her arms wrenched behind her back. Her shoulder blades scream with pain and she gasps in shock.

'That fucking hurts!' she yells, hating that she sounds whiny and weak; beaten down. Even though she knows she is.

'You just calm down, alright?' The yelling copper's face is so close to Angel's she feels hot breath on her cheek and smells coffee. Then the handcuffs click around her wrists, and the knowledge of what is happening makes her knees buckle. *Someone is really putting handcuffs on her.*

She's hauled, roughly, to her feet. Her knees knock together and she is suddenly so cold that her teeth clatter together. Her head spins before her eyes hungrily search for Lucas, who is making guttural sounds on the floor as though he is dying. She tries to pull towards him and is yanked violently back by the wrists.

'Just stay where you are!'

'Where's the baby?' barks a bald, muscly policeman to Nina, who is standing in the middle of the room with her hands over her mouth, her eyes stretched wide with horror. She doesn't reply and the man says, 'Nina!' sharply, and she jumps visibly.

'Where is the baby? Where is Zach?' he repeats and she seems to come to life then, blushing, which is a bit weird. Of all the emotions right now, embarrassment is bizarre.

'Oh, he's over there.' She scurries out of the room and emerges a few moments later, clutching a – silent for once – Zach, who looks around the room with his alien, depthless eyes, small skull resting against Nina's shaking hands. He is swiftly taken from her by the burly copper and the baby looks comically small in his beefy arms. Angel feels a sharp stab of resentment towards the infant. If it hadn't been for him, they could have got away. They could be in Scotland now, feeling cool, soft rain on their faces.

'Sir, look at this,' says the female copper. She's holding the replica gun up by a blue-gloved finger to show a tall, thin man with grey curly hair. He nods at her and she puts the gun into a see-through evidence bag.

Angel wants to say, yet again, 'It's not even a very good fake,' but senses now is a time to keep quiet. Is this really happening? It can't be real. Can it? She can't keep track of the people swarming around the room now. More police seem to be appearing all the time. She's having trouble getting her breath. It's like there is a finite amount of air and she can't get her share.

'Angel Munro,' says the female copper, 'I am arresting you on suspicion of possessing an imitation firearm with intent to cause fear of violence; false imprisonment; child abduction; and assisting an offender. You do not have to say anything, but it may harm your defence if you do not mention when questioned something which you later rely on in court. Anything you do say, may be given in evidence. Do you understand?'

The feeling of unreality seems to be seeping deep into Angel's bones now. She has the urge to laugh at hearing these words spoken in real life. And then she does, a shaking, hysterical giggle that rumbles so deep inside her it feels like her organs are chafing and grinding together. She knows there is something meaningful she is expected to say but what comes out is, 'That sounds like a long list,' and then she starts to cry, loudly and with a wrenching pain in her stomach.

The grey-haired copper is leaning over Lucas and barking, 'Lucas Munro, I am arresting you on suspicion of murder; child abduction and false imprisonment. You do not have to say anything, but it may harm your defence if you do not mention when questioned something which you later rely on in court. Anything you do say, may be given in evidence. Do you understand?'

Angel hears her brother respond. *Always been so fucking polite*, she thinks. Even now when he's just been zapped like a troublesome fly, he feels the need to respond to an authority figure.

Murder, child abduction, false imprisonment.

They sound like such terrible acts. The kind of acts done by cruel, bad people. That's what people are going to say, that they are rotten.

They were trying to do the right thing.

She only ever wanted to help her brother.

She meets Nina's eyes at last and Angel wants to communicate so many things.

But she doesn't know how, even if she had all the time in the world, so she drops her gaze and stares at the floor as she's led roughly out of the kitchen and through the front door.

37

Nina

I'm numb as I'm led out of the house with a gentle grip on my arm, by a policewoman with a flushed complexion and auburn hair. She has the soft beauty of a Thomas Hardy milkmaid.

But I saw the way she slammed Angel onto that table and handcuffed her, as though Angel's long limbs were as powerless as a puppet's. I feel a little frightened of her, even though I haven't done anything wrong. Have I?

The policewoman is saying something now but I can't focus on it. My attention has been sucked towards one of the four police cars parked on the road outside, along with an ambulance. A slim, tall man with cropped grey hair is standing there, leaning against the bonnet, with a strangely insouciant expression, smoking a cigarette. It might be the senior police officer, perhaps watching with satisfaction as his team carry out a job well done. But wouldn't he come inside? Is that what they do in real life?

Something is bothering me about this but I can't grasp it. Then, as though the dial on a radio has been tweaked, turning white-noise static into comprehensible words, I hear the policewoman saying, a little too loudly, 'Nina?'

'What?' I say, flinching, and sending a silvery shiver down my arms. The sunlight out here is so bright I'm freezing cold.

'I said,' repeats the policewoman, more quietly now, 'do you need any medical assistance?'

'I'm not sick.' I feel baffled by this question.

The policewoman gives me a new, kindly look then, as though I'm a little bit simple and says, 'What I mean is, did *they hurt you* at all?'

I think of Angel's slap across my cheek, just after Lucas arrived. It feels like a lifetime ago. I should probably tell them.

'No,' I find myself saying, 'they didn't.'

The policewoman gives me a curious look and then says, 'We'll just pop you over to the paramedics to be sure. We'll get you quickly checked out before we go down to the station for a chat.'

Her talk of 'popping' and 'chatting' is entirely at odds with the steely look in her dark blue eyes. I'm aware that I am a victim, to be spoken to in a particular way. To be handled carefully.

But it all feels off kilter. The boundaries between aggressor and victim don't feel so clear cut. I picture Lucas lying on the ground, limbs twitching and spasming after the pain zapped blue through his body. Of course, it wasn't really visible at all. But I somehow felt I could see the violence of it inside him. I shiver again, a hard, muscular tremble from head to toe, just as if I had been Tasered too.

'Will he be alright?' I say and the policewoman regards me again, thoughtfully.

'They're checking him out now,' she says. 'He's too little to know what was going on, which is a great blessing.'

This is baffling for a couple of seconds. We are at the

ambulance now. My thoughts seem to be moving like slowly shifting mud. Then I understand.

'No, no,' I say. 'I know Zach's OK because I've been looking after him all night. I mean Lucas. Will he be alright, after being Tased . . . Tasered?' I don't know the correct term and for a moment think that's behind the odd look from the policewoman now.

'I'm sure he'll be fine,' she says crisply. 'Now let's get you checked over, shall we?'

I'm greeted briskly by a paramedic, a shortish black man with wide shoulders and serious eyes.

There is a second paramedic – a white woman with a black ponytail and glasses – inside the ambulance, who is evidently checking Zach over. I can hear his miserable, tired cry and the gentle shushing of the paramedic. There's a wash of intense gratitude that someone else has this job now and it isn't all on me. Compliantly, I sit down on the step at the back of the ambulance, as directed by the man, who then starts to probe me with questions.

Have I been assaulted?

Can he just have a little listen to my heart?

He's just going to take my blood pressure, is that OK?

Is it alright if he looks at my hands?

I endure all this and am then encased in a silver thermal blanket, which has a rapid effect on the shivering. I find myself saying, 'I can pretend that I'm a runner now too, can't I?' then realize this would make absolutely no sense to the paramedic, even though he smiles kindly.

The policewoman is back now, peering at me. She says, 'Do you feel up to giving your statement now? Much better to get things down while they're still fresh.'

'OK,' I say, because I feel I should comply.

We walk towards one of the police cars. The burly bald policeman is already waiting in the driver's seat.

'Mind your head as you get in,' says the policewoman. 'That's the way.'

I climb into the back of the car, pulling the blanket around me gratefully. I can see Lucas in one of the other cars, head bowed, and the proud Cleopatra profile of Angel in another.

As the engine starts and the car does a smooth three-point turn to head back towards town, I glance out of the window and see the good-looking policeman walking in an unhurried away towards the paramedic carrying Zach in a bundle against his shoulder.

Then it hits me.

That's not a policeman. It's Nick Quinn.

My heart starts to thud, hard. Something is wrong about this scene, like the colours are off or something. What is it? It's just out of reach. I'm too exhausted to work it out. Why is my body reacting before my sluggish mind can catch up?

He was presumably allowed to come, told to wait in the car until the situation was under control. I would have been frantic if Sam was a prisoner somewhere. Ian too.

Yet he had been calmly smoking a fag and waiting, in no evident hurry to be reunited with his son. His expression had been completely calm, like a man in control. Not one who had just lost his wife to a murderer and had his son snatched away.

I crane my neck, watching Nick Quinn recede.

As he slips out of sight, I turn back to face the front, freezing cold once again.

38

Lucas

As Lucas was getting into the police car, he'd seen Quinn, standing there. Watching.

It was the first time ever that Lucas hadn't felt frightened of him. After all, what more could he do? Their eyes had locked and Quinn had given him the smallest smile, probably undetectable to anyone else, but full of triumph and a strange sort of curiosity. It seemed to say, 'I've finally destroyed you. How does it feel?'

It wasn't the first time Lucas had seen that toxic mix.

Lucas is now lying on the narrow, smelly bed in a police cell. It feels like every five minutes that the metal flap opens and closes. He guesses he is on suicide watch. Wishes Angel hadn't said anything; hadn't told them about what he'd done earlier. About the road.

The look in her eyes had been terrible. So much pain, caused by him.

He can't get anything right.

All he'd wanted was for the noise in his head to end. To stop all thought and have some peace. He didn't really want to be dead. Did he? He wishes he knew the answer to a question like that.

After a cursory examination by a brisk, tired-looking female doctor, who he assured that he wasn't going to tie his bed sheet to the light fitting, he has been told that along with a solicitor he is going to be assigned an Appropriate Adult. Lucas thought it was only children who got these in police custody, but his actions earlier now qualify him as a 'vulnerable adult'. He knows he ought to feel ashamed. Doesn't, really. The numbness from earlier has returned. It's quite pleasant, like his ragged, throbbing nerve endings have all been cauterised. Maybe he can stay like this. It would be so good not to feel.

Some time passes – it's hard to say how long – and the door to the cell opens.

An attractive man in a dark blue suit comes in and tells Lucas he is Dev Shah, his appointed solicitor.

He shakes his hand and they sit. Shah asks him some questions and explains what is going to happen next. Charges, remanded in custody, bail, blah. Meaningless words that buzz and fly inside his head, bumping against his skull. Shah's brown eyes are on him all the time; bright with intelligence but there is a kindness there too.

Lucas nods but can't really take in what he says. Shah regards him for a moment, and when he speaks again his voice is slower; more measured.

'Look, Lucas,' he says. 'I know you have seen the Forensic Medical Examiner and that in her opinion you are fit to be interviewed. But I can see that you are still in quite a distressed state.' He pauses. 'I'm not convinced you are able to provide the full picture of events to work with and, in the light of this, I'm concerned that you might harm your chances in the interview. My advice to you is to exercise your right to silence.' Another pause.

Silence. It sounds like a beautiful, silvery thing. Lucas longs for it. He'd wrap it round him like a silk shroud and stay there forever.

He nods. 'Alright,' he says in a murmur.

'I have to warn you that this can be held against you by a jury,' Shah continues. 'But that might be better in the long run than giving an interview you are not mentally prepared to deal with. Do you understand?'

Lucas nods again. He feels like one of those Churchill dogs you see in cars.

'Right,' says Shah, wearily. 'I'll tell them you're ready to start. But remember what I said. Beyond the most basic questions, say nothing or that you have no comment.'

Inside the interview room, Lucas is greeted by an Afro-Caribbean grandmother type, clutching a shiny, black handbag like a shield. The Appropriate Adult, he's told. She is very large, but with curiously thin legs that disappear into patent black shoes that match her bag. She reminds Lucas of a sparrow. She says she is Alfretta . . . something; he doesn't catch it. Her lips make a dry, clickety sound when she speaks, as though she needs to drink some water. She clears her throat a lot.

Lucas sits between Alfretta and Shah, feeling sandwiched by flesh. The room smells of sweat, coffee and Alfretta's pungent perfume. It irritates Lucas's gritty eyes, making them sting.

Two people come into the room; a man and a woman Lucas remembers from earlier.

The man, in his fifties with a tired air and grey curly hair, introduces himself as Detective Sergeant Colin McKinney and the red-haired woman as Detective Constable Rosanna Gilbey.

They start the tape and say all the stuff he recognizes from the telly.

Lucas is finding it hard to concentrate. It's so hot in here.

They ask Lucas for his name, date of birth and address. He looks at Shah, who gives the smallest incline of his head. This is the bit he should say. But pushing enough air up through his voice box and out of his mouth feels like the most enormous effort. He can't imagine how he has spent all these years speaking as though it is nothing.

'Can I get you to speak a little more loudly, please, for the benefit of the tape recorder?' says Gilbey in a flat tone.

'It's very hot in here. Why don't you have a drink of water?' says Alfretta, in such a loud, confident voice that Lucas, surprised, takes a sip from the glass in front of him. It does help. He glances at her and she gives him the smallest smile in return. He's suddenly glad she is there, pictures himself nestling against her shelf-like bosom and never coming out again. He wants to wrap his arms around her substantial waist, hold her squishiness tight to stop himself from drowning.

McKinney's talking to him again and he says, 'Sorry, what?'

'I said I'm aware it's very warm in here so if you need a break or need more water, you can tell us, OK?'

'OK.'

'So, Lucas,' he continues, 'you're here today because you've been arrested this morning for the offences of murder, child abduction and false imprisonment and that is what we are going to be questioning you about. Do you understand?'

Lucas nods. His body is turning to wet sand. It's too heavy to cart around. He's so tired.

Zach is probably worn out now. He hopes he gets a good, long sleep. He hopes Zach has some silence. He hopes he isn't missing Alice already.

'Before we start,' says McKinney, 'I'm going to ask you if you are responsible for the murder of Alice Quinn?'

Lucas doesn't reply. He focuses his attention on his hands, which are hanging loosely between his knees. He can hear the slightly laboured breathing of Alfretta.

What a question.

No comment, he thinks but the words seem to echo inside his aching head.

Responsible. The murder of Alice Quinn.

She's never coming back. He may as well have stabbed her. He can't even save Zach now. It was stupid to take him. Zach will end up with Alice's parents because Quinn won't want the hassle of a baby. He wasn't interested in him before. Why would he care now?

I'm so sorry, Alice.

The silence stretches on and on until the female one says, 'Lucas, can you please answer the question for us. Are you responsible for the murder of Alice Quinn?'

He raises his head, his huge, heavy head, and looks at Alfretta. He gives her a small smile. He wants her to know that he's grateful she came here today and made him drink some water. His Appropriate Adult.

He doesn't want to have to make any decisions for himself any more. He wants it all to stop.

'It's all my fault,' says Lucas, finding his voice at last.

He hears the sharp intake of breath from the solicitor next to him.

'Lucas—'

Gilbey leans across the table a little closer.

'You're saying you are responsible for the murder of Alice Quinn, Lucas? Is that what you're saying?'

Lucas feels as though he is far away from the room as he hears his own voice again.

'No comment.'

39

Angel

Angel climbs into the car. The white Range Rover is so high, she must pull herself up by holding onto the leather strap hanging just inside the door.

Typical Leon car. A cock on wheels.

She looks at him as she pulls on her seatbelt. He is watching her, a wary but soppy expression on his face. She wishes he would stop looking at her like she is a bomb that might need defusing. People have looked at Angel that way her whole life, it seems.

She feels disgusting; smelly and coated in cell filth. Uncomfortable too because he brought the wrong clothes for her. Sighing, she tugs the too-tight trousers away from her crotch, where they are digging in. It's so *him*, to have brought an outfit that he likes, rather than something comfortable.

But he was the only person she had to call. The reason she has bail.

How sad is that?

The conditions were that she report to the police station twice a week. Stay away from anyone involved in the 'events', including her brother.

Angel looks at Leon and tries to give him an approximation of a smile. It's the best she can manage and she's not sure it doesn't look more like a grimace.

'What do you want to do, babe?' he says. So far, he hasn't asked her about what had happened. Maybe he's waiting for her to tell him. Well, he can wait.

He has pushed his sunglasses onto his head, like a girl. Angel looks away quickly and faces the front. The weather has turned cooler, finally, and the sky is grey. People come and go into the squat red-brick square of the police station.

What the fuck does he think she wants to do? She's been in a cell for the night. Does he think she wants to go for a picnic? Go dancing?

'I just want to go . . . home,' she says. He doesn't quite manage to hide the little crinkle of satisfaction at the corner of his mouth. Home.

So much for getting away.

Angel sighs again and leans her head back against the high head rest. It might be a stupid gangster car, but it's very comfortable. She hurts all over.

Her body felt like a bag of right angles last night on that thin mattress. It was impossible to get any sleep, especially after she had been told by that ginger bitch that Lucas had given a no comment interview. It was like he had given up. Angel had shouted her head off that she had to see him but no one was interested.

She couldn't understand it. How could she let Quinn get away with what he had done? Again?

For a moment, Angel feels a quiver of something sour inside. Her brother is so weak. He's always been the one who crumples into a ball and lets the blows rain down on him. Why can't he just fight back for once, like she does? Why?

'Ange . . . baby, do you want me to stop the car?'

188

Leon's voice floats into her ears and she turns to him, distracted.

He leans over, eyes on the road still, and gently touches her cheek. His fingers are so gentle that she closes her eyes and sighs. Maybe she can lose herself in his body once she has had a shower. Try to blot it all out. It is only when she feels the wetness spreading down her jawline and into the crease by her ear that she realizes her face is wet with tears.

40

Nina

I've been staring into a cupboard for several moments with absolutely no idea what I'm doing here. Then it comes back to me. Carmen's coming over.

I reach for the bag of Portuguese custard tarts and then find a plate. I've already eaten one of them, and I know Carmen will probably decline hers, because she is always watching her weight. I'll finish them off later, alone. They can be pudding. Or maybe dinner, I don't care.

In the five days since what I think of as That Night, it isn't just mealtimes that feel back to front.

The first time I went into town afterwards, it felt like being in one of those strange dreams, the ones where you are completely naked in a public place. I was convinced everyone was staring at me; that they knew what had happened. I felt like I was having a heart attack when a woman said, 'Excuse me?' in the Post Office. My heart banged wildly in my chest and I was breathing heavily when I turned to her with a wary face. She said, 'Can I just get my buggy through?' and I realized I was standing in her way.

The police told me that as a vital witness in a case like

this the press wouldn't be allowed to contact me. I'm grateful there was no photo of my house on the news. The Quinn house was shown, with white-suited CSI people coming in and out. It was chilling, and brought home with even more force what I had been caught up in.

I'm so confused about it all.

When I made my statement to the police, I tried to tell them about the stuff Angel told me. But they very gently kept asking me – telling me, really – to 'stick to what happened' and to leave the rest of it to them.

There was practical stuff to deal with. They organized the repair of my battered front door and suggested I stay with a friend for a day or so. I thought about calling Carmen, or a couple of good friends from work, but somehow I couldn't bear the thought of all the questions. So, I checked myself into a Premier Inn for twenty-four hours, which added to the surreal nature of all this. I feel untethered; floating in the darkness like an astronaut.

Even the house looks different now. It's no longer my home, and Sam's only home. It's the place I was held hostage.

Normal life feels like something that I once had, but has gone forever.

Mealtimes may happen at three in the morning or not at all.

As for sleep . . .

I keep waking up from vivid nightmares that revolve around blue, wrinkled babies and various rodent-like animals. Last night I dreamed that Sam had stamped on a mutant mouse as big as his hand and said, 'I hate spiders.' Try as I might, I couldn't make him understand that he hadn't squashed an insect, even though he had hair and gore on his Converse shoe. Horrible, horrible. I woke gasping for breath and slick with sweat.

I find myself wandering into rooms and forgetting why

I am there. I wonder if I have Post Traumatic Shock Syndrome and obsessively Google the symptoms in the middle of the night.

I can't stop thinking about little Zach. Wondering who is looking after him. Nick Quinn? What if everything Angel told me is true? Is Zach even safe with his father? I find myself remembering the precise weight of his warm, dense body in my arms. The dark eyes that seemed to understand everything and nothing all at once.

Until yesterday only Ian – well, and I suppose Laura too – know what happened here. I was adamant that Sam was not to know of it until a much later date. Ian had panicked and got into such a flap I hadn't known whether to be happy that he cared so much, or pissed off because he had no right to care any more.

But I'd managed to persuade him that there was no need to come home, which was the important thing. I told him I was going to visit my old friend Sal in Devon for a few days. I'd half meant it too. It's weird though. I don't like being here, but I don't want to be anywhere else either.

But I couldn't carry on with this strange half life I've been living the past five days. I need to do normal things again. So I screwed my courage to the sticking place and phoned Carmen, who had left three messages now.

When I told her what had happened, she cried, making me feel guilty. She thought this was why I hadn't been in touch, when actually, it was forcing me to break my strop with her. If Angel and Lucas hadn't burst into my home, I may well have not talked to Carmen for the whole summer.

Frankly, though, I could do with a friend right now. Carmen, with her no-nonsense Yorkshire attitude, is the most straightforward person I know, and I need that. I think I'm turning a bit strange.

The doorbell trills and I get up, wiping sweaty hands on

my jeans. It's only Carmen, for goodness' sake. No reason to be nervous.

She doesn't say anything at first, merely envelops me in a J'adore-scented hug. She has to bend down, being so much taller than me. She's like my opposite, physically. Tall, with blonde straight hair. Always immaculate, spending time and effort on manicures and pedicures every month. I'm what you might call more DIY about these things, with a tendency to drop food down my clothes.

'I'm alright, Carm,' I say in a strangulated voice and peel myself away. I force a bright smile because she is looking at me with such a stricken expression it's sort of annoying. 'Come on,' I say, 'let's have some coffee.'

'Oh, sod coffee,' says Carmen and I see she is brandishing a bottle of Prosecco. 'I think we both need a proper drink.'

Three-quarters of an hour later, the bottle is almost empty. Carmen, who is driving, has only had one glass. I feel stone-cold sober, but I suppose the rest of it must have gone into me.

I try to tell the story in the order it happened, but already, the details are starting to be muddied in my mind.

'God,' says Carmen when I finish, blowing out so that her carefully blow-dried fringe puffs up and falls again. 'I hope they throw the book at the pair of bastards.'

I can feel my brow pinching and my mouth turning down. I don't know why I react like this. It's just it feels as though Carmen has failed to absorb half the story. Like the police. But what can I do? I can only presume they will do their job. If Quinn really was guilty, they'd get him, wouldn't they?

'What do you think about all the abuse stuff?' I say,

leaning closer over the table. 'And the idea that it was Nick Quinn who killed Alice?'

Carmen regards me for a moment. 'Neen,' she says carefully, 'these people barged into your *home*. They held you at gunpoint and, before you say anything, it makes no difference that it was a fake.' She pauses. 'People never want to believe that their loved ones can commit terrible crimes, do they? And this . . . Angel,' her lip curls a little when she says the name, 'sounds like she would do anything for her brother. She isn't going to want to believe he is a murderer, is she?'

It's very hard to deny this. But I can't seem to *feel* it. It's the cold logic of someone who wasn't there. I picture Lucas sliding down the cabinet onto the floor, liquid with grief. The way he looked at Zach. The story about finding his dead mother in the bath.

'Yeah, but it just sounded . . .' I hesitate.

'Sounded what?' says Carmen carefully.

'Sounded real,' I say in a small voice. 'Like the truth . . . Oh, I don't know.'

'Well, I expect the police are very used to people like that,' says Carmen. 'Good liars.' She seems to be thinking for a moment, frowning, then she clicks her fingers. 'Got it. Been trying to remember the name all day. Remember the Menendez brothers?' Her eyes are shiny now, indecent with triumph.

'No,' I say warily, wondering where this is going.

'Killer siblings,' says Carmen with satisfaction. 'Murdered their parents then went on a spending spree.'

My hands start to shake so I gather up our glasses and move away from the table. I'm aware that Carmen is staring at me as I wash them at the sink.

'What's wrong?' she says now, voice dripping with a concern that feels like nails on a blackboard to my senses. 'Have I said something?'

I don't know how to explain it.

I turn and force a smile. 'No, not at all,' I say. 'I'm just not sleeping all that brilliantly. I'm sorry . . . I'm not very good company right now.'

Carmen gets up from the table and comes over to the sink. 'Look, Nina, why don't you come and stay with me until the guys get back?'

I feel like I have just stepped on a live cable.

'The *guys*?' I say, in much the same way I might use words like 'vomit' or 'diarrhoea'.

A blush smears across Carmen's cheeks, darkening her subtle tan. 'I meant . . . I just meant Sam, and, and . . . his dad, even though obviously, Ian will be . . .'

She seems to finish on a gulp, as though trying to bite the sentence off at the end.

Heat builds in my chest. It feels good, like a cleansing burst of steam inside.

'Only,' I say quickly and a bit too loud, 'I know that you are all good *chums*, aren't you?'

Carmen flinches visibly, then her expression settles into something harder. 'Nina, look,' she says, 'we're not going to go back over that again, are we? We all have to get on, don't we? I mean, Laura is part of Sam's life now and she really isn't so bad when you get to know her.'

I stare at my friend, my supposed friend, and the beseeching yet defiant expressions struggling for dominance on her face. Carmen takes off the large, ever-present, sunglasses balanced on her head and puts them on the table, very much as if trying to find something to do with her hands.

'Maybe she *is* so bad,' I say. I know I'm raising my voice but can't stop it now. 'Maybe,' I say, 'she is actually a bit of a bitch.'

God, that felt good.

One of Carmen's hands flies to her mouth, as though she is the one who has said the unkind, disgraceful thing and she wants to shove it back inside where it belongs.

I, Nina, who hardly ever swear, who has worked so *very* hard at saying positive things about Laura in front of Sam, have shocked her deeply. I feel an infusion of pleasurable righteousness spread through me, liquid and sweet. I could get used to this. Saying what I think.

Carmen looks away, as though I am a tiny bit disgusting. Well, good. I'm disgusted with *her*, Carmen, and her disloyal ways. I'm sick of the lot of them. I only wish Sam were here. I don't need anyone else.

As suddenly as it came, the fight drains out of me. I pick up the tea towel for something to do and sort of flap it at the table, pointlessly. Maybe I'm drunk after all. I have the start of a headache beginning to pulse behind one eye. Oh dear. Carmen's eyes are swimming.

'Carm, I'm sorry, love,' I say at last. 'I just need to get back into the swing of things. I need some sleep. I'm not meaning to be difficult.' I pause. I can't do this. 'In fact, I think I'm going to go for a lie-down. Do you mind?'

Carmen blinks rapidly and begins to rise awkwardly from the seat. I feel a queasy rush of guilt.

'I'm just worried about you, that's all,' she says thickly as she fusses with her handbag, head lowered to hide her flushed face.

I force myself to cross the kitchen and give my friend a hug. Carmen responds by putting her arms around me and giving me a heartfelt squeeze. It seems to go on forever.

'Look,' she says, pulling away at last and regarding me. 'I think you've had a horrible, traumatic experience and it is going to take time to get over it.' Her voice wobbles and then she continues. 'I'll get out of your hair now. But please know I am here for you. Call me any time, day or night, OK? Promise?'

I nod and endure having my curls pushed gently back from my face.

'I promise.'

We walk to the front door together. Carmen says, 'I'll check in with you tomorrow, OK?' and I nod, suddenly desperate for her to go. I feel a bit pissed, the Prosecco hitting me belatedly. I'm so tired.

She's only trying to help. But how can she possibly understand? How anyone who wasn't there? Carmen just feels like the wrong fit today, that's all.

'I do love you, Carm,' I say and she hugs me again, a bit gratefully, and I feel even guiltier.

After she has gone, I walk slowly back into the kitchen. I've been forcing myself to spend time in here, determined that the room won't have been spoiled by That Night.

Nonetheless, my brain keeps pulling cruel tricks on me, so that I'll suddenly picture Lucas jerking in agony on the tiled floor, or the little frog-shaped body of Zach, lying on the table, his chest rising and falling at speed. I glance at the tea towel on the table now and see Angel rubbing her bird's nest hair, eyes glittering with something I couldn't identify then. I thought it was madness; malice perhaps. But now I think she was terrified and trying to pretend she was in control.

It's as though I can't seem to leave it all alone, even though it has finished. Which makes absolutely no sense.

The gentle tap at the back door makes me jump and, for a minute, I'm back to the strange, almost dreamlike moment when I was woken from my uneasy sleep.

Then I notice Carmen's oversized sunglasses lying on the table.

I grab them and hurry over to answer the door.

Opening it, I start to say, 'Knew you wouldn't get far without th—' but the words are stolen from me.

The sunglasses fall from my hand.

41

Angel

The door hasn't been slammed in her face within three seconds so Angel reckons she is already winning.

It could still go either way, though.

Nina looks as though someone has just punched her in the stomach. Her eyes are wide, her mouth hanging slightly open. She is very pale.

Angel can see straight away that the other woman has lost weight. Her curly hair is making a bid for freedom from a red scrunchie and there are violet shadows under her eyes. If she looked 'beaten down' before, now she looks . . . haunted. The truth is, Angel feels a squeeze of regret when she thinks about saying that 'beaten down' thing. She did it partly to wound because she felt criticized about her own choices. In fact, she'd thought Nina could be gorgeous, with a bit of work.

But now, she does look awful.

Nina still says nothing.

Angel has always been able to tolerate awkward silences better than most so she simply waits, glad she thought to come to the back door and not the front where she might be seen from the road. She's not a fool. She knows what she's risking by doing this.

When Nina finally speaks, the words burst out in a rapid gunfire of outrage.

'*What the hell are you doing here?*'

'I just want to talk, that's all,' says Angel, raising a hand in supplication, palm up. Nina looks at it as if she has been presented with a dead fish.

'Talk?' she says, voice skidding hysterically at the end. 'That's exactly what we can't do! I'm going to be the main witness in your trial! Haven't you been told to stay away? This is illegal! Don't you know this? Don't you even know this from the *telly*?'

This last bit gives Angel the inappropriate urge to laugh, but it's only because she is thrumming with stress right now. She could seriously fuck up her trial doing this, not to mention going to prison for breaching conditions of her bail. She knows, alright.

'Just five minutes,' she begs. 'Please, Nina. I promise no one knows, or *will know* I'm here. I walked the whole way. Look?' She twists her leg and lifts a foot half out of one of her dusty grey ballet pumps, revealing raw, red skin and a yellowish blister.

Nina hesitates and then her shoulders drop.

'God's sake,' she says, pulling her by the arm into the room. Her hand feels hot against Angel's skin.

Angel wants to sit down but Nina doesn't offer, merely stands in the middle of the kitchen, arms folded and face closed. Angel is suddenly so tired and sad, and her feet hurt. She doesn't know where to start. She can't stop her brain from replaying those thundering boots coming into the room, and all the shouting. The sheer, electric terror of it all.

'Why are you *here*, Angel?' says Nina and Angel fancies something has softened in her.

'Can I have a drink of water?' says Angel, seizing on this. Nina hesitates and then sighs.

'Go on,' she says gesturing towards the table, 'you may as well sit down but you need to drink it and then go.'

She pours Angel a glass of water and places it in front of her. Angel takes it, hoping Nina won't notice the slight tremor in her hand, and takes a long draught. Nina stares down at her own hands spread before her on the wooden surface, as though grounding herself in some way.

'So,' says Angel after a few moments. 'I know I'm risking everything by coming to you like this, but I wanted to say, first off, that I'm really sorry about what we did.'

Nina looks up sharply. This is evidently a surprise and it pisses Angel off a little. Of *course* she's sorry. What did Nina think? That Angel and Lucas were scumbags who did that kind of shit all the time? That this wasn't a big deal for them too?

She makes herself take a breath and tries to focus again on what she has come here for.

'I was only trying to keep my brother safe,' she says. 'But it was all wrong. I know that now. We both messed things up really badly and none of it was your fault. You were just unlucky enough to get caught up in it all.'

Nina meets her eyes and then gives a small incline of her head. It may be an acceptance of the apology, or it may just be a gesture encouraging her to go on, she's not sure.

'The thing, is,' Angel continues, leaning forward earnestly, 'he has completely given up now. He's not even bothering to fight back.' She takes in a breath, audibly. How can she explain this? She should have practised.

When she was little and getting wound up about something, unable to get her raging emotions into words, her mother would sometimes tell her to say the words in her head first; to put them in order before letting them out into the world. It was advice she seldom took but now wishes she had prepared a little better.

She presses on, anyway.

'Look, Nina,' she says, 'I think I know what happened. I really do. But I have no way of even telling him that it's OK, I understand, that it really isn't his fault.'

Her voice cracks at this. Angel's nose fizzes and her vision blurs. 'Shit,' she says and produces a grubby bit of kitchen towel from her handbag. She was determined to be calm and in control. This woman already thinks she is a fucking fruitcake. Angel swipes angrily at her nose.

'What happened then?' says Nina, her voice steady.

Angel is still for a moment before she speaks. It's so important to get this right. To make her understand.

'You have to understand first how frightened Lucas was of Quinn,' she says. 'I mean,' she pauses, 'I was too, don't get me wrong, but with me it was more . . . about anger. I've always been a stroppy bitch, you'll be dead surprised to know.' She barks a short laugh at this and it helps her onwards. 'One time, a few months before . . .' she swallows, '. . . before we were sent to boarding school, Lucas actually wet himself because Quinn started shouting at our mother. Right there at the kitchen table.'

Nina lowers her eyes and toys with a mug of something, surely cold now, in front of her.

'My brother really is a gentle person,' Angel presses on. 'I think he wanted to be the tough guy who would protect Alice, but when it came down to it, he was just too fucking frightened. And he thinks I don't know. That I haven't guessed. He thinks the absolutely last person in the world who is there for him will . . . turn away.'

It's no good, a ridiculous quantity of tears is now cascading down her face and she can't scrub the wetness away fast enough. Angel can't bring herself to tell Nina about the row, about the awful thing she'd said to Lucas a few months back, the last time she'd seen him until that night.

They'd gone for a drink. She'd been angry with Leon over something, she can't even remember what now. Lucas didn't have anything in common with Leon but had defended him, saying something about him being 'decent' and how maybe he was good for Angel. He hadn't seemed all that interested and was distracted all evening. She knew why now.

It had enraged her, anyway. So she'd mumbled something under her breath and when pushed, as she'd known she would be, she'd said, 'I don't know why I always have such weak men in my life.'

Lucas had looked as though she'd slapped him. She'd tried to make it up, but he left the pub without another word and didn't speak to her again until the night everything kicked off and his life depended on it.

Nina gets up from her seat now and a moment later Angel feels a hand on her shoulder. Looking up, she sees that Nina is offering her a box of tissues. She murmurs her thanks and takes several, blowing her nose loudly.

They sit there for several minutes, the only sounds in the room the ticking of the clock and Angel's snuffling. She feels hope quickening that she may be getting through to Nina. After all, she hasn't thrown her out yet, has she?

'But Angel,' says Nina now and Angel is conscious of the careful tone. 'What is it that you expect *me* to do about this?' She gives a small, mirthless laugh. 'I mean,' she says, 'I'm not going to *lie* in court about what happened, am I? I'm going to answer all their questions as they come. What do you want from me exactly? *I* can't do anything, can I?'

Angel looks at the other woman. She is genuinely confused, her brow creased.

She doesn't get it at all. Yes, that's exactly what Angel wants.

She wants Nina to change the whole narrative of that

203

evening. To say that Lucas told them everything straight away, and that the whole gun thing and not letting Nina go was only because they were scared. That Nina knew all along Lucas wasn't a murderer.

These are all the things she wants her to say.

This is hopeless. Nina looks as likely to agree to this as to jump off a tall building. It's an impossible thing; literally not an option in her universe.

It all seemed like a good idea this morning. When she had been lying, sleepless since five am, mind churning with it all, the idea of speaking to Nina felt like a bolt of clarity amid the fog and muddle.

But Nina isn't the sort of person to stand up in a court of law and tell a lie.

She is the sort of person who has never stolen anything, even as a child; the sort who would hand in a twenty-pound note she found on the floor.

Angel has to at least try, though. Doesn't she owe Lucas that?

'You could,' she says in a tiny voice. 'You could lie.'

There's a sharp intake of breath.

Hopelessness bears down around Angel like a rapid change in air pressure and her heart begins to thump.

Nina can't, won't save them.

No one can.

'I'd never have really hurt that baby,' she says in a tiny voice.

42

Nina

I had no need to worry that Angel would outstay her welcome.

After she had made her extraordinary request, which I'm still struggling to comprehend, and I told her emphatically what I thought of it, she left quickly.

Just before she went, she wrote down her number on a scrappy piece of paper and shoved it onto the table in the hall. I eyed it warily and then opened the door. I said nothing as I watched her dark bowed head moving away, shoulders slumped, and the raw, blistered heels slipping in and out of her crumpled shoes.

I then spent a jumpy evening convinced the police were going to come to my door at any moment. It would be much the way it happened before, I was sure. With drama and violence.

I'm not even completely sure that *I've* done anything wrong, having not invited Angel. But I did let her over the threshold. I once read about a woman going to prison for contempt of court after speaking on Facebook about a trial when she was a juror. There are strict rules about trials. As a major witness for the prosecution I should not have allowed Angel into my home.

There's a lesson I don't seem to learn.

I contemplate telling the police . . . for about five seconds. Then I decide that nothing will be served by it. Angel is already in enough trouble.

I manage to doze from midnight until two am but am only skimming the edges of sleep. I have an earworm of a song from a television advert circling in my mind and I keep thinking my heels are bleeding and that I need plasters.

Now I'm staring up at the occasional light sweeping across my ceiling and marvelling again that Angel had the nerve to come here and ask me to lie. In *court*.

Why would she think I'd agree? Waves of outrage keep breaking over me, heating me up from the inside.

Angel and Lucas are responsible for one of the most frightening experiences I've ever had. We are *not on the same side* here. How can she be so deluded as to think we are?

I keep turning it all over in my mind.

Her talk about 'giving up' sounds as though Lucas is going to plead guilty. I want to know more, but didn't want to press her and encourage the conversation any further.

Maybe Lucas really did murder Alice Quinn. I think about what he looked like when he arrived. The wild, almost unfocused eyes. The animal smell of fear and the blood literally on his hands.

Shivering despite the heat, I pull the duvet up around my chin, eyes darting about the silent bedroom.

I hate being here alone. I'm longing for Sam to be home again and for some sort of normal life to resume. It feels like everything is still turning in slow circles since that night, and it might not stop until it begins to spin out of control.

My thoughts are yanked back, inevitably, to Angel's visit.

'My brother really is a gentle person,' she'd said. Women are forever defending violent men; claiming them misunderstood. I have no real reason for believing a word that comes out of her mouth.

But I can't stop thinking about the images she has planted in my mind. I wish I could shake them loose and out of me.

Nick Quinn beating Angel and Lucas's mother and driving her to suicide.

The guinea pig.

The small, skinny boy sitting in a pool of urine because he is in mortal dread of an adult . . .

'Bugger it.' I violently throw the duvet off myself. There is no way I'm going to sleep.

I owe it to Zach anyway. I need to know he's safe with that man.

I'm in the study, turning on the desktop computer, before I even decide to do it. My eyes are too tired and sore for the iPad.

The trial hasn't started – I'm told it will probably be in the autumn – so there's no harm in looking now, is there? I have to do something, find some way of funnelling this nervous energy outwards, instead of inwards.

As the computer comes to life, I wonder why I haven't done this beyond the most cursory glance before. I think I was trying to *move on*. But how can I, really?

I ignore the news stories in the aftermath. I've already seen them.

But I'd somehow missed a press conference that was held during the breakfast news, while it was all still happening here.

The two police officers from that night are there, along with Nick Quinn, who looks terrible. His eyes are puffy and his cheeks are grey-stubbled. He keeps wiping his hand across his face and then looking around, as though he can't quite believe what is happening to him.

So strange to think that he has yet to open Twitter on his phone and to find my message waiting there. The police told me, after, this was how they found Zach.

I shiver and pull my cardigan around my shoulders as I watch the female officer begin to speak.

'Around eleven pm last night, a twenty-eight-year-old woman was stabbed to death. Her six-week-old baby, Zachary, was stolen. We want to appeal to whoever has the child to come forward so we can make sure he is safe and well. I am now going to hand over to Zachary's father, Nicholas Quinn.'

Quinn has been sitting with his head down and there is a delay before he looks up, as though he might have missed his cue. He blinks several times, then swipes the back of his hand across his eyes. His hand, I notice, is trembling visibly. I find myself softening, despite myself. There is something very vulnerable about a big man with shaky hands, I always think.

'I, uh . . .' he starts to say and then breaks off to cough. I find myself leaning closer to stare at the monitor. 'I am devastated about the death of my beautiful . . . my beautiful wife.' His voice cracks and he looks down, before wiping his eyes again. 'But,' he continues, shakily. 'But, I just want to say to whoever has my little boy, please, *please* don't hurt him. He's all I have now and I just want to know he is safe.'

He pauses and then his final words seem to be squeezed out of him. 'He's so very tiny.' It is barely a whisper. Then he hangs his head and covers his face with one hand. His shoulders begin to shake and the press conference comes to an end.

208

My own hands are shaking now. I don't know what to think.

I have known a few liars in my time, and, whatever part he may or may not have played in all this, that was a genuinely devastated man. I think about the strange energy from him when he was outside this house, when the police came. I'd thought he seemed cool and together. But perhaps what I was looking at was a sort of numb exhaustion?

I try to imagine what it would be like to spend a whole night wondering whether Sam had been harmed. Hours and hours of corrosive terror. It almost makes me want to throw up.

None of this sheds light on whether Lucas is really guilty of murder.

With a big sigh, I sit back in my chair.

I need to know more. I'm not going to be able to rest until I have further perspective on what happened within these walls that night.

I go to make a cup of tea and bring it back to the desk. The steam rising from it feels comforting and, combined with the warm glow from the lamps, I feel enclosed in a small, safe place. For the first time, it seems, in ages.

There are loads of clips of Nick Quinn on YouTube. He seems to have been in every war zone and troubled place in the world over a period of twenty-five years.

But the most recent clip is of him on *The Graham Norton Show*, promoting his book. I lean in, studying him closely. Now that I am seeing him in happier times, I can see that he's an attractive man; there is no denying this. The weather-beaten face, crinkly blue eyes and thick curly hair add up to someone who wears middle age with style. He has authority but smiles a lot too. He looks like someone you would trust in a crisis.

Easily over six foot, he has a powerful build. I think of

Lucas's slight frame; his slim fingers. Again, I wonder. If it had been anyone but Angel who told me that awful story . . .

Clicking play again, I find myself staring at Quinn's large, strong hands as he uses them to emphasize a point he is making. I try to picture them smashing into a woman's face, or striking a child. I can't seem to do it. I think of his shoulders shaking at the press conference; the terrible distress on his face.

The next most recent is a story about the kidnap of schoolgirls by Boko Haram in Nigeria. There's little from Iraq and Syria. I suppose that's because he was taking time to write that book. I zone out much of what he's actually saying. I want to get a sense of him; what he's like as a person. But it's very hard to tell. He just seems professional, intelligent and sober.

I think of Angel and the wild energy that seems to crackle off her. About how far she can really be trusted. But that guinea pig story; it feels too horrible and bizarre to be fabricated.

With a sigh, I go to Google Images next and look at the many pictures of him there. In the field in flak jacket and fatigues; suited and bow-tied at various events, sometimes collecting awards . . . he looks like a man who understands how the world works.

Like someone who is never frightened, even when someone actively wants to kill him.

The printer makes a whirring sound as it comes to life in the still room. I find it easier to think on paper. I start printing out pages: the Wikipedia on Quinn, an interview with him in the *Guardian* from a few years ago, and other bits and pieces. And photos, several photos.

Lost in my research, it's only when I start to shiver that I realize I've been sitting like this for over an hour. I feel . . . easier. It has been good to focus my energy on something, even if I would struggle to explain it to another person.

I go to the kitchen where I open the fridge and find the uneaten Portuguese custard tarts from earlier. I eat them both, quickly, standing. Then put my plate in the sink.

When I go back to the study I stare at the print-outs I've scattered across half the floor. I have a wobbly moment of wondering if this way madness lies.

The thought of going back to bed is appalling, though. So, I turn back to the screen, and begin reading about Quinn accepting a National Journalism Award in 2009.

Described as 'the Pulitzer Prize of UK journalism' it sounds like a prestigious event. I quickly find it on YouTube. There's an interview, conducted by a television presenter I vaguely recognize but can't name.

'So, you've been on our screens for many years,' says the presenter, 'reporting from some of the most dangerous places in the world. How does it feel to accept the award for Best Foreign Reporting tonight?'

Quinn's cheeks are flushed and he looks slightly drunk as he gives a slow smile in return.

'Well, I work as part of a team, always,' he says in that honeyed voice. 'And even when I am out there in the field, I'm conscious of all the people who have helped me get there.' He looks distracted for a moment and then says, '. . . And not least my team of producers, such as this amazing lady, Marina Goldman.'

Quinn grabs the arm of a thin, dark-haired woman who is passing and pulls her in to the frame. She blinks and looks uncomfortable for a moment. Then smiles and pushes a strand of hair away from her face.

I lean forward and hit pause.

Something about this exchange has given me a jolt. Something about it feels wrong. What is it?

I back up a little on the video, going too far.

'Damn it.'

This time I successfully reach the moment just before Marina Goldman appears in Quinn's sightline. When she is on camera for the first time, she appears to . . . what? Draw back a little from his touch? And what is it about her eyes . . .?

I rewind again and then pause that exact moment. The woman is a little blurred but her eyes are wary. No, more than wary.

A little scared?

I stare at this frozen image until my eyes begin to sting. I try to screenshot it, but it doesn't work. Sam would know how.

I open another tab and type in 'Marina Goldman, tv producer'.

She has a Wikipedia page.

'Marina Goldman is an experienced television producer working in current affairs. Her job includes planning and producing live broadcasts, pre-recorded content and location shoots for the channel and the website. Marina is currently working for Channel 4 News.'

There is a picture of her. She looks plumper here than in that clip. Very pretty, with thick dark brown hair tied up and warm eyes, smoky with make-up. Looking back at the video clip, it's odd, but she looks older there than in this, presumably, current photo.

I Google 'Nick Quinn and Marina Goldman' and find a picture from *Hello!* magazine of an event held at the Natural History Museum for a charity. They are smiling widely for the camera, Marina in an elegant black dress and her lips painted scarlet. Clearly a couple. I check the date – July 5th 2008. So, the year before that awards night then.

I really want to screenshot these images and print them

212

out. I open yet another tab to see if I can Google how to do this . . .

. . . and then a bolt of clarity seems to pierce my intense, feverish state.

I see myself as if from above: a rumpled middle-aged woman, obsessively Googling a man in the middle of the night whose wife has been murdered. A highly respected journalist who hasn't had a whiff of scandal attached to him in these celebrity-obsessed times.

And why? Because a young woman who has no real regard for the way things should be done, who *held me hostage* for Christ's sake, thinks her word counts for more? It's insane. I don't know what the hell I'm doing.

If Ian saw this, he'd probably tell me to go straight to the doctor.

Maybe that night's events are having a worse effect on me than I realize.

I turn off the computer and, shivering with exhaustion, force myself to climb the stairs to bed.

43

Lucas

He wishes they would just let him sleep.

It's as though he has lived a lifetime in deficit.

Now, he can easily spend most of the day curled up on the bed in welcome oblivion. It feels like a kindness he doesn't deserve, that he can sleep like this. But he doesn't feel guilty enough to tell them to stop the daily dose of diazepam. Unlike his sister, he has never been much of a one for narcotics. His friends used to laugh at the rapid speed at which a few tokes of a joint would knock him out. He just has a low tolerance, that's all. It's proving to be a blessing now.

Lucas is on the top bunk and, apart from trying to ignore the frequent grunts and bed squeaks from his Russian room-mate's vigorous masturbation below, it is better than he might have expected. It's a step-up from his first destination here anyway; a room with a barred plexiglass door designed for close monitoring of vulnerable prisoners. The constant eyes on him began to feel like insects burrowing into his skin.

He was interviewed by several people on arrival, who told him they were putting together some kind of 'care plan'. It seemed to be because of what he had done on that road. He answered in monosyllables. Talking feels so exhausting.

And they needn't worry. Lucas isn't going to try and kill himself here. At least, not yet.

He knows he doesn't have the guts to do what a bloke did the other day on his corridor; attempted to hang himself with a pair of trousers tied to the top bunk.

He'd heard the frantic shouting then seen three prison officers racing down the corridor.

Lucas has exchanged no more than twenty words with the Russian.

It suits him just fine.

He can go to a place in his mind where all that is muted; no more than a vague background buzzing. He can go to Before. To when there was still time.

The first time they had spoken, the rain started just as Lucas had finished mulching the new flower beds. Miserable with the fuggy feeling inside his waterproofs and the clammy sweat clinging to his back, Lucas was thinking about calling it a day when he became aware of a rhythmic banging sound. He turned to see Alice at the French windows in the kitchen, making the gesture of a cup of tea with her hands.

He'd shaken his head with a small smile and then she had mimed shivering, her arms around herself, her eyes raised in mock horror at the sky, which had made him laugh. So, hating that he was so wet and that he could smell his own heat rising up from inside his damp clothes, he had entered the house for the first time.

'I don't think we've ever spoken properly, have we?' said Alice as he stood awkwardly at the windows. He knew that Quinn was away because the car wasn't out in the driveway. But he still felt a thrill of fear as he stood there.

'Come in, come in!' Alice insisted now.

She stood so beautifully, her spine perfectly straight and her shoulders back. Lucas would have known she was a dancer from her posture alone.

She didn't seem to notice, or mind, that he was being weird, that he couldn't find the words he wanted to say.

'Tea? Coffee?' she said, and this time her bright smile slipped a little because he still hadn't said a word.

'Tea, if that's OK,' he said and she smiled.

'Man after my own heart.' She filled a kettle at the sink and then placed it on the cooker before turning and gesturing that he should sit.

'Take off those wet things and I'll get you a towel.'

Hesitating for a moment, Lucas pulled off his wet boots, fretting that his soggy socks smelled, and shucked off his waterproof coat, which he laid neatly over the boots and then walked to the table, conscious of the damp footprints he left in his wake on the stone floor.

'What a filthy day,' said Alice with a little shiver, as she dropped teabags into a red teapot and found milk from the fridge. Her dark hair was piled onto the top of her head in a bun, with tendrils of hair falling around her face. She wore dark grey workout trousers that hugged her narrow hips, and a soft pink cardigan that crossed at the front and tied at the back of her waist. Her feet were in sheepskin slippers that made a shh-shh sound as she walked around the tiled floor.

'I'm surprised you came today,' she continued. 'Is there anything that urgent that needs doing?'

Lucas felt a flare of panic then. She knew, he thought. She knew he had been watching her. He had to say something, something that would stop him from coming across as a freak, but just as he opened his mouth, which felt stiff and underused, she spoke again.

'Mind you, I've seen Bob out there in all weathers.

Suppose that's the thing with gardens, isn't it? They need a lot of care?'

'Well,' he said, finding his voice at last, 'composting those new beds is much easier on a damp day like this.'

She grinned and murmured, 'Damp?'

Lucas found that he laughed, easily. 'Yeah, maybe "damp" doesn't quite cover it,' he said. 'But you don't want to be digging in when the ground is hard.'

Alice seemed to consider this and then she did a little side-to-side thing with her head that would soon become familiar.

'I guess that makes sense,' she said with a grin. 'I swear that if I was in charge I'd kill the lot. I even managed to kill a cactus once, and aren't they supposed to be indestructible? It feels like there's some magic formula I just don't understand with plants.'

Lucas laughed and it felt good. 'People always worry about that,' he said, 'but really it is more about knowing the right environment for things to grow. The right soil and so on.'

He accepted the mug of tea she handed him, which was the colour of beechwood. He looked up to see Alice making an apologetic face.

'Sorry,' she said, 'I should have asked how you take it. Not everyone likes their tea so strong you could stand your spoon up.'

'It's perfect,' said Lucas with a smile.

After they had both sipped their tea, he felt emboldened to say, 'You make tea just right. And I'm sure you're not that bad with plants really.'

Alice made a face. She did this a lot, pulling her pretty features into mock horror, or exaggerated surprise. It was as though she felt her face to be uninteresting as it was, when it was anything but.

217

'Well, let's hope I get a bit better at looking after things,' she said, and laid her hand on her belly.

Lucas paused with his mug halfway to his lips, slow to pick up her meaning. Then, when he understood, the shock made his face flood with heat. Alice was looking down at her belly now as she took a surprisingly loud slurp of her tea.

Lucas forced the required words out of his mouth.

'When is the baby due?' he said. 'Sorry, I hadn't—'

Alice waved a hand airily. 'Oh please, no one seems able to see it, although I feel as though I'm enormous. It's due in three months.'

Lucas stared at where she was rubbing her stomach. Now he looked closely, he could see the slight curve there. But it was barely noticeable unless pointed out.

She caught his gaze and he gave what he hoped was an apologetic smile.

'Don't worry,' she said, leaning forward. 'It's because I'm a dancer, or so I'm told. The old stomach muscles are unwilling to go against years of training to behave a certain way. The doctors have assured me there will be room for the little fella in there.'

'It's a boy then?' said Lucas, his smile plastered onto his face in a way that felt so unnatural, he was sure it was obvious.

'Yeah, I wanted it to be a surprise but Nick,' she paused, 'he's my husband, he really wanted to know. So . . .' she shrugged and looked down at her cup, before taking another drink of her tea. The rest of the sentence was left to hang and an awkward silence fell.

Of course, he did, *thought Lucas. It's all about control, with him.*

His heart was banging almost painfully in his ribcage now. Surely, she could hear it? He flailed about in his mind for something socially acceptable to say, but instead blurted out something entirely different.

'I bet he's excited,' he said. 'Your husband. About the baby.'

Alice looked up and beamed but her eyes were clouded with something now.

'Yeah,' she said. 'It will be his first too.'

'He hasn't had kids before then?' says Lucas, forcing tea into his mouth to hide his oddness.

'No,' said Alice. 'Think his ex-wife did but, well, he won't talk about that,' she said. 'Said it was a part of his life that was difficult. Wants us to make a fresh start.'

Then she let out a small laugh. 'Bloody hell, get me, opening up like this! I think you must have that sort of face, which makes people confide in you.'

'That's alright,' said Lucas. 'I don't mind at all.' He looked outside and saw that a thin band of blue was splitting the bruised clouds. 'Clearing up out there. Better get back to it.' He stood up. 'Thanks for the tea,' he said.

'I don't even know your name!' said Alice with a laugh.

He hesitated. 'It's Luke,' he said. 'My name's Luke.'

44

Angel

Leon has started to complain about Angel lying around watching telly all day, like she's some sort of housewife who's going to cook his tea.

Still, she thinks, maybe he has got a point. She isn't even sure she had a shower yesterday.

Angel swings her legs around from the sofa and picks up her cigarettes from the coffee table. Leon had swept up the wine bottle, glasses and pizza boxes this morning, grumbling all the while. But there is still a sticky red circle where the bottle rested.

Her head throbs and her mouth tastes foul. She lights up a cigarette and leans back again.

For the millionth time, she tries to picture what is happening to Lucas right now. The fact that she can't speak to him boils painfully inside her.

Every cliché she has ever known about prison keeps playing endlessly around her head. Her unhelpful imagination is very good, it transpires, at presenting her with a whole series of horrific images: Lucas curled, bleeding and naked on the dirty floor of the showers; Lucas being stabbed in the dinner queue; Lucas being forced to suck off some bald, tattooed ape . . .

This cigarette tastes disgusting. She jabs it out into the ashtray, then rises quickly from the sofa.

She's going to have to do something about this . . . situation. She can't pretend it isn't happening any more. At some point Leon, thick as he may be, is going to wonder why she nearly jumps through the ceiling if he touches her breasts, or why she can only face one drink. Why she is so tired. She tells him it's the shock of everything, still catching up with her, and he believes her. So far. At least she hasn't been throwing up. You would think everyone did this, from watching telly. It's different to that other time, when she was a teenager and took that stuff someone gave her in a club. That didn't have time to root in. She'd had no symptoms at all then.

She gets up from the sofa now and goes to the bathroom. Stripping off her T-shirt and tracksuit bottoms, she stands in her knickers and looks at the full-length mirror.

Her nipples look huge; darker than usual too. Her stomach is still flat though and she stands to the side, trying to imagine what it would look like, rounded and full, her hand on her belly.

She had been so close to telling Nina yesterday. It may have made a difference to her decision, perhaps, had she known. But there is something else too; deep inside her, Angel had just wanted to tell her for . . . what, advice? Sympathy? A little motherly tenderness? Nina seems to find it effortless to be warm and kind. As if there is nothing difficult about it at all. Angel marvels at this.

Fuck this. She can't sit around stewing in fear and resentment.

221

She gets into the shower and lets the hot water pound on her head and down her face, where it mixes with the sudden tears. This is where she does her crying, largely. Always has been.

This time she can't seem to stop, though, and her whole body shudders with the spasms of grief. It's only now, belatedly, that the truth is properly sinking in; Quinn has won, again. Lucas is broken. Forever? He never could fight back.

She might actually go to prison.

Prison.

For all her supposed rebellions – taking every drug going, generally putting two fingers up to authority all her life – she'd never been arrested before. In the back of that police car . . . she'd never felt smaller or more alone in all her life.

Angel leans against the wall with both hands and bows her head, letting the water run over her face and off her chin. She stands there for so long that the water starts to run cool, then cold, as the hot water tank empties. *This is such a shithole*, she thinks. *Can't even get a decent shower.*

When she dries herself, shivering a little, she can feel sparks of her ever-simmering anger starting to return. She grasps onto them; anger is better than this pathetic crying.

She's getting dressed in the depressing murky light of the bedroom when it comes to her.

She's already in terrible trouble. How much worse can it get, really? Nina will probably tell the cops about her attempts to, what is it called, pervert the course of justice?

Angel makes a face at no one and then finds a pad of writing paper and a pen.

Luckily, she still has a note of the address in her phone from the night it all happened and Lucas needed help finding his way.

It's nice to actually write something properly, rather than dashing off a vague bit of communication with two thumbs.

Angel, much to certain people's surprise, has nice hand-writing and she takes pleasure in the process of sweeping pen on paper as she writes.

You probably think you will get away with this, as you get away with everything else. And yes, maybe my brother will be too broken to fight back.

But I am not broken.

I won't go to prison for very long. And it will be worth it to have my time in court. I think the press are going to be all over this case, aren't they? I'm looking forward to telling the world about what a monster you are. Remember all those times Marianne went to the doctor about walking into doors and falling down stairs? People might start to wonder if they look into that a little deeper. Not to mention the bruises and bumps that Lucas and me always had (clumsy old us). Plenty of mums at our old school who might have wondered too.

I bet other women will come forward if this becomes news.

And even if there is no proof of your crimes, it might just put off all those publishers and telly people from featuring your pig-arrogant face.

You wouldn't be the first national figure to be shown up for what he really is to the British public. It's quite the trend, news-wise!

I hope you rot in hell, you piece of shit. See you in court.

Angel feels calmer than she can remember for some time as she goes to find an envelope. Hard to imagine that he will really want to show *this* to the police.

Next, she can get her job at Gioli's back for the time being. It will stop her sitting around and obsessing about the things she can't fix. Stop her picturing her broken brother and worrying about what to do about this thing burrowing deep inside her.

45

Nina

I sleep more heavily than I can remember for ages. When I emerge from the thick, slow mass of it, I see it's after two pm.

After showering and getting dressed, I eat breakfast in front of the telly. But I don't really take in what's on the screen. I'm staring at the female news anchor, with her sharply cut hair and professional smile.

Then the content of what she is saying begins to filter through my consciousness. It's a story about a woman being murdered by her ex-boyfriend as she walked home from work one night. Her fresh, pretty smile shines out from the screen and I feel a chill at the thought that she never managed to be free of this man.

I start thinking about all the things that Angel told me about her childhood. If it's true that Quinn is an abuser like this, then it is unlikely it was only that once. What does that mean for Zach?

The spoonful of cereal slows on its journey to my mouth and my heart beats a little harder. I have to know, you see. I have to. I think of that tiny boy, who will never remember his mother, and the sadness inside me, which I think I've

225

been carrying ever since Ian left, feels different. Like the soft bruises are finally hardening. Scar tissue is forming and I'm angry now, determined.

I try ringing the number I find online for Channel 4 first.

After being kept on hold for a while and then transferred twice, I'm told that Marina Goldman has just gone on maternity leave.

The disappointment cuts deep.

I sit back on the sofa and sigh. What now?

Then I get thinking. I bet someone like her keeps an eye on her work emails.

It's surprisingly easy to work out her email address. I find out online that ITN controls Channel 4 News and that the email addresses are first name.lastname@itn.co.uk.

I write:

> Dear Marina,
>
> You don't know me but I am the woman who was held hostage with Nick Quinn's baby. You might have seen it on the news.
>
> I know this is out of the blue and a strange request, but I wondered if I could talk to you.
>
> You can reply here or call me on 07700 900789.
>
> I really hope you will be able to reply.
>
> All very best,
>
> Nina Bailey

I feel a surge of adrenaline that isn't unpleasant once I've hit send. Then I sit back, wondering what to do next.

Again, I ask myself what I am hoping to achieve.

When my mobile rings with an unknown number about five minutes later, I stare at it as though it has just caught fire, heart hammering in my chest. It can't possibly be her.

It's probably someone claiming I've had a car accident in the last few weeks or offering to sort out my PPI.

I answer and a clipped, well-spoken female voice says, 'My name is Marina Goldman. You sent me an email just now.'

'Oh!' I say. 'Gosh, yes, I did.'

There is a brief pause and then, very coolly, she says, 'And how is it that I can help you?'

I feel as though she is a grown-up and I am a silly teenager, even though I think I'm probably a decade older than her. I don't know where to start, so I decide to get to the point.

'Look, Ms Goldman,' I say tentatively, 'I'm very sorry to contact you out of the blue like this, but as I said in my message, I'm the person who got caught up in that whole thing that happened with Nick Quinn recently . . . the, um, murder of his wife, and the kidnap of his son, Zach.'

Silence.

'Did . . .' I falter, 'did you see that?'

There's another pause then, 'Naturally. I work in the news.' Then she adds, in a stilted tone, 'I'm sorry you had to go through that, but I'm still not sure why you are contacting *me*?'

I take a deep breath. I've got this far; I may as well see it through.

'Well,' I say, 'the thing is, Ms Goldman, er, Marina, I believe you used to be together with Nick Quinn. At one time, I mean.'

I never knew silence could have such an Arctic chill. After what seems like a very long time she says, 'Look, that really was a long time ago. I don't see what it has to do with anything.'

'But it might,' I say quickly. 'Because that night, Angel . . . Did you know about Angel?'

'No,' she says crisply, after a moment's hesitation. 'Not until I read about her and the man, her brother. Ni— he never talked about that time in his life.'

'The thing is,' I say, desperate to get this out before she – quite understandably – hangs up on me. 'Angel told me things about Quinn. About terrible cruelty from him when she lived with him. Said he effectively killed their mother. Drove her to suicide by breaking her down and bullying her.'

I hear a sucking-in of breath on the other end of the phone and she says, 'I really don't think I can . . .' but I rush onwards; suddenly terrified she will hang up on me.

'Please, Ms Goldman,' I say. 'Please listen. Angel thinks it was Quinn who murdered Alice,' I say, 'and her brother was only trying to get the baby away, through, I don't know, some kind of saviour complex.' This all comes out in one long breath.

There's another pause before she speaks. Her voice sounds thick now and I wonder whether she might actually be holding back tears.

'And did you tell the police this?'

'Well, yes,' I say. 'I tried to. But I'm not sure how much they took that on board. I mean, oh God,' I sigh, 'I don't even know if I believe it myself!'

This time the pause drags on even longer and I'm about to say, 'Marina? Are you there?' when she speaks again.

'Look,' she says, her voice almost inaudible. 'Nina. I am having a baby in three weeks. I have a loving partner, a beautiful home, a career . . . I'm a very lucky woman. I don't want to re-visit the past.'

'No, no,' I say hurriedly, 'I completely get that. Of course. But I'm frightened that a huge injustice may be about to happen or something. Oh, I don't know. I don't really know why I contacted you. I'm sorry.'

I run out of steam and, as the adrenaline leaves my body, a tired lethargy comes in its wake.

I sit down at the table, feeling old.

There is a silence on the other end and then Marina Goldman speaks again.

'When I saw that story on the news,' she says, 'I . . .' she pauses, 'I wondered whether there was something more to it. It took me back to a very dark time in my life. Nick Quinn is two things above all else. He is a very, very bad person, but he is also one of the cleverest men I have ever met. He can manipulate the people around him until they start to doubt their own sanity.'

'Right,' I say, heart beginning to beat harder again. I don't really know what to say to this.

'But I managed to escape him once,' she continues. 'And I cannot be sucked into his orbit in any way again. Do you understand? There's nothing I can do for you here.'

'Oh,' I say, shocked. 'I don't think I'm asking you to *do* anything. I mean, all I want to know is . . . well, do you think it's possible Angel was telling me the truth?'

I can hear her fast breathing now down the line and for a second I imagine that I am sending her into labour with this. I'd never forgive myself.

'Marina?' I say a little too sharply. 'Are you alright?'

'Yes,' she says in a barely audible voice. 'I mean, yes – I can believe that might be the truth.'

'Oh,' I say. 'God . . .'

'But I don't want you to contact me again, alright?' she adds in a rush. 'I'm not getting involved in any way. Please. I just can't . . .'

'Marina?' I say. But the line is dead.

I sit there for several moments when I come off the phone, trying to absorb what I have just heard.

So many emotions are fighting for dominance inside

me, I feel almost dizzy with them. There's a strange exhilaration – a triumph, almost – that my amateur detective work online actually helped me to find out valuable information. But pitched against that is another, more complex worry.

Now I have this information, what exactly should I do about it?

I sit there for a few moments, staring down at the phone in my hand.

Marina Goldman seems quite clear that Angel may not be lying. But her refusal to go on the record feels absolute and just because Quinn is a domestic abuser, it doesn't mean he is a murderer, does it?

Am I really any further forward?

I groan and drop the phone onto the table. It immediately buzzes with a message and I jump, before snatching it up, suddenly sure, illogically, that it is Marina Goldman.

It's a WhatsApp from Ian.

I sigh.

You home?

I hesitate, then reply, Yes. Why?

Coming over. Be there in fifteen.

My hastily tapped reply, What mean??? Surely in France? doesn't show the blue ticks that signify he has read it.

I don't want to see Ian but the thought of seeing my boy makes my heart swell in my chest. Sam's home!

Joy suffuses me as I race round trying to tidy up the kitchen, shoving newspapers that have been piling up into the recycling bin, and dumping the cups and plates into the dishwasher. Sam won't care, but I don't want Ian judging me . . . thinking I've fallen to pieces because I've been on my own.

I hope she isn't coming too – Laura. I look awful . . .

I'm hurriedly slicking on mascara and fluffing out my hair, clean, thank goodness, when the doorbell goes.

I do a quick teeth-check in the mirror and try to stop myself from shaking by breathing deeply as I head for the front door.

Opening it quickly, the anticipation of seeing Sam almost makes my knees weak.

But there is only Ian.

Ian, *without Sam*.

His face is grave.

'Where is he?' I say, momentarily convinced he is about to tell me something awful; something I won't be able to bear hearing. 'What's happened to him?!'

'Nothing, nothing!' he says, hands up in placation. 'He's in France still. Having a lovely time.'

My whole body turns icy cold now.

'In France?' I say, a little hysterically. 'Why is he in France? When you're *here*?'

'Look, don't freak out,' he says, enraging me further. 'But I've been worrying about you ever since I heard about what happened. I needed to see that you were alright. Carmen told me you didn't go away to Sally's like you said you would.'

'Oh, did she now,' I say flatly. My face is tight; my jaw almost locked.

He looks at me until I sigh and say, 'Come in then.'

When we go inside he wanders over to a cupboard and starts rooting about.

'What are you *doing*?'

Evidently surprised at my tone, he turns with wide eyes.

'Didn't we have a bottle of whisky in here somewhere? I feel like one.'

'Oh, do you now?' I say tightly. 'Sit down.'

He obeys, a bit meekly. I go to where I keep the whisky now.

There is one glass and one plastic cup on the drainer. I slosh some into each and then bang the beaker down in front of him, keeping the glass for myself. It's so childish, but it feels good as I meet his gaze defiantly.

'There you are,' I say, 'a drink.'

I'm so angry I'm struggling not to smash mine down on the top of his head, so instead, I make myself take a swig, which seems to scald my throat on the way down.

He starts to speak, 'Look, Nina, I—'

'I can't believe you came back and left Sam there,' I interrupt. 'What the hell were you thinking?'

'What was I thinking?' says Ian, wide-eyed with outrage. 'You get held hostage at gunpoint by some kind of . . . I don't know, Bonnie and Clyde couple, and I'm not meant to be worried?'

'It's none of your business,' I snap. 'It's got nothing to do with you.'

'Nina!' he cries, forcing me to look at his stupid face. 'You're the mother of my child! We were married for eighteen years, for Christ's sake! You're my . . . you were my best friend.'

His voice breaks a little at this and I frown, noticing the brightness in his eyes. All the bitter sentences inside me begin to gather and whirl together, an internal tornado. Like, if I was so great, why have you run off with someone else? But I make myself remain silent. This is ground we have been over so many times. I don't have the stomach for it.

'Anyway, of course I have a right to care,' he trails off.

I sip my nasty drink again before replying.

'But to leave Sam there on his own with Laura,' I say.

'I literally cannot *comprehend* why you thought that was a good plan.'

My own eyes burn now and I look down and blink furiously. Buggered if the bastard is going to see me cry ever again.

'Look,' he says, voice gentler now, 'Sam's having a really brilliant time. His swimming has come on loads and he has completely fallen for the dog there. I know you want him to be happy more than anything, and I didn't want to drag him away early from an enjoyable holiday and scare him half to death. He thinks I'm here for a work meeting.'

He fills up our empty glasses. I can't be bothered to protest.

'He sends his love,' he says softly. 'And says he's dying to drive you insane about getting a dog.'

I'm too furious and upset to laugh. When I feel his hand softly covering mine, my brain wants to tell me to snatch my own away. He's lost all right to touch me, after all. But my skin responds on its own, traitorously. I almost involuntarily turn mine and we clasp hands across the table. It feels good, the familiar shape of it in mine. Something tight inside me slackens.

'Are you alright?' he says. 'Can you tell me what happened?'

I pull my hand back again and force down another mouthful of the whisky. Gathering myself, with difficulty, I go through the whole thing again.

This time, having learned my lesson with Carmen, I give the barest details about what Angel told me. I merely say she is convinced her brother is innocent and that Quinn was abusive as their step-father, but I don't offer any opinions.

But to my surprise, when I finish, Ian sits back and

puffs out his cheeks before saying, 'God, you'd never think that about him when you see him on the telly, would you?'

A strange rush of relief washes over me that he hasn't dismissed all this like Carmen. I find myself smiling at him. He may have cheated on me, but the fact remains we were always friends. He gets me like no one else. It's like putting on a comfortable hoodie after a long day in tight clothes.

There's a silence during which we both contemplate all this.

I don't want to talk about it any more. Not now.

'Please,' I say, 'please let's talk about Sam. Tell me what he's been doing.'

I find a bottle of red and pour us glasses. Ian protests about drinking, but I find myself almost forcing it on him and he mumbles that maybe he can get a cab.

He tells me about Sam's love affair with Bisou the dog and shows me pictures that make my whole chest fill up with love. Sam looks so happy. Tanned and grinning in a variety of different places; but mainly by the swimming pool, or with one arm slung about Bisou's neck.

'Why didn't you send these to me?' I ask, after a while.

It's dusk now. I haven't put the lights on inside so the deep blue twilight is soft against the windows.

Ian is sitting next to me now, the phone between us in his hand. His arm, in the rolled-up blue shirt, is tanned and covered with fine, dark hairs. I always liked his arms. I can almost feel the heat of him, seeping into my own skin.

Something I shouldn't be feeling fires up low down inside me.

'I don't know,' he says, softly, bringing me back to myself. 'I kept wanting to, then I panicked about it making you feel shit to see them. I spent quite a lot of time debating this in my mind rather than enjoying the moment.'

He gives a small chuckle and I look at him. Our eyes lock together and I hold my breath. He's feeling this too.

We've never been the 'angry sex' sort of couple. Too comfortable with each other. But now I suddenly want to pull his hair, bite his lip until it bleeds, rake my fingers down his spine.

People say, 'I don't know who started it,' about illicit sex, don't they? But it's me. I'm starting it. I want this.

I lean in to kiss him, hard, and after what feels like two seconds of hesitation, he responds, his mouth pressing against mine, his taste so familiar.

Then we are stumbling over to the sofa like one person. There's a flurry of unfastening and pulling down of clothes and in no time, he is inside, pushing into me and murmuring, 'Nina,' into my hair. It's something that has happened a million times before, yet it is so very different.

It's so strange and fast that I'm not even sure I'm enjoying it.

When it's over we both rush to put on our clothes, eyes averted. I can feel the pressure of his guilt like the headache before a thunderstorm.

'Nina . . .'

I shush him so harshly he visibly flinches.

'Don't,' I say. 'Don't *say it*. I know exactly what you want to say and I don't want to hear it. I know this was a mistake. I'm not going to be getting any hopes up. I won't tell Laura. I'm not a complete bitch.'

He looks down and says, 'Thank you.' There's a long silence and he says, 'Well, I'll just . . .' gesturing to the door. I nod. Our eyes don't meet once.

*   *   *

While he's upstairs I tidy up my hair and take the dirty glasses over to the sink. Putting on the lights brings a harsh reality into play. This happened in a dreamlike state and now it is over.

I call him a taxi from the card we keep on the fridge. Or, I should say now, I keep there. Ian doesn't live here any more. He won't ever live here again. I know this now, more than ever.

I'm told it will be fifteen minutes.

When he comes back into the kitchen he's frowning and holding a bundle of sheets of paper. I get a sinking feeling as I recognize what they are.

'Um, what's all this?' he says. 'I wanted to pick up something from the study and saw it there.'

I clench my jaw.

'You can't just wander about in this house,' I say tightly after a moment. 'You don't live here any more. Remember?'

His expression sours and he waves the papers at me.

'Yeah, OK, sorry, but what *is* this?'

'Just some research,' I say, avoiding his puzzled gaze. 'Anyway, I've called a cab. They said fifteen minutes, which might be ten now.' I can't stop myself from adding a sarcastic sign-off. '. . . You never know your luck.'

He steps a bit closer, holding the bundle out to me. Nick Quinn's eyes look out at me from the top sheet.

'But why, Nee?' he says and I want to tell him not to call me that any more. He doesn't have the right, even if we have just screwed on the kitchen sofa. 'What purpose does this serve?'

I force myself to look at him. The kind concern on his face makes me want to smack it. It's the same expression Carmen wore the other day. The 'oh poor Nina is behaving weirdly' look.

236

I'm so very angry with everyone. Was this there, dormant, before that night? Or did the experience of being held hostage cause some fundamental change inside me?

'Ian,' I say in a low, controlled voice. 'It was a very, very strange night. I don't think you can really understand it if you weren't here.' I pause and draw breath. 'I just wanted to get a sense of this Nick Quinn. Whether he might be capable of, well, doing the things Angel and Lucas said he did.'

Ian's frowning deeply as he waves the bundle again before throwing it onto the table.

'Do you really believe he murdered his wife?' he says, his voice rising in incredulity. 'Even if he's a horrible man, it doesn't mean he's a killer, does it?'

This is the exact thought I had earlier but hearing it from him makes me feel more entrenched, rather than less.

'Well,' I say carefully, 'according to Angel, he already is a killer. They think he drove their mother to suicide.'

There is a long pause. I pick up my phone and pretend to check messages, all the while feeling the heat of Ian's gaze on me.

'Look, darling,' says Ian, 'I think you ought to try and get away or something. It can't be good staying here obsessing when you've had such a scary experience. Why don't you go to see Sal until Sam comes home? It's only a week.'

I can feel the stiffening of my spine, spreading up to my shoulders, as if I'm slowly turning to stone.

'First of all,' I say, 'I'm not your "darling" or "Nee" or any of those things. Not any more.'

'I'm sorry,' he starts to say, 'it slipped out and . . .'

But I talk over him. 'And secondly, I'm not some obsessed *nutter* who, who,' I cast around, hearing my voice rising, 'who is being *weird* about this. I'm not being weird! I just wanted to find out more about this man who may or may not be a total monster!'

'And did you?' he says in a gentle voice that enrages me further.

'Yes, I did,' I say, chin raised defiantly. 'I found out lots of useful things actually. And,' I start to say this before I have even consciously made the decision, '. . . I'm planning to go back to the police to talk to them about it.'

I can't tell whether it's scepticism I see written on his face, or that he thinks I'm quite mad.

Then I hear the toot of a car and, with great relief, I say, 'Anyway, there's your taxi.'

He lets out a big sigh and rubs his hand over the top of his head.

'Is there anything I can do to help?' he says, reasonable bastard that he is. 'Do you want me to hang around?'

'No thanks,' I say crisply. 'Just get Sam home safe and sound in a week's time, that's all.' I pause as he moves towards the door. 'And don't worry,' I say, so he turns to look at me again, '*that* . . .' I make a vague gesture at the sofa, 'never happened.'

Ian looks anguished for a moment, like he wants to hug me, then he nods and opens the door.

A few minutes later I think about what I said to him; about going to the police.

Apart from my recent experience, I know about the police only from crime dramas, but I've watched an awful lot of them. Plus, I read the news.

I know that they are short on officers on the ground and resources. They have what seems like a clear-cut case, I imagine. And anyway, maybe Lucas did murder Alice after all.

But my instincts are starting to scream at me. Flaky and

unpleasant she may be, but is Angel telling the truth? What if Lucas is a very damaged boy who is guilty of nothing more than panicking and trying to do right by Zach?

However, I know that instincts are not enough.

If I'm going to go back to the police, I need to find out more.

46

Nina

Press reports about the night Alice Quinn died refer to the couple's home in 'a leafy Hertfordshire village' but I found one report that said it happened in a place called Mirestone. I've never been, but I don't think it's that far from here.

The front of their house was shown in several of the tabloid accounts I find online, usually with grim, salacious headlines involving descriptions like 'murder house' or 'house of horrors'. There are pictures of white-suited CSIs milling around in front of the house but I try to focus on the other details; what the house looks like from outside.

I study the images carefully, looking for any distinguishing features.

It's a substantial, detached Edwardian property with a wide driveway. Stone urns with bay trees sit neatly by the front door. But there are probably loads of houses in that area which look similar. I need something else . . .

There's a large magnolia tree in the front garden. But again – it's not enough.

I keep looking but I'm close to giving up on this no-doubt-stupid idea when I spot what looks like a bus stop just to the left of the house.

I sit back, drumming my fingers on the table. Could I find it by looking at the houses near all the bus stops in that village?

There are no doubt all sorts of clever ways to find people's homes online but I'm going to have to do this the hard way.

The next morning, I dress carefully, in the silky black shirt I wear for important school evenings, my best jeans and boots with a heel. I carefully dry my hair so it's wavy rather than full-on bubblehead, and apply a little eye make-up. I want to look trustworthy; whatever that looks like.

Outside, the sky is stone-coloured with a threat of rain in the air. The temperature is still muggy and oppressive.

It doesn't take long and when I get there I drive around to get a feel for the place.

It's much bigger than I thought; obviously wealthy. The village square has two delis, several restaurants and cafés and some high-end designer shops. A whitewashed pub with tumbling baskets of flowers advertises artisanal gin and wood-fired pizza.

There are many white people in Boden clothes pushing Bugaboos.

There is only one bus that goes through the village and I painstakingly plotted its route, as much as I could, online. I follow the instructions I've written for myself and slow down at each bus stop, checking the houses nearby.

It's boring work. I worry that I look odd and that someone will report me but I press on.

I finally find it on the far side of the village, in the opposite direction to where I live.

As I pull slowly up at the side of the road, it strikes me that Lucas walked miles and miles to my house that night. No wonder he looked so dreadful when he arrived. It must be at least seven miles from here to mine.

I park a little way away and sit in the car for a few moments, gathering myself. I'm not completely sure I have the bottle to do this.

I pull down the driver's mirror and look at myself, wiping away a smudge of make-up under my eye. Then I snap the mirror back decisively, grab my handbag and get out of the car.

I don't even know that anyone will be there, I tell myself. I'm just taking a look. No harm in that.

But my knees are trembling as I start to walk towards the Quinn residence.

I might finally meet this man, who has been living in my head for the last two weeks, along with Angel, Lucas and Zach. And, of course, Alice. I wish I could get them all to leave me alone, but there is no chance of that. Not when I know there is going to be a trial at some point in the future.

I pause at the entrance to the driveway and look up at the house. The windows are all closed, so I'm guessing no one is home. I picture blue lights washing the front of the house. A stretcher with a body bag emerging through that front door.

I shiver and I'm still standing there when I hear someone coming along the pavement behind me. I turn, startled, and see a woman, maybe in her thirties, pushing a pram. Alongside her is a small girl of about five. The woman and the girl both look Middle Eastern, with thick black hair and dark eyes. The mother wears a hijab and the little girl is in a pink T-shirt and shorts. She is holding onto the pram and hopping from one foot to the other, happy curiosity on her face as she looks at her mother and then at me.

The woman is frowning, and I can't work out what she wants from me when she suddenly speaks.

'Excuse me,' she says carefully. 'I go in here.'

'Oh,' I say stepping back, as I realize she is going into the Quinn house. As she passes, I glance down and recognize the little face in the pram.

'Oh!' I say again, stupidly. 'That's Zach!'

Her body language visibly changes and she scrunches over the pram, grabbing the hand of the little girl now and hurrying into the driveway. I have an irrational but nonetheless powerful desire to see Zach again, to see him healthy and well-looked-after.

'Please!' I say. 'Stop! I just want to talk to you, that's all.'

'No journalist,' she says, or rather hisses, pronouncing the word, 'journaleest', and almost runs to the front door. She knocks on it hard and turns to look at me, almost fearfully, as I follow her up the driveway.

'I'm not a journalist!' I call out in desperation. 'I'm Nina. I'm the woman who, who . . .' I cast around, suddenly unwilling to use the word 'hostage'. I settle on, '. . . Who was with Zach on . . . on, that night.'

I'm not sure whether she understands me, because her expression doesn't change at all.

The door opens then and another woman appears there. She's perhaps in her sixties; elegant, with silvery blonde bobbed hair and clothes in various shades of cream and taupe. She's wearing a long, soft cardigan despite the muggy warmth of the air today. A pair of glasses are balanced on her head. She stares curiously at the other woman and then at me and says, 'Nooria, who is this?'

I realize, as if waking up from a dream, that I've made a terrible mistake in coming here.

47

Nina

My instinct is to turn on my heel and flee but I can't bring myself to behave in such a cowardly way. Not with this woman.

Despite my embarrassment and panic my brain throws up the concept that this is Zach's grandmother – it is Alice's mother. I'm here now and I have nothing to lose. Bar getting into trouble with the police, that is, for speaking out of turn before a trial. Best not to think about that.

I try to smile but it is met with stony gazes from the two women, while the little girl looks with curiosity between the three of us, as though there is a puzzle to be deciphered.

'I'm so sorry,' I say. 'I shouldn't be here, but, well, I'm Nina. I'm the woman who was with . . . was with Zach on that terrible night. I just wanted to know that he was alright.'

The two women exchange glances. Alice's mother's face seems to slacken, with a gravity pull of grief perhaps, at the mention of what happened. Then she gathers herself and almost visibly straightens her spine.

'He's fine,' she says and begins to help the other woman, Nooria, I think she said, in with the pram.

I have no idea what to do and, feeling quite flattened, I turn away. What a waste of time. What was I thinking?

'Wait!' The call back takes me so much by surprise that for a second I genuinely think it must be aimed at someone else.

'Please, wait a minute!'

I turn around to see the woman, now holding Zach up against her shoulder, coming down the driveway towards me.

She turns the little boy so he is sitting on her arm, against her chest and facing me. He kicks his legs and gives a happy little squeal. An uncomplicated feeling of warm pleasure floods my chest. I wish I could hold him. We went through a lot together that night, Zach and I.

'Oh Zachy!' says the woman, her voice almost breaking. 'You like this lady, don't you, darling?'

I reach out tentatively and let him grab hold of my finger. He kicks his legs again and gives me a gummy smile; the first I have ever seen from him.

'How are you doing, little guy?' I say and then I remember that his mother is dead and my eyes fill with tears. I look up at his grandmother and see that hers are swimming too.

We both go to speak at the same time.

'Look . . .' I say.

'I'm not sure . . .' she says. We laugh politely, like the well-brought-up women we are, even in this very bizarre and painful situation.

'You first,' she says and I jiggle my finger in Zach's hot little fist to get myself together. It's so very good to see him safe and well.

'I shouldn't have come,' I say, 'but I wanted to tell you how desperately sorry I am about,' I falter, '. . . about Alice.' I pause. 'Am I right in thinking you are her mother?'

245

She nods, tightly, and it seems that she holds Zach a little closer.

'. . . And well,' I say, suddenly letting out a torrent of words. 'It was such a strange night, you see, and I can't seem to . . . I can't seem to . . . move on. I'm sorry!' I extricate my finger and go to turn away. 'I should go.'

I'm struggling not to cry. I think if I start, I may never stop and so I'm reduced to taking deep, gulping breaths as a semblance of keeping control.

'No, please,' she says quickly. 'No one will know if you come in and have something to drink, will they? Please.'

The woman, Nooria, snaps a quick, sharp look at me then lowers her head to her daughter and speaks in a low voice. I wonder what her role is here. A nanny, perhaps.

We walk through a hallway scented with flowers and I see that there are several large vases filled with lilies, roses and gerbera crammed awkwardly on a table. The floorboards gleam golden from a sudden soaking of sunshine through the stained-glass window of the front door.

In the large kitchen, there are more vases of flowers. Some are still wrapped in cellophane and sit looking sad and droopy on the side. Too many flowers. The scent is almost sickly.

I stand awkwardly by the door as the women move comfortably about the space.

Nooria takes Zach and holds him expertly against one shoulder while she starts to prepare a bottle. The little girl, who has been silent the whole time, skips over to a baby doll that is lying on a long sofa and begins to play with it, holding it and crooning quietly in perfect mimicry of a mother.

I'm wondering where Nick Quinn is right now. What I'll

246

do if he walks into the room. My heart starts to thud uncomfortably hard.

Alice's mother washes her hands at the sink and then turns to look at me.

I find that I have been staring down at the floor, wondering whether this is where Alice died. I can't stop my brain from conjuring dark blood against the creamy stone tiles.

Our eyes meet and I start, as if caught out. It feels as though my thoughts were written on my face, like some prurient gawper. My cheeks flush.

'I'm Jennifer Sommerton,' she says. 'And I believe you are . . . Nina, is it?'

I smile eagerly, grateful to move on from the awkward moment. 'Nina Bailey,' I say.

'Come in and take a seat,' she says easily. 'What can I get you to drink?'

'Just something cold if you have it,' I say. I'm sweating, partly from stress, and it's making it hard to think through how I should handle this.

'Orange juice?' offers Jennifer and I nod gratefully.

She pours a glass for me and water for herself and picks them up. As she walks towards me she turns briefly and says, 'Nooria?'

The other woman looks up from the sink, where she is testing milk from the bottle against the back of her hand.

'Can you bring Zach's stuff to the front door so I can get everything in the car?' says Jennifer. 'I'm intending to leave after lunch to beat the traffic on the M3.'

Nooria nods and turns back to the sink. Zach grumbles and turns his little face into her shoulder. My body reacts, remembering exactly how he had felt, this poor, cross little boy who didn't even know about the immense hole that had been torn in his life.

She leads me into a large, comfortable sitting room with the same oak floorboards and tasteful grey sofas. The floor is taken up with a kilim, no doubt from Quinn's Middle Eastern travels, shot through with shades of blood red, gold and pea green. On the wall, there is some sort of ancient-looking Arabic writing in a frame and over the fireplace is the most beautiful mirror, surrounded by lapis lazuli tiles. It's all so tasteful and beautiful in here. Hard to imagine that this is a house in which a murder took place.

On the mantelpiece, there is a large black and white wedding photo; a close-up of Alice and Quinn's faces. She looks stunning; so fresh and pretty, vivid lipstick on a mouth stretched into a wide, happy smile, showing perfect teeth. She is turning to him and his face is lowered towards hers. You can't really see much of his actual expression. Again, he feels just out of reach, even in this special moment.

Jennifer gestures for me to sit and places the orange juice on a tile mat on the coffee table in front of me.

There is a brief, awkward silence and I feel a hot surge of panic about being here. Quinn could surely walk in any moment. It feels crucial that I get this right.

'Thank you,' I say, after taking a sip of my juice. 'Are you taking a trip?' I feel bold and blush a little as Jennifer Sommerton coolly meets my eye.

'Yes,' she says after a moment and lowers her eyes. 'I'm taking Zach back to Devon with me for a while.'

I'm desperate to ask why. But I have to be careful. My 'Oh yes?' is met only by a cool nod.

'I'm so dreadfully sorry about your daughter,' I say, glancing up at the wedding photo again.

Jennifer follows my gaze and I see a quick frown pass across her face; almost a wince. I presume it is the sight of her daughter's face on what must have been one of her happiest days. But maybe there is something else? Her eyes linger there for a moment before coming back to rest wearily on mine.

'I'm glad I got to meet you,' she says, with a small, tight smile. 'I know that Zach was clean and well looked after that . . .' she swallows, 'that night. The police told me that you went to great lengths to care for him.'

I return her smile, gently. 'I only did what anyone would,' I say and she frowns again.

She lifts her glass of water to take a sip and her hand shakes a little.

'I'm not so sure,' she says when she has drunk and replaced the glass back on the table. 'It doesn't sound as though much was done by those . . .' I can hear the quickening of her breath even from here, 'by those other two.'

I'm not sure how to respond to this. It is, after all, the truth. But I'm beginning to think there may have been more complex factors at play.

'He's a beautiful little boy,' I say pointlessly and, just for a moment, her face lights up with a proper smile.

'He is,' she says. 'He really is. And probably too young to understand what he has lost.' She says this with admirable control. Her eyes are dry and it's only the deep grooves at the sides of her mouth that give away the grief etched into her.

I decide to be bold. I can't sit here all afternoon.

'And how is,' I pause, nervously, 'his dad? Mr Quinn? How is he doing with it all?'

Jennifer lifts the water and takes another birdlike sip, avoiding my eyes. I can't tell if I have imagined the slight stiffening in her shoulders.

'It's rather hard to tell,' she says, with a false, bright tone. 'We have barely seen him since it happened.'

'Oh,' I say, wrongfooted by her sudden openness. 'I'm sorry to hear that,' I add carefully. 'Where is he now?'

Jennifer looks at me sharply then and my stomach clenches. I hope she doesn't think I am here because of Quinn's fame; wanting to grab a little bit of the dim lime-light surrounding a celebrity tragedy.

'I wish I could tell you,' she says. 'The BBC seem to have required his services out of the country almost constantly since my daughter was killed.'

I don't know what to say to this. It sort of thuds onto the floor in front of us. She suddenly looks weary, and draws her cardigan around her shoulders before getting to her feet.

'Now I really must get on,' she says. 'I hope you won't think me rude. I do want to have lunch and then beat the traffic.'

'Oh, of course, of course,' I say, getting hurriedly to my feet. But now I've got this far, I'm reluctant to leave.

'It must be hard for,' I pause, 'Mr Quinn. He's lucky to have you to help with Zach.'

Jennifer frowns at me and is about to say something when, on cue, Zach begins to cry in the kitchen. She rises and I follow her out of the room.

Damn. I feel like she was on the verge of saying something important then.

I am thinking of how I can coax more information from her without directly discussing the trial as I follow her through to the kitchen, when I see her swipe at her eyes. A bolt of hot guilt goes through me. I'm only upsetting her, being here. Reminding her of the night her own child was stabbed to death.

'Let me take him,' she says to Nooria, 'and you can show Nina out.'

The message is clear. I've overstayed my welcome and need to go.

Nooria looks at me with the same frank assessment as before. There's something oddly defiant in her eyes that I don't understand. The little girl now playing on the floor looks up, as though automatically connected to her mother's movements.

'It was good to meet you, Nina,' says Jennifer, rocking Zach in her arms and managing a thin smile. 'And I do appreciate all that you did for Zach.'

I don't know how to respond, other than to say, 'Take care, Jennifer,' and then I touch Zach's hot little back for a moment and say, 'Bye Zach. Be good for your grandma.'

I can hear Jennifer singing in a low voice to Zach as we reach the front door. Nooria is about to close the front door on me without saying a single word so just before the door closes, I hiss, 'Wait!'

She pauses, suspicion tightening her brow.

'What do you really want?' she says in a low voice.

'I want,' I pause, trying to think how to frame my thoughts. 'I want to know whether you think Lucas did this.'

Her eyes flare wide for a moment, melting her otherwise haughty expression.

She gives the slightest shake of her head and my heart seems to jerk inside my chest. Then she says, 'I can't . . .' and, 'I'm sorry. I have Asefa to think of.' She begins to close the door.

'Wait!' I say, too loud. 'I just want to—'

'I said no!' The strength of her reply makes me flinch and when I go to respond I find I'm talking to a closed door.

48

Nina

I walk slowly down the driveway, my thoughts seeming to knock against each other like snooker balls, crashing and swerving in new directions.

What have I gained from this?

I'm so lost in thought, I almost bump into the swarthy man coming the other way. He looks Arabic, with thick black hair and a neat beard that looks fashionable rather than religious. We both apologize and then he disappears up the Quinn driveway. Delivery man, perhaps.

I give him no more thought as I try and analyse that moment with Nooria.

I don't know whether she was agreeing with my statement or it was more of a 'I can't believe your lack of tact' sort of head shake. I mean, I don't *know*. But I do strongly suspect that she was saying that, no, Lucas wasn't capable of murdering Alice Quinn.

It feels like some kind of evidence.

And where was Nick Quinn? Alice's mother was far too well-brought-up and controlled to badmouth him but I could tell there was something dark there; a frisson of bad feeling when she talked about his absence.

But what does it all *mean*?

I'm on the pavement now and I emit a small shriek of frustration, before looking around wildly to see if anyone is looking at me. A car with blacked-out windows is coming along the street and I find myself watching as it pulls up outside the house opposite the Quinns'. The rich really are a different species.

Large gates open slowly to let it in and I notice the swivelling eye of a CCTV camera on the corner of the gate.

As the car disappears behind the grandiose gates, it strikes me that whoever lives there is very concerned with their privacy. It's unlikely that it would be able to monitor the front of the Quinn house because the driveway is hidden behind hedges. But maybe it's something to go on?

A light rain begins to patter about me, lifting a warm scent from the pavement.

I feel a bit sick when I see the red-brick building of the police station. I've parked in the multi-storey and walked here, hoping to prepare myself as much as I can on the way.

Rehearsing what I'm going to say in my mind for the tenth time, I walk inside and go to the main desk there. I can feel myself shrinking a little, remembering that queasy early morning when I came here to make a statement.

I'm asked what I want and for a moment I get in such a flap that the name of the relevant officers goes right out of my head.

The young police officer, his face studded with acne, looks at me with a tired expression until one of the names comes to me.

'Can I speak to Detective, er, Gilbey please?' I say. I'm sure that was his name, the big man with the curly grey hair.

'What's it regarding?'

I make myself stand a little straighter.

'The murder of Alice Quinn,' I say in a clear voice and he frowns, then tells me to take a seat on one of the broken plastic bucket chairs opposite.

I don't know how much time passes, but let's say it is long enough for me to need both a wee and a drink of water, and for my coccyx to start to throb from the unforgiving seat.

Various people come and go; mainly police officers with bursts of static from their radios, and the occasional member of the public coming in to have earnest conversations with the policeman on the desk, most of which he parries with the same efficient but deeply world-weary air.

When the doors to my left swing open for what seems like the millionth time, I look over to see the red-haired policewoman who was part of the raid on my house. I remember thinking that she had an extraordinary physical confidence for someone who must barely reach five feet four.

Her eyes are like bright chocolate buttons in her face as she regards me.

'Nina,' she says. 'What can I do for you?' Her voice isn't unfriendly, but there is a sense of forbearance in her tone. As if whatever I have come to say is only adding to an annoying day.

A few minutes later we're at her desk in a busy office. There's a *Game of Thrones* mug that's spiky with pens and a place mat that reads: *I'm no good at advice . . . can I interest you in a sarcastic comment?* Her screen saver is of a little girl; clearly her child judging by the red curls tumbling around the impish face.

She offers me tea or coffee ('To be fair, they look and taste much the same here') and I decline.

As she regards me with her quick, sharp eyes, I feel myself

liking her. I decide she isn't the sort of person to muck about. So I don't either.

'I'm concerned that Lucas is innocent of Alice's murder,' I say, clenching my fists discreetly so she can't see the tremor that has begun in my hands.

Her expression doesn't change as she reaches for a pad of paper and a pen on her desk.

'And why's that?' she says in an even tone. Not dismissive. But not intrigued either.

I pause for a moment. I am determined not to come across like a fruitcake.

'Well,' I lean forward a little for emphasis, 'I keep thinking about what I was told that night about Nick Quinn. What Angel told me.'

Gilbey frowns. 'Yes, that was all part of your statement, I believe.'

'I know that,' I say, carefully. 'But I have been looking into him a bit and I think there's definitely something that's not right.'

She's really giving me the dead eye now, and gently tapping her pen against the pad. She hasn't written down a single word yet.

'When you say you've been *looking into him*,' she says, 'what does that mean exactly?'

It's impossible not to squirm. I feel like I am fourteen and in the headmistress's office or something. I force myself to stop being so pathetic and meet her look with a stern one of my own. I have good reason for being here.

'Look,' I say, 'I know how this works.' She manages to raise a single eyebrow at this, quite impressively. I go on regardless. 'You've got very little resources these days and it appears that this case is straightforward. I wish it was. Believe me when I say I don't want to be having this conversation either.'

Something shifts in her expression and it encourages me, even though I can't read what she is thinking.

'But what I'm saying,' I continue, 'is that I know for a fact Quinn has a history of domestic violence and you ought to at least check him out a bit more thoroughly before assuming that someone as damaged and vulnerable as Lucas is the person who should be in prison.'

She's silent for a few minutes and then says, 'How do you know for a fact about this supposed violence?'

To my irritation I feel a slight heat in my own cheeks then. I maybe stretched that a little bit.

'I spoke to an ex-girlfriend,' I said. 'And she basically said Quinn ruined her life for a while. And that he was dangerous.'

Gilbey pulls the pad closer. 'So, she'll go on the record with that? What's her name?'

I give a frustrated sigh. 'Well, no, I'm certain she won't. She's moved on, you see, and told me she wouldn't talk about it again.'

I can almost feel the energy seeping out of the policewoman in front of me.

She puts the pen down and uncrosses her legs.

'Look,' she says, 'Nina . . . I'm grateful to you for trying to do the right thing here, but sometimes . . . when someone has . . . gone through an event like the one you did, there's a strange sort of kinship that develops with the people who have all the power.'

I look back into her eyes, which are kind. Irritatingly so.

'Are you suggesting I have Stockholm Syndrome?' I say, barely able to contain my disgust. 'That's the most ridiculous thing I've ever heard!'

'Please, don't raise your voice,' she says reasonably. I wasn't even aware I had and the chastisement gives me a cold jolt in my stomach. The pause is useful though because

I was just about to mention Nooria and who knows what trouble I might be in, if they find out I have been to the Quinn house today.

'Look,' I say, trying to smile in what I hope is a reasonable, not-mad way. 'Can I just say one more thing? Make a suggestion?'

She nods her assent, then wipes a hand wearily across her face.

'Well,' I say, 'have you checked whether Quinn was at the house at any other time that evening? If he only arrived back and found his wife dead, then he wouldn't be seen on any CCTV cameras just after the murder happened, would he?'

I can't stop myself from beaming with excitement as I say this. I feel so clever. Unstoppable, actually.

'Right,' says Gilbey in a reasonable tone, 'so you're suggesting that in a *murder* enquiry, we haven't already checked all the relevant CCTV, is that it?'

I can feel the slow creep of a horrible embarrassment for the second time this afternoon.

'No,' I say, blushing. 'But I just wanted to be sure, you know.'

Gilbey switches on a bright smile and stands up, clearly signifying I've wasted enough of her time.

'Right, well thank you for coming in, Nina,' she says, as I stand up miserably. 'I'll certainly take your thoughts into account. Now let me show you back to reception.'

We start to walk back down the narrow corridor and I feel so defeated I can barely drag myself along.

As we reach the doors to reception again, I turn to her.

'Please,' I say desperately. 'I think he's one of those men who gets away with it. I think he might be the kind who stays under the radar for years and destroys women's lives.'

For a moment, I think there is some spark of interest in

257

her eyes and then she holds out her hand and thanks me for coming in again.

That's it. There's nothing more I can do. I just have to trust the criminal justice system now and try to pick up the pieces of my life.

49

Angel

Angel stares down at the red droplets dotting the toilet paper and then wipes a little harder. There is only a little bit. Hardly anything, really.

She's almost as surprised to see that her hand is shaking as at the sight of blood. Leaning over and opening the bathroom cupboard, she rummages for the package of sanitary towels at the back. Better to be safe than sorry. Humiliating enough to have to go and report to the police station in the first place without worrying about bleeding everywhere.

Plus, she has to work later.

Ron-the-creep had pretended he needed persuading to have her back; going on about criminal elements and how he *reads the news like everyone else.* But she had made sad eyes at him and even touched his fat arm as she assured him she was going to be a 'really good girl'. He'd almost come in his pants as he pretended to reluctantly agree to a temporary contract.

Leon is getting up in the bedroom next door and she hears his loud yawn and then humming as he looks for his running gear.

She hasn't told him yet. Maybe she won't even have to now.

Breakfast is swift.

She still doesn't feel sick exactly, but most food feels a bit alien in her mouth. There are so many textures and smells in food that she hasn't noticed before. She is particularly off the various forms of meat that Leon favours for breakfast, lunch and dinner. Angel has mainly been living on Coco Pops and plain crisps.

Outside, the world feels oppressed by the thick, white cloud encasing the sky and the air is unpleasantly sticky. Angel realizes she has come out without an umbrella – again – and grimaces as she makes her way to the bus stop, hoping it's not going to piss down.

She has to take two buses to get to the police station, which is at the opposite end of town to the restaurant. As she strap-hangs on the first bus she looks down at a woman about her own age who has a baby in a sling against her chest. The baby is one of those unattractive ones with a big, bald head that's laced with something yellow and crusty. But the woman keeps looking down at it as though there has never been a more beautiful creation.

Angel can't stop watching her. She wonders if the woman is having to work at this love, like making sure you get your five-a-day or flossing your teeth. Or maybe it really is coming naturally to her. Then she thinks about her own mother – something she allows herself to do only in small, swift curtain-lifts in her brain – and concludes that, for some, love is easy.

Too easy, perhaps, when you think where it got her.

She has a two-hour slot to do the business at the police station and is in no hurry. It always makes her feel like some scumbag, the whole process. Like someone who belongs among the drunks and thieves and prozzies traipsing in and out all day.

Plus, it only highlights the fact that she is free; to an extent. And Lucas is in prison going through stuff she is too frightened to think about.

She's asked her solicitor to find out how he is but not heard anything back yet. She decides she will chase him later.

Once off the first bus, Angel looks up at the sky and sees there is a brightening beneath it, the sun starting to burn through.

She has plenty of time and the smells of other humans on the bus were starting to get to her, so she decides to walk the rest of the way to the police station, along the canal. This morning's weirdness seems to have stopped anyway, which is either good news or bad news. She has no idea which.

Maybe a walk will help her clear her head about it all.

Angel crosses the road and heads down the stone steps to the towpath. She slowly ambles along the river and under the bridge, her footsteps ringing out.

The heavy footfall behind her seems to come from nowhere.

She doesn't even have time to turn round before the blow lands.

50

Lucas

When Lucas was five and Angel eight, his sister had gone for her first sleepover with someone from school.

She had been annoying about it for days, telling her brother that she was going to be given as much cake and chocolate as she wanted to eat, and be allowed to stay up until one in the morning if she wanted to. Lucas remembered how brightly the envy had burned at his sister's exciting life.

This was in the time before Quinn entered their lives. Lucas remembers only a normal dull evening of fish fingers and spaghetti hoops in front of *Brookside*, which Marianne loved because she came from Liverpool.

Those kind of good/boring evenings, lacking in drama, became something he craved later. But at the time, they were the fabric of his day-to-day existence. Later that night, though, Lucas had woken with sharp pains in his stomach. He hadn't made it across the coarse blue carpet of his bedroom before the sour sick was pumping out of him.

He called for Marianne and she came quickly, looking sleepy and concerned, before swiftly getting Lucas into the bathroom and beginning the process of cleaning him up.

But what he remembered most, as he sat shivering in the bathroom that was never warm enough, was that he felt instantly better in his stomach after the evilness had been expelled. What was worse, though, was that he suddenly wanted his sister more than anyone in the world and had begun to cry in a way that Marianne couldn't understand or begin to placate.

He hadn't been mortally scared before then. That was a feeling he would wear like a heavy coat in the years to come, but for now, this corrosive dread was something new.

Marianne had been annoyed with him when he said, 'Something's wrong with Angel.' It had frightened her and once she was sure he wasn't going to be sick again, she had told him off for being silly and then brought him into bed with her, where he lay wide awake, like an ice block for most of the night.

When the phone rang at five am, Lucas hadn't been surprised at all. He had quietly gone back to his room and got dressed, while his mother spoke on the phone to the mother of Angel's friend, Soraya.

She said that Angel seemed to be very sick and they had called an ambulance and Marianne should meet them there.

Marianne had given Lucas a strange, wild-eyed look, then kissed the top of his head and called him a clever boy.

Lucas is now lying awake on the top bunk in his cell, shivering so hard his jaw hurts. His body is coated in a slimy cold sweat and his stomach is roiling as though he is at sea.

He had been dreaming about his sister. She had been sitting in the cell with him and taking the piss about how lazy he was lately. It was nice. It felt so real, especially when she grimaced at the toilet in the cell and made jokes about what she called the Wanking Russian.

But then, out of nowhere, she opened her mouth and began to scream at the top of her voice. Lucas couldn't make her stop. She just carried on screaming, her face quite impassive, almost curious.

He rubs his sweaty face now. He can't shake the dirty remnants of the dream away, like they are cobwebs that cling to him.

Angel.

He sits up in bed, as far as he can without banging his head, and leans on his elbows. He is wide awake and can hear the loud nasal rumble of his room companion's snoring below so the whole frame of the bed vibrates with it.

What has he done? He has disappeared inside himself here and let his sister deal with everything alone. And now he can't shake off the feeling that something bad is happening to her. Something he should be able to stop.

The feeling is intolerable and the room seems to shrink around him, encasing him in a tomb. He throws his legs over the side of the bed and dangles his feet down, leaning forward with his head in his hands and trying to slow his galloping heartbeat and shallow breathing.

The sharp slap against the sole of his foot is a surprise.

'The fuck you doing?' says the Russian, his already gravelly voice even coarser with sleep. 'Is middle of fucking night. Lie the fuck down before I cut you throat.'

Lucas forces himself to lie back again and stares up at the ceiling. Lights stream in around the edges of the door. It's never dark here.

He starts to think about that night. How Marianne had been full of wonder the next day and claimed Lucas had a

264

'premonition' about his sister's appendicitis. It had only happened that one time.

But he can't get it out of his head now.

Angel. There's something wrong.

51

Nina

Sam's almost home.

Only an hour until they touch down at Heathrow. I think they will probably get here about three, allowing for traffic on the M25. I thought about meeting them at the airport, but concluded it would be too strange, seeing them looking like a family. So, I decided that the best thing would be to make the house feel as welcoming as possible.

I can't wait to see my boy. The fridge is stuffed with all his favourite things, from Pepsi Max to fresh mango to jumbo hotdogs for dinner.

I don't care if he's had unhealthy stuff on holiday. If anything, he's more likely to have been force-fed sophisticated adult food from what I've heard. Well, there will be no moules or fois gras here. It's going to be wall-to-wall comfort food if that's what he wants. He's not the only one who might be craving it.

I need all the comfort I can get, right now.

I've been busy cleaning bathrooms and hoovering and now I'm having a quick sandwich in front of the lunchtime news on the telly. It's just for company, really; a new, rather tragic habit. The local news reporter talks about a robbery at a betting shop and then about a violent mugging on the canal. The suspect was captured on a CCTV camera and there is a shot of his face, quite clear, but I am distracted and don't pay much attention. They move on to a story about a woman celebrating her hundred and tenth birthday.

I switch it off. I'll stop having this need for noise when Sam's home. It will be so good to have him back under this roof again. I need normality and a boy's chatter to exorcise the ghosts still lingering after That Night. Hopefully it will stop me obsessing about it all.

I've already put all the paper from that strange feverish research in the recycling bin. I'm telling myself that if I do ordinary things, then I'll stop thinking about it all the time. It isn't really working, but having Sam home will help, I'm sure it will. I just need to resume my life, and to stop going over things I can't change and don't really understand.

That's not even to mention the ridiculous thing that happened with Ian. I bitterly regret what we did. But more than anything, I find myself despising him a bit for it. *Make up your mind about what you want.* Stupid man.

In Sam's bedroom, I dump the pile of clean bedding on his chair and then lift off his blue and white Chelsea duvet from the bed. As I begin to unsnap the buttons on the cover, something flutters to my feet. I reach down and pick up the unfamiliar photo, puzzled for a moment. This isn't Sam's. Then realization dawns.

Lucas lay down in here. That night, or rather morning.

It's a Polaroid picture, which gives it even more of a retro feel than its mere age should. But there is something about the lighting too, bleached a little and faded by handling.

It shows a woman perhaps in her thirties and two children; quite recognizably Angel and Lucas. Angel is mugging furiously; standing on one leg and thrusting the other out to the side, bony knees emerging from red shorts. Her hair is short and bushy and she looks like a handful, but also enormous fun.

Lucas was clearly an adorable little boy. He is giggling; his two front teeth are missing and the curve inwards of his skinny little chest suggests the woman's hand on his chest is tickling him. He looks like he is squirming with pleasure. There is a shaggy old Golden Retriever at his feet.

I sit down on the bed and study the woman. Marianne, I think Angel said she was called.

She was very beautiful, with thick honey-blonde hair and wide eyes. Dressed in a short pink sundress she looks so fresh and young. A slow wave of sadness washes over me at the thought of her taking her own life. And for Lucas to find her. No wonder he is such a messed-up person, and Angel too.

This photo must be very special to him and I hate to think that he was lying in this bed looking at it, maybe before he did that crazy thing on the road. I wish there was some way I could get it back to him. Maybe when the trial happens, I might find a way to pass it to the defence team . . .

The very thought of going to court makes me want to be sick. I've been warned it may be months and months until it happens. With a sigh, I put the photo in the pocket of my jeans and start changing Sam's bed. But all the energy I had for his homecoming is turning in the wrong direction now and I can feel my mind being yanked obsessively back onto its usual hamster-wheel.

What if Lucas goes to prison for a murder he didn't commit? And Nick Quinn gets to carry on as he has always done, possibly going on to hurt more women and ruin more lives? Zach might be living with his grandmother for now, but the time may come when he goes back into that house.

When he learns how to be a man from Nick Quinn.

I quickly stuff the duvet into a new cover and pillows into fresh cases. After snapping a new fitted sheet onto the bed, I pick up the dirty bedding and take it to the laundry basket on the landing. My mind is whirring with an idea that has brought a storm of butterflies to my stomach. I know I must leave it alone.

But there's still ages until Sam gets back. I've got plenty of time.

The thing is, I'm certain that Nooria woman knew something she wasn't saying.

I can just make one last attempt to speak to her. She may not even be there now that the baby has gone off with his grandmother. If she is there, she might slam the door in my face. I have to try, though.

I'll have one last go. There's no harm. Then I'll leave it alone and wait for a chance to speak in court. Move on with my life.

As I hurry down the stairs, I decide this will be the dividing line of my summer; a demarcation line between the horrible dark events of that night and my normal life as a schoolteacher and mother to Sam. I'll be able to enjoy hanging out with my son much more if I know I really did try to make this right.

Grabbing my car keys and handbag, I make for the front door. As I'm about to leave, though, I think of something.

It's still there; the scrap of paper with Angel's mobile number on it.

I know I shouldn't contact her – for all the reasons she couldn't be here in my house. But I need her to know that things have changed in my mind. It feels important that she knows someone is at least beginning to believe her.

I'll send her a quick text, let her know that I am going to speak to Nooria, and then I'll go over there and have one last attempt at making things right before Sam comes home and my life is able to move on.

52

Lucas

Lucas can see the slight surprise on his solicitor's face as he is led into the room. He hopes it is because he is properly awake and on his game. But, equally, it might be that he looks even worse than when they last met.

Shah looks immaculate in a charcoal suit and pale blue shirt, smelling of an aftershave Lucas recognizes but can't name. Lucas feels disgusting in comparison and hates that his body slightly reacts with attraction to the other man. Another consequence of coming off the drugs, he supposes.

For the last couple of days now he's been refusing the diazepam he has been offered and, even though the panic is swirling like an oily pool just below the surface, he knows he must stay on top of things.

'Did you find out anything about my sister?' he says after they shake hands and sit down at the Formica-topped table.

Shah frowns as he pulls papers out of his brown leather briefcase and places them neatly before him.

'I'm afraid all I know,' he says, frowning, 'is that she didn't check in to the police station yesterday as she was due to.'

Lucas feels an icy tickle up the back of his neck.

'What do you mean, *didn't check in*?'

Shah's dark eyes look serious as he gazes back at Lucas. 'As part of her conditions for bail,' he says, 'she is required to report to the police station twice a week. It seems this didn't happen yesterday. I expect if she doesn't go in today, then she's going to be in serious trouble.'

Lucas sits forward and places both his hands down on the table to stop them shaking.

'I think something has happened to her,' he says. 'I can feel it.'

Shah's expression doesn't suggest that he thinks Lucas is an idiot, for which Lucas feels immense gratitude.

'Well,' says Shah after a moment. 'I'll find out for you whether she goes in today. Let you know if I hear anything, OK?' He pauses. 'Try not to worry, Lucas,' he says. 'There's absolutely nothing you can do from here. I'm sure she's OK. But your sister will find herself in prison if she breaks the terms of her bail, I'm afraid.'

Lucas's mind is whirring. It would be just like Angel to stick a finger up to the police and take off. At least it would if it were just *her* in trouble. But when he is already in prison and about to go on trial for a murder he didn't commit? No. Something isn't sitting right here.

Shah begins to sort through his bundle of papers, lifting a sheet to the top.

'So,' he says, 'we have the date of the plea hearing. It will be next Monday, the twenty-fifth.' He slides the paper towards Lucas, but Lucas doesn't look at it. Shah continues, patiently. 'At this hearing,' he says, 'the charges against you will be heard and you will get the opportunity to make a plea of guilty or not guilty, which we can talk through. The date for the actual trial will be set then too.' He pauses. 'Do you want to ask me anything so far?'

Lucas's stomach is churning. He nods slightly.

'Yes,' he says. 'There's still time then?'

Shah frowns. 'What do you mean, exactly?' he says. 'Time?'

'To tell you the truth,' says Lucas. 'About what really happened that night.'

53

Lucas

Lucas wasn't working that day, which was just as well because the van was in the garage waiting for a new gearbox. All day he had felt restless and couldn't really settle to anything. The ever-pressing heat didn't help. He'd only seen her once or twice since the little boy had been born. She had stayed with her mother for a while afterwards. He'd made all the right noises when she showed him Zach for the first time, but it had felt too strange. He had quickly made himself scarce, citing urgent garden jobs.

When his phone buzzed with a text at seven pm he was lying on his bed, desultorily flicking through Facebook; something he did only very rarely.

It was from Alice. He sat up quickly and swung his legs round to sit on the side of the bed.

You here tomorrow? Ax the message read. Lucas had pressed his number on her some time ago, without explaining why she might need it, and they had exchanged a few texts about his working hours, but the kiss was something new. *Entirely possible that it was a mistake and she was right now kicking herself*, he thought.

He hesitated and replied. Sorry. Van knackered and it

wasn't in the diary anyway. He added an *L* and contemplated adding an *x*, but decided against it.

The message showed as 'read', then Lucas watched the grey speech bubble with three dots pulsing on the screen, signifying that Alice was replying. But no message arrived. He waited for several minutes but still there was no response.

He let out a frustrated groan and glared down at the screen as if he could will the message into existence.

Had she deleted it before sending?

Before he could talk himself out of it, he tapped out another message:

Everything ok?

An agonizing few seconds passed before the bubble appeared again, this time followed by the words: Not really.

Lucas's heart was thumping. He knew he may be overstepping the mark now, but he replied: Want me to come over?

He stared down at three floating bubbles for several long seconds then read, just: Yes x

It took almost two hours to get there, on three different buses. On the way he wondered whether he was making a terrible fool of himself.

When Alice opened the door, she gave a wan smile and said, 'I shouldn't have dragged you all the way over here,' but without much conviction. She was wearing a baggy white jumper with a roll neck, even though the heat had been an assault all day. Her face was pale and drawn, her lips dry-looking and chapped. She kept gnawing on them and bringing her hand with its small blunt fingers to her cheek and then away as though brushing something unseen away. Her hair looked greasy at the roots.

They went through to the kitchen, which looked so clean it was though no one had used it for days.

Zach was in his Moses basket on the table, his face turned to the side, so he was all curved cheek. Alice grimaced and lifted a finger to her lips and then seesawed her hand. Clearly, things could still go either way on the nap front.

She gestured for Lucas to go with her through to the sitting room, a place that had put Lucas on edge the few times he had peered in there. He much preferred the large kitchen, generally Alice's favoured place to hang out too, it seemed, from the amount of time she spent there.

Lucas felt uneasy as soon as they entered the room. It smelled strongly of cleaning products and was far too hot. The room had an oddly unused feel, like no one had ever slumped on the sofa and relaxed in here, despite all the comforts on offer. There was more evidence, too, of Quinn's life than in the kitchen.

He averted his eyes quickly from the large wedding photo on the sitting room mantelpiece, but there were other things too: copies of an Arabic journal underneath the coffee table, plus some artefacts and art. In fact, the framed Koranic script on the wall was something that had been hung for the first time in Lucas's childhood home. It had been some kind of gift he'd received on his travels.

Alice sank back onto the sofa and waved for Lucas to sit too. She didn't speak. The clock in the hallway thunked the passing seconds with laboured significance.

'He's away for a couple of days,' she said, 'in case you were wondering.' It brought the unspoken issue right into the room, which was a relief and also a surprise to Lucas. He waited for her to elaborate but she was quiet, staring downwards as she worried at a fingernail with her thumb. The room was so quiet he could hear the *thwick-thwick* sound this made.

'Alice,' said Lucas tentatively after a few moments had

passed. 'Has something happened?' He took a breath. Had to handle this properly. 'Are you . . . are you, hurt?'

Alice's head had snapped up at this and when she met Lucas's eyes, her own were blurred and brimming.

'I'm so selfish, Luke,' she'd said in a small voice. 'I have all this . . .' she swept her arm around to encompass the house before going on, '. . . and I have Zach and I have Nick. But I'm still *ungrateful*.'

Hearing her use this word – the very one Quinn had liked to lob into their faces like a rock whenever he was in one of his drunken rages – had the effect of shooting Lucas full of crackling, fizzing adrenaline. His breathing became shallow and he had to take a moment to steady his voice before replying.

'Why would you say that?' he said. 'You're not.' Alice covered her face and started to cry, her narrow shoulders shaking.

Lucas could hold back no longer. He'd been watching and waiting for five months now, trying to protect Alice from the side-lines. It was too much, seeing her like this.

He found himself down on his knees in front of her, the wooden floor hard beneath him. She looked at him as he took hold of her hands, a hopeful look on her face. There was no surprise or wariness at all at his audacity, which spurred him on.

'I have to tell you something,' he'd said in a low voice. 'And it might be hard to hear but I need you to understand that everything I've done has been for the best reasons.'

Alice's hands had jerked out of his. She looked a little scared now. But she had to know.

So, Lucas told her that her husband had been his step-father and that he had driven his mother to her grave. He told her that he had tried to put the past behind him, but when he learned about Nick's return to Britain and

277

marriage to Alice, he'd felt he had to find a way to warn her. The words tumbling out of his mouth felt so inadequate to the task required of them. How could he possibly make her understand? It had never gone down quite like this in his imagination.

Alice had followed it all without speaking; her brow was furrowed, and her jaw kept clenching and unclenching as she studied his moving lips carefully.

Finally, he had run out of words.

There was a moment's pause, an elastic feeling of time stretching between them, and then Alice had jumped to her feet in one swift movement.

'So, what, you're some sort of *stalker*, is that it?' she said in a loud, quavering voice.

Lucas clambered to his feet, more awkwardly, so he was standing opposite her.

'No, no,' he'd said desperately. 'It's not like that! I just wanted to make sure he wasn't doing it again . . .' he swallowed, '. . . the thing he does. And when I got to know you, I wanted that even more.'

He was searching for what else to say when, in a clear, hard voice, Alice had said, 'Who even are you? Is Luke your real name?'

Lucas had made an anguished face, beseeching her to understand. 'It's close enough,' he said. 'My name is actually Lucas.'

Alice had walked abruptly out of the room then and gone back to the kitchen. Uncertainly, Lucas had followed. She had her head down and was breathing hard, her chest rising and falling at speed as she pointed to the French windows.

'Get out,' she'd said. 'Get out right now before I call the police on you.'

'But Alice . . .' he'd started to say, and she had screamed

at him then, grabbing his arm and dragging him across the room.

'Get out, get out!'

He began to walk, as fast as he could in the opposite direction.

He found a bench by the churchyard and sat down, sinking his head into his hands. His body felt as though it were made of lead.

He couldn't believe he'd played it so badly. What was he expecting? That Alice would greet his revelation with *gratitude*? He was an idiot. His sister would have told him that within minutes of him embarking on this enterprise, he was sure. If only he'd told her.

When his phone beeped with a message he almost ignored it. He was too upset to deal with anyone. Then he saw Alice's name on the display and his stomach twisted with hope.

Please come back.

That was all it said.

Alice opened the door quickly. He came inside and enveloped her in his arms, without even thinking it through.

She had clung to him, and Lucas had felt a sense of wonder at holding her. There was no thought of Zach at this moment, but all was quiet anyway.

Then Alice was pulling him through to the sitting room and drawing his face down to hers.

He started to say, 'Alice, I don't think we should . . .' but he was overtaken by the feeling.

Apart from some experimental teenage fumblings, it was his first time with a woman and, despite the strange otherness of this whole scenario, Lucas had felt a sense of wonder that female lips were really no different. The softness of her body was unfamiliar though after the harder male angles he was used to but he felt himself getting lost in her as they sank onto the sofa, tugging at clothes.

Afterwards, they'd lain there in silence for a moment and then, in a quiet voice, Alice began to tell him what life had really been like in that house while Lucas watched and waited in the garden.

There hadn't been any physical violence, not yet. It was the psychological assaults that sounded so horribly familiar to Lucas. The small cruelties: ignoring her when she spoke to him; mocking her and saying she disgusted him; leaving evidence of having been with other women right under her nose. Telling her that she was useless, that her career was over. Even though they had a cleaner, he insisted on the house being kept in a constantly spotless condition and told her she was revolting if he saw any signs of baby sick or milk on her clothes. But when she said she would leave him, he'd looked her coolly in the eye and said he wouldn't ever let her humiliate him. The implication of what he might do if she left seemed to linger like a bad smell, Alice said.

Quinn hadn't wanted a baby. He lacked any real affection for Zach, while constantly criticizing what he called Alice's 'lax' mothering.

She talked and talked, and that was when she made her request.

'If something happens?' she'd said. 'I want you to get Zach out of here. I don't care where you go. Just get him away. Do you promise?' He'd felt the hot breath from her fierce words against his neck where she was still curled.

He'd said only, 'Nothing's going to happen to you, Alice. Not while I'm here.'

'No,' she'd said. 'I hope not. But I'm not sure I've got the strength to leave him, Luke . . . Lucas. He told me he'd always find me. Wherever I went.'

'I'll look after you,' he'd said. 'Both of you.' He meant it. 'I'm going to help you get away from him.'

They had gone upstairs to the bedroom then and lain curled together on top of the bed, in silence. After a few moments, rain started to thrum against the bedroom window. It was very peaceful, lying there, although Lucas had to force himself not to think about Quinn being in this bed with Alice.

Zach had been so quiet downstairs that Lucas had almost forgotten he was in the house. But now he started to cry with gusto. Alice sprung up from the bed.

'Should I go?' Lucas said uncertainly and made a move to get up, but Alice placed her hand on his leg.

'Please,' she said. 'Stay with me. Stay the night. I don't want to be alone.'

Lucas sank back against the pillow and nodded.

A little while later, Alice came upstairs with the baby; Zach was apparently in a milk stupor – eyes glassy – against her shoulder. She smiled at Lucas and laid the baby down in the cot at the end of the bed, then rocked it with her hand and made gentle soothing sounds. The baby quietly chuntered away and eventually went silent.

Lucas lay with his head resting on his hand, watching her. He was feeling something strange and wonderful; a sense of stillness and peace entirely at odds with the situation he found himself in.

When Alice came over to the bed, she took off the robe she had been wearing and slipped in beside him, a small smile on her lips.

He never intended to sleep. He wouldn't have thought it possible that either of them could, in the circumstances.

But somehow, it was very late, and he was waking up to the most terrible sound of his life.

The front door opening.

'Alice?' The sharp, clipped tone felt like a punch in the side of the head. 'The trip's been cancelled. I got as far as fucking Heathrow before the brainless publicist told me. Had a few drinks on the way home.'

They had leapt to their feet, both yanking at clothes. Alice frantically began to pull on the robe on the floor, while Lucas tried to zip his flies with useless fingers. They looked at each other with expressions that might have been comedic in different circumstances. Circular mouths, circular eyes.

Faster than seemed possible, Quinn was right there, in the room. In Lucas's mind, the other man had always been a kind of giant. But now it seemed he really was still huge in real life, dominating the doorway with his frame.

'What the fuck is happening here?' he said, his voice low and quiet. Then, 'Who is that?' He came closer and his eyes widened. 'Jesus fucking Christ! What's that little shit doing in my house?'

'Nick . . .' Alice said, stumbling to her feet.

Quinn didn't respond, just roughly lifted the baby, and walked out of the room and down the stairs. Zach began to cry.

Alice called, 'Nick, what are you doing?' and hurried after him, closely followed by Lucas.

'I don't think you're a suitable person to be a mother,' Quinn said. He put Zach into the carry cot – again, without much gentleness – and said, in an almost conversational tone, 'God knows I never wanted him. I might just leave him somewhere at the side of the road. What would you think about that, hmm, Alice? Leave him for someone who can look after him properly?'

'Stop it, Nick!' Alice cried and rushed to Zach, but Quinn swatted her around the head and sent her flying onto the floor, as if she weighed as much as a rag doll. She crashed into the side of the cabinet and cried out in pain.

Lucas was finding it hard to breathe. The time had finally come.

He was no longer a little boy. He was a grown man of wiry strength. He launched himself at Quinn before he was able to pick up Zach.

Alice was screaming. Zach was screaming.

But Quinn had been so fast. Before Lucas had even been able to make contact, his arm was twisted, and then he was on the floor, ribs exploding with pain as he was repeatedly kicked, Quinn's spit arcing and flying at him.

He wanted to get up, go at him again, but Quinn was yelling that he was just like his 'neurotic, useless mother' and that he was so worthless and unlovable that she couldn't even 'be bothered to stay alive and mother him'. He kept on – 'She didn't love you enough, Lucas. You just weren't good enough' – and the words seemed to bloom in Lucas's mind until they blotted everything out and something shattered inside him.

He was ten years old again, a small boy frozen with terror, while the monster grew bigger and stronger and more furious above him. He couldn't seem to make his limbs work as Quinn dragged him to the front door.

'Now get the fuck out of my house, you useless little shit.'

It felt like seconds later that he was staring at the closed front door.

He heard shouting inside and then piercing, terrible screams. The sounds brought him back into himself and he was on his feet, hammering on the front door and yelling, 'Alice! I'm coming! Let me in!'

Silence inside now.

He leaned his sore, hot face against the wood and moaned, banging uselessly on the door. When it suddenly opened, he almost fell inside.

Quinn was right there, his eyes unfocused and his cheeks flushed. He pressed something hard into Lucas's hands and it took Lucas a moment to understand what he was holding.

A knife, smeared bright with blood.

'She's all yours,' Quinn whispered and then he was gone. Lucas dropped the knife and stumbled into the house, shouting Alice's name.

He found her on the floor, her eyes open and already turning opaque as the blood spread around her.

Lucas had stared down at Alice and began to shake.

He knew he should call the police. But his fingerprints were on the knife. Who would believe the truth? He was the man Alice had called a stalker. Quinn was a national treasure, trusted by millions to be the calm voice of reason.

He was going to end up being blamed for this, he knew it.

But that wasn't even what was killing him now. It was the fact that he didn't save her, when he was *right there*; the younger, stronger, fitter man. He'd allowed himself to be thrown out of the house like a binbag of rubbish.

His sister was right. He was weak and useless and now another woman he loved was dead.

He couldn't call the police. But there was one last thing he could do for Alice.

54

Nina

It starts to rain as I make the journey back to Mirestone.

I've chosen the worst time to do this; the beginning of rush hour. The dual carriageway is at a standstill and I drum my fingers impatiently, thinking about the window of time available for this mad enterprise. I crawl along with intolerable slowness. It's only one junction and I should have tried to go by the back roads. But getting lost would be all I need right now.

Finally, I'm able to pull off the dual carriage and take the turning that will eventually lead to the village.

As I wind round the country road and into the village, it's hard not to picture, once again, Lucas stumbling through the rain with Zach stuffed inside his coat like a bag of shopping. I look anxiously at the time on the dashboard. But it's still ages until Sam gets home.

The thought of him arriving back and me not being there is so dreadful I can't even contemplate it. I know that I already have work to do, after the awful lie I was forced to tell when he wanted to come home that night. I still haven't decided whether to tell him everything or not. I haven't been named in the press but what if one of his mates somehow hears anyway and tells him first? No, I need to do it, but in my own time.

When I pull up near the Quinn house, the rain is beating down like a tropical storm. I wait it out in the car for a while until the intensity lessens but I don't have time to sit here for hours. Of course, I didn't think to come with a coat or an umbrella. I'm just going to have to make a run for it and hope the bedraggled look might elicit some sympathy.

There is no car in the driveway and relief is warm in my chest. Jennifer Sommerton had said Quinn was away and I doubt he would be here without a car, if he was in the country at all.

There are no lights on inside despite the gloom of the rain, but it's still only early evening. There is every chance no one is in at all. But that's a risk I'm prepared to take. If Nooria isn't here, I will draw a line under this and go home to wait for my son. I need to try though; just one last time.

I press the doorbell, then bang the metal doorknocker, for good measure.

Nothing happens, although I swear I hear some sort of movement inside.

I knock again, harder, as rain forces its way down the back of my top and pools miserably there.

The door opens a tiny bit and it takes me a second to look down and see the little girl peering out at me with big brown eyes and a thumb planted firmly in her mouth.

There's a burst of rapid-fire language I don't understand, and the little girl looks behind her and runs off, leaving the door open like a gift.

I don't know what comes over me. I don't even consciously decide to do it but, somehow, I am stepping right inside the house and closing the door behind me.

Nooria appears at the end of the corridor, holding a tea towel. Her face goes from shock to fury in about one second.

'What are you doing?' she demands. Her English is very clear. 'What do you mean by coming in without invitation?'

I take a step back, so I'm almost leaning against the wood of the door, breathing heavily.

'Nooria,' I say, holding out a placatory hand, 'I'm so sorry about this and I really hope I haven't alarmed you in any way. I would never normally dream of just barging into someone's home, but this is really important, don't you see?'

She says something in her own language, her tone disgusted, and then behind her the little girl appears, wailing suddenly and holding up a finger she has obviously injured in some way.

Nooria shouts something I don't understand but the meaning is clear. 'What have you done?' Then she goes back into the kitchen at the end of the hallway.

I hesitate briefly and then follow her down there.

The little girl is crying as her mother holds the finger under the tap and speaks to her in a low voice, cross but not unkind.

When she sees me she says again, 'Get out!'

'I'm sorry, I . . .' I start to say, then sensing a movement behind me I turn, starting when I see a man lurking towards the French windows. It's the same one I'd seen coming to the house the other time I was here, the one I'd assumed was a delivery driver. There's something else about him . . . I feel like I know him from somewhere else.

He looks considerably worse than he did then. His jaw is black with speckled stubble, his eyes slung with bags, his skin grey. He fumbles in his pocket and pulls out a packet of cigarettes. He's attempting to light one with badly shaking hands when the little girl rushes over to him and says, 'Baba! I squished my finger!'

He gathers her up in a hug, murmuring endearments while Nooria says something sharply that makes them both stop and stare at her rather balefully. So he's the little girl's dad, then.

Nooria grasps her daughter and says something in an angry voice before lifting her up, so she sits on her hip, despite her size.

The man is sniffing now and wiping his nose with the back of his arm and Nooria says something that makes him nod and leave the room, looking like a man condemned.

I don't even know what I'm doing here. I have no business witnessing whatever private drama this family is going through.

I must get out of here . . .

And then I hear the front door open.

Seconds later, Nick Quinn, the man I've heard so much about, walks down the hallway and into the kitchen.

55

Angel

Angel is made from water. This seems like an amazing revelation and she can't believe she has gone all these years without this basic knowledge.

She's part of the loch, looking up at the sparking sun dancing on the surface. She can hear Lucas's high-pitched little voice as he tries to skim stones the way Grandad is showing him.

Then she's in different water. This time it's brown and dirty and it fills her mouth with poison.

With a strange mewling sound, she turns her head and feels sourness slipping out of her mouth and down into her neck. Someone says, 'Oh, let's get you cleaned up,' and the light is so bright it feels like it's splitting her head open.

She tries to speak but her voice feels broken. Her mouth is so dry that her tongue feels as though it is two-and-a-half times its normal size, at least. The person in the room, coming into focus as a thin blonde woman in nurse's scrubs, helps to lift her head and gently tips a little water into her mouth. Angel drinks greedily until she starts to cough.

Her head hurts so much.

'My 'n hospital?'

The nurse seems to understand anyway because she nods and says, 'That's right. Can you tell me your name, lovely?'

'Angel,' she says in the remnants of her voice. 'It's Angel.'

'Right, that's brilliant,' says the nurse. 'I'm just going to get the police lady who wants to have a little word, OK? They didn't find your bag at first, but I'm assured your wallet and phone are in there. I'll bring them to you in a mo.'

There's a flare of panic in her chest and she tries to sit up. There's something very bad that's connected with the police, if she can only get it. 'Prison,' she says, 'I'm 'n trouble,' and the nurse gently pushes her back down.

'I don't think so,' she says. 'Please just try and rest while I go get someone.'

She leaves the room before Angel gets the chance to protest further.

Angel closes her eyes and winces as she begins to remember what happened. Today? Yesterday? How long has she been here?

She'd been on her way to the police station to report in.

And she'd decided to walk by the canal. That was it . . .

It was quiet down there, with only an occasional runner and, once, a boy on a bike with a Yorkshire terrier running along beside him. She'd been under the bridge when there had suddenly been the sound of loud footsteps behind her and there had only been a moment for her to turn to see a bearded man in a baseball cap before her head exploded with pain and she was falling. She vaguely remembers the tilted world showing her handbag being slid off her shoulder and then that's the last thing she can remember.

290

Opening her eyes again now, Angel sees a couple of police officers, one male and one female, standing by her bed.

'Hello, Angel. You've been in the wars, haven't you? Are you up to talking?'

She turns her head to the wall and closes her eyes.

56
Nina

He says, 'What the fuck is going on?' and then he spots me and his face is a mask of pure surprise. 'I'm sorry, do I know you?' he says, brow scrunched. And then recognition dawns.

'Oh! Goodness,' he says and puts a hand to his chest. 'You're . . . you're the person who . . .'

'Yes, I'm Nina,' I say in a rush. This is all so peculiar. He's not what I expected.

He's dressed in pressed khakis and a deep blue short-sleeved shirt. He's both taller and slightly less good-looking than he appears on television. He looks tired, his eyes a bit bloodshot and baggy. He looks like a man grieving.

My overwhelming feeling now is one of embarrassment. My cheeks start to flame. What the hell am I doing here?

Nooria speaks to him in her own language and he replies the same way. She nods and hurries out of the kitchen, dragging the whining little girl by the arm. The man goes too, head bowed.

I should get out of here right now.

But I feel as though my feet are made of lead. I can't seem to move.

Nick Quinn takes a step closer and I don't move as he holds out his hands.

'Nina,' he says gently. 'I don't really understand why you are here. But in a funny way I'm glad you are. The police told me how you cared for,' he swallows, visibly, 'for Zachy that night. I want to thank you from the bottom of my heart.' His eyes are shining, his shoulders slumped. I find myself taking his hands, almost without consciously deciding to do so. 'My wife is,' he pauses again, and a wave of pain passes over his face, 'my wife would have *been* so grateful for your care.'

'That's alright,' I say foolishly. 'I only did what anyone would do.'

'Look,' he says, 'you'll have to forgive us for being in chaos. I've been away and our nanny Nooria seems to be having some sort of crisis.' He makes a rueful face. 'I've been trying to help her and her husband with their application for asylum but I think something must have happened on that front. Can I ask you to take a seat so we can speak properly? I would like to talk to you.'

'I really should probably—' I start to say but he interrupts.

'Please, Nina,' he says. 'Have a drink with me? Just one.'

He looks so beaten down and sad that it feels like the very worst manners to leave now. He hasn't asked why I'm here yet and I have no idea what to say if – when – he does. But I nod stiffly and take a seat at the table.

He presses his palms together in a little praying gesture and mouths, 'Thank you,' before leaving the room.

All I can think about is seeing him in news reports, relaying stories of terrible suffering with what seems like compassion and gravitas. Then I think about the guinea pig. About the small boy so terrified of an adult he wets himself.

This is a mistake. I should go, but I can't seem to make myself get up. Is it this desire to understand that is pinning me to the spot? Do I really think I will be able to peer into this man's heart and see the darkness there?

I can't believe I am in any danger, but that's not the only reason I shouldn't be here. Ian and Carmen would have a field day if they knew I had done this, let alone the police. It might even be contempt of court or something. With a small internal groan, I lean my forehead on my hand as I try to think what I can say to enable me to leave quickly.

A rustle in the doorway makes me look up sharply. The little girl is standing right on the threshold of the room, one foot twisted behind the other. Her skirt has got caught in her knickers and she has a doll under her arm. Her large dark eyes are fixed on my face.

Flushing, I attempt to smile. 'Hello,' I say, then, 'how's your sore finger?'

She holds it up to show me a printed plaster wrapped around it and I make a sympathetic face. 'I bet that will do the trick,' I say.

The little girl stares hard at me and then comes over to the table, where she places the doll. It's a Barbie, dressed as a mermaid, with an extravagant, sparkly tail. The doll's hair has clearly been cut on one side, giving her an odd, punky look.

'Is that your dolly?' I say a bit stupidly. I've forgotten how to talk to small kids. She nods solemnly though and slides the doll across, indicating permission to pick it up. I do, and begin to fuss with the hair a little.

'You've made her look very pretty,' I say, and she doesn't reply but I can see the pleased flush of her cheeks.

'My daddy bought her for me,' she says airily and I make an appreciative noise. She takes the doll back – clearly,

I have had it for long enough – and begins to fuss with the mermaid tail, crooning a little as she does so.

I look at my watch. It's just after one pm. I still have plenty of time. But this is all too weird. I wonder if I should just slip out quietly without saying anything. The little girl starts to murmur something and I don't catch it, but she is looking right at me, a sly expression on her face.

'What was that, sweetie?' I say, a bit distracted.

'My daddy hurt an angel and he is very sorry,' she says.

I stare back at her. 'Pardon?' Something begins to stir uncomfortably in my stomach. What an odd thing to say.

She looks down at her doll and says, very quietly, 'My daddy didn't want to hit the angel but Nick said he had to and now everyone is really cross.' She scrunches her brow. 'And angels can fly so why didn't she fly away?'

But Nooria is standing in the doorway now, glaring. She calls sharply to the little girl, who hurries out of the room.

An angel.

Angel?

My mind is filled with shards of information that I can't seem to connect.

Angel has been hurt. By this man, who is connected to Quinn's nanny? But why? And hurt in what way? Seriously?

Understanding flashes bright in my mind then as I think about that news report, from earlier. The man's face on the news.

It's him. The man upstairs right now. Was it Angel who had been attacked? But why? The little girl said, 'Nick said he had to.' But why would Quinn do that when the police seem to have such a strong case against her and Lucas?

It doesn't make any sense. One thing is certain, though. I have to get out of here.

Right now.

I can hear movement and quiet murmuring in Arabic

between Nooria and Quinn in the hallway. The man says something louder and is shushed. There's the sound of a bag being dragged across the floor and then the front door closes with a bang. My hands are shaking. He doesn't necessarily know what I heard just now, does he? Did Nooria hear what her daughter said?

I grab my bag and move to stand up but Quinn comes into the kitchen just then and gives me a friendly smile.

'Right, Nina,' he says. 'Let's have that drink, shall we?'

'No,' I say, trying and failing to suppress the panic making my voice an octave higher than usual. 'I really have to go. My son is arriving soon, and I need to be there.'

'Please,' he says, so reasonably. 'Just stay for a minute.' He closes the door. 'It's so draughty in this room,' he says. 'Can never seem to get this house warm enough.'

I can't tell if this is a normal thing to say. I eye the closed door. I'm too agitated now. I can't believe he can't see how desperate I am to leave. I should just walk straight out, but I don't want to alert him to the fact that something has changed since I got here. I feel like there is a wasps' nest in the room and I am going to have to get past it to get out of here.

He is still between me and the door as he goes to one of the cupboards, where he gets out a bottle of Macallan whisky, tipping it towards me with a raised eyebrow. I shake my head, a bit too vigorously. My hands are shaking hard and I grip the bag tightly to try to hide it. He gets a cut-glass tumbler and pours a generous measure into the glass.

He is still looking at me so pleasantly, as though there is nothing strange about any of this at all.

'You really shouldn't be here, you know,' he says. 'We are both key witnesses in a murder trial, not to mention the other terrible business those people put you through.'

'I know, I—' I start to say but he carries on speaking.

He is leaning back against a cupboard, one arm slung across his waist, the other holding the tumbler of whisky. He looks completely at ease.

'Don't you want to see justice done?'

I swallow. I'm finding it very hard to meet his eyes, so I just look down and nod. 'Yes, of course,' I say. 'I don't really know why I'm here. I'm sorry. I really do have to go now. I don't mean to be rude.'

His next words come as a shock.

'I don't think you should go anywhere, *Nina*,' he says, drawing out my name. 'First, I think you should tell me why you are really here.'

I swallow and force myself to meet his eye.

'I really don't know what you're talking about,' I say as I stand up. 'And I haven't got time to—'

The violence happens in what seems like a split second. The glass he had been drinking from explodes against the far wall, sending shards everywhere. The effect is like someone has attached a couple of charged defibrillator panels to my chest.

He smiles, oh-so-reasonably.

'Come on, then,' he says, still sounding normal. 'What did that poisonous bitch Angel say about me?'

There's no point pretending. I'm scared, but I'm angry too. This well-spoken, cultured bully thinks he has all the cards.

'She told me about their childhood,' I say tightly. I must clench my jaw to stop my teeth from chattering.

Quinn shakes his head slowly.

'You don't have a fucking clue what you're on about,' he says and then his face tightens. 'Marianne was a flaky mess when I met her. Those children were practically feral when I came into their lives. No discipline . . . eating when they felt like it. It was a disaster of a household.' He goes into the cabinet and gets out another glass, which he fills half full with whisky.

'I did the world a favour,' he says after taking a sip. 'She was a drain on us all.'

My neck prickles. 'What do you mean, a *favour*?'

He gives me a strange, disappointed smile. 'I'm sure you are a smart lady. You can work it out.'

'You killed her?' I say. My breath is coming fast now. 'Made it look like suicide?'

He wags a finger at me. 'You shouldn't go making accusations like that, Nina. It's very impolite.'

He takes another sip and bares his teeth as it goes down. I don't like the vulpine look it gives him before his face is in repose again.

'Go on, then,' he says. 'What else have you got?'

I lift my chin and force myself to meet his eyes. 'I think you killed Alice. And I think you got that man to attack Angel.'

He shakes his head and makes a loud 'tut'.

'What a flight of fancy,' he says after a moment's silence. 'Are you one of those people who likes to blame everything on the Arabs, eh? Is that what's going on here?'

'Not at all,' I say in as calm a voice as I can muster, even though my knees are shaking now. 'I'm simply going by the fact that his face was all over the lunchtime news.'

Finally, something seems to have penetrated his smooth outer layer. His brow folds and a flush creeps up his face.

'What do you mean?' The voice is sharp now.

'They caught him on a camera,' I say. 'And there was a witness.' Then, pretending to be about a million times more in control than I am, I say, 'I have to go now. My son's coming back from his holiday and people are expecting me.'

I force myself to put one foot in front of the other and move towards him and the door. It is so hard; like wading through a substance made of mud and my own terror. But – and I can't believe it – he does nothing as I open the door and walk through.

I am suffused with such sweet relief it's all I can do not to break into a grin.

Maybe this has all just gone too far now. He's letting me go!

I hurry into the hallway on shaking legs. The front door is only about three feet away. I can see rain running down the stained glass of the window outside and it's a beautiful sight. I want to be out there so badly, I don't even care if I get soaked through.

I take two or three steps almost at a run and then there is sudden movement and I'm slammed against the wall. The back of my head explodes with pain and I cry out.

His face looms down over mine. He was only toying with me, I think. He was never going to let me go. His hands close around my throat as I look into his eyes. I fight with everything I have, legs kicking ineffectually, fingers scrabbling at his big hands.

And then—

57

Nick

Nick catches Nina as she begins to slide down the wall to the floor. She's unconscious, but breathing. He lays her gently down and runs his hands through his hair.

'OK,' he says. 'Shit. *Shit.*'

He tries to slow down his breathing. This is all he needs right now.

'Fuck!'

He kicks out at a delicate table that holds the telephone and a pad of paper. One of the legs snaps and it lists sideways, so the phone crashes onto the wooden floor. He stares at it for a moment and shakes his head.

'It's OK,' he says. 'It's OK.' He just needs to *think*.

Thank God, he didn't go too far. He knew when to stop. He just needed to stop her, temporarily. He is still in control, even if everything is a total fucking mess now.

Breathing heavily, he manages to heft Nina up and over his shoulder. It's awkward and he feels twinges of pain in his back. Slowly making his way upstairs, he grimaces. She's heavier than she looks, but it's also harder because he is so exhausted too.

He hasn't slept more than three hours for as long as he can remember.

In the bedroom, barely occupied since he was last there with his wife, he lays the woman face down on the bed and turns her head to the side.

He's not a monster. He doesn't want her to die, even though he could feel the violence twitching inside when she had looked at him in that superior way in the kitchen.

Stupid interfering *bitch*.

It was a puzzle, that she was here at all, but he really thought he could get her to leave without too much fuss. Middle-aged women like her were usually easy to charm. Then Nooria told him what she had overheard and he *still* thought that maybe – just maybe – it was alright.

But the minute Nick had walked into the kitchen and seen those startled-rabbit eyes, he'd known. He could smell it on her, the fear. It was a bit of a turn-on, that was the truth, but only for a second. The stakes were high here.

'Oh, Nina,' he says. 'You silly woman.'

He pulls her arms, gently, behind her back and rests them against her bottom. Then he looks around the bedroom. He needs to tie her up.

Nick goes to Alice's wardrobe and opens it, pausing for a moment at the sight of all her clothes still neatly hanging there. It looks as though Jennifer couldn't face this task either on her recent visit, although he had told her to take what she wanted.

His chest begins to ache as he reaches for one of those soft, pastel jumpers Alice favoured from the neat pile there. He holds it to his nose and his knees almost buckle as he breathes in the smell of her. A dry sob of anguish wrenches its way out of his body. It should never have happened like this. She should be *here*. Zach too. A family.

They would have found a way to make it work.

He could have got used to fatherhood in time, especially when the boy was older and not glued to his mother's breast. It would only be seven years until he could go away to boarding school, just like Nick had. She would have adjusted. In time. There was so much they hadn't done yet. Nick had so many places he had wanted to show her.

He closes his eyes tightly and breathes heavily until the waves of pain recede.

An image of Lucas and her, scrambling to get their clothes on, still flushed with sex, unrolls in his mind and he has to clench his fists to stop himself from punching the wall.

Lucas, that whining little bastard he thought he would never see again, had to come back into his life and fuck everything up for him.

And the sister . . . well, never had anyone been less deserving of the name they had been given at birth.

He had believed her absolutely when she said she would tell the world about him. She was right that she didn't even need proof. Mud sticks, especially in the current climate.

Nick sighs. It had been such a mistake to get Sahar to do a job that required balls. He'd paid him well, even though he didn't really have to do that. One phone call is all he would have needed to make and the whole family would have been on the next plane back to Hamid Karzai International. But he couldn't do that to Nooria. They had been through such a lot together, and he was glad she had found Sahar, even though he was a poor excuse for a man.

Not many would be prepared to take on Nooria and a child that wasn't his. The question of Asefa's paternity has never been discussed and, as far as Nick is concerned, it never will be. There are some things that don't need to be dragged out and pored over, not when things are working as they are. Or had been, anyway.

He grabs a couple of scarves from where they hang on

302

a bar inside the door, one red and black silk he bought on one of his trips, and another, older one in light blue. He also grabs a brown leather belt with a plaited pattern.

The woman on the bed is still out cold. Nick carefully separates the thick curly hair at the back of her head to check her scalp. No blood from where she hit the wall. It is pretty; her hair.

For a second, he feels a stirring. She's so vulnerable, lying there, and she's got one of those curvy, soft bodies that women are so anti these days. Nice tits. But no. That's not who he is. He was never that.

Taking the black and red scarf, he ties her wrists together with his best Boy Scout knot, and then wraps the leather belt tightly around her ankles, binding her legs together. He thinks about wrapping the other scarf around her mouth. Might she be sick? He doesn't want her to die. But he can't have her yelling her head off. He'll do it for now, then untie her when he leaves.

There's something unreal about all this.

Nick can't believe he, a highly respected professional man, is being forced to take part in such squalid activity. It disgusts him.

He pours another glass of Macallan and drinks it in one go. He barely tastes it as it goes down. Then he goes to his bag and pulls out his laptop, before sitting down at the kitchen table.

His mind spins. Where to go? There is no reason to think he's under any suspicion. Nina had clearly only made the connection about Sahar when she was here. But best to go somewhere where extradition procedures are less than straightforward.

Kuwait?

He has friends in Kuwait City who will let him stay in comfort while things quieten down here. And getting him back to be interviewed is going to be complicated, at the least, for the Met Police.

Nick feels his heart rate begin to slow down for the first time since he came into the house. He quickly finds a flight leaving for Kuwait City from Heathrow in four hours.

That should do it.

Nick pours himself another drink.

58

Nina

I'm looking at a corner of a bed and a dangling foot in a sandal reflected in a full-length mirror. I have shoes like that.

That's me.

Understanding rushes into my mind and I try to move but pain and nausea come crashing over me. My head hurts. My throat hurts.

Quinn's house. He tried to strangle me.

And now I'm tied up. There's something in my mouth.

Tears squeeze hotly over my lids and down into the cloth wrapped around my mouth. I try to chew it to drop below my lips but the dry rasp of the material against my tongue prompts a dizzying wave of nausea. I must not be sick. Oh God, if I'm sick I'm going to choke. I manage to make some strangled sounds and buck against the bed but it's hopeless.

A surge of sheer *unfairness* hits me; I didn't deserve this. I'm just an ordinary woman. Why did I have to get caught up in all this?

I cry helplessly until the cloth feels damp against my lips. At least it helps with the dryness. But my shoulders hurt from being pulled behind me and the back of my head throbs. I picture the cartoonish lump that is no doubt lurking there.

I try to look around the room to see if there is anything that can help me.

The walls are covered in that very expensive silk wallpaper in a colour that is somewhere between grey and turquoise, printed with images of delicate, long-necked birds. There is a wardrobe and a large mirror on the wall.

I turn my head and see the nightstand on the other side of the bed. It contains a beautiful black and white photo of Zach – new-born, I think. A copy of a thriller everyone was reading last year is next to it, with a bookmark poking out at an angle.

Alice slept in this bed.

Until he killed her. The man downstairs.

Is he downstairs?

Fear courses through me again and I buck against the bindings, but I am helpless here.

I can't hear anything at all apart from the heavy ticking of a clock coming from somewhere in the room. Have I been left here? Is he coming back? I know exactly what Nick Quinn is capable of now. There is no element of doubt about anyone trying to do the right thing.

Tick-tock, tick-tock.

And then I remember. I cry out, my breath hot and damp against the fabric of the gag.

Sam.

I desperately look around for a clock. I don't know how long I've been here. But there is a strong chance that Sam has arrived back and I wasn't there.

I wasn't there . . .

The despair rips at my insides.

Soon the heavy grey eiderdown is soggy against my cheek.

I picture them driving away again, Sam's sad face against

the window. I let out a stifled scream of pure frustration and thump my feet up and down so the bedframe rattles.

Then I see the tall frame of Nick Quinn filling the doorway and my eyes open wider. I'm breathing uncomfortably hard.

'You're being very noisy,' he says.

He comes closer and my whole body seems to cringe in on itself. I don't want him to touch me.

With surprising gentleness, he pulls the material away from my mouth and the gratitude is immense. He stands back, hands raised in supplication.

'Let me go, you bastard,' I say, my voice croaky. 'They know I'm here. People, I mean, my husband knows I'm here.'

Nick ignores this and gives me a small smile.

'I am not a bad person,' he says, his voice a little slurred now. He's drunk, and I don't know whether to be grateful or more scared. 'None of this was meant to happen.' He pauses. 'Anyway,' he says, 'I've come to tell you I'm going away. Once I reach my destination, I will call someone to come and let you go. I'll leave water. It won't be more than a day at the very most.'

'A day?' I manage to croak. This – the terror of being left, tied and helpless – is such a strange echo of what happened before that it makes my head spin. Except that was never the same, really, as this. I understand it now. Angel and Lucas were two damaged people who were trying to do the right thing.

Quinn is regarding me and, to my surprise, his expression seems to contain real contrition. He's either an excellent actor or it's something more disturbing. Perhaps all those years of seeing terrible things have broken something inside him and he no longer understands the boundaries of good and evil.

'Look,' he says, letting out a heavy sigh. 'You may not believe me, but I *bitterly* regret the way things have turned out. We should never even have crossed paths. But we are where we are, and I don't really see any other way out now.'

His reasonable, self-pitying tone enrages me and I'm grateful for the heat of this feeling, which cuts cleanly through the fear. I despise this man, with his easy charm and the ready fists, which he is so quick to use against weaker people. He makes me sick. I want the whole world to know the truth about him.

'You're a monster,' is all I manage. He blinks for a moment and then almost winces.

'Well,' he says, 'that's as may be, but . . .'

He is interrupted by a series of sharp raps on the front door.

'Fuck,' he says. I pull in a breath to scream but he is too fast, his large hand pressing against my mouth as he fumbles for the cloth thing again. I manage to bite his thumb, hating the taste of his skin. He cracks a blow across my cheek that shocks me so much I lie uselessly, dazed. He stuffs something inside my mouth so hard my gag reflex shudders convulsively and then he runs out of the room, dragging the door closed behind him.

My cheek is throbbing from where he hit me. The manic pounding of my heart is making it difficult to hear but I strain to make out what's happening downstairs. Wriggling so my head is a little off the bed, I find I can hear the voices being raised somewhere below me.

'I'm sorry, I really don't have any need for dishcloths or your other tat,' says Quinn. 'So if you'll kindly get off my doorstep . . .'

I can't make out what the other person says. I think it might be someone on one of those homeless schemes. It's exactly how I imagine Quinn would treat someone like that.

In one awkward movement I roll myself sideways, wriggling until I thump down from the bed, cracking onto the wooden floor with a sickening pain in my right arm. I've broken it, I'm certain. I swallow nausea and gag on the sourness.

I have to do this. It's all I've got.

I make myself bang my head and drum my feet against the hard floor, despite the pain that shudders from my scalp to my toes. I'm screaming into the gag, saliva flooding my mouth, and I cough and choke; tears streaming down my cheeks. I crack my head and my toes against the ground one more time. Darkness is creeping in around my vision and a spinning in my head makes vomit begin to rise. I'm choking. Again. I'm choking. I'm going to die.

Then the gag is roughly wrenched off my mouth and my stomach spasms. Dazed and disorientated, I feel wetness and smell the sour tang of my own sick by my cheek.

'You stupid woman, what did you think you would achieve by that?' Quinn's voice is a booming, painful thing. It seems to ricochet in my ringing skull.

I can't reply. Weak with despair; sore and dizzy.

I can hear him moving around and then he says, 'You're too heavy to lift. Come on, let's get you up.'

I feel his hands on my arms and I groan as I am dragged onto my knees and then to my feet. He unties my wrists and I think, *I must fight back now*, but I have nothing. My head throbs and my arms ache as he re-ties my arms at the front of my body.

For a second I am close enough to look into his eyes, but he won't look at me. He is focusing on the bed behind, where he lays me down and pushes me onto my side. A pillow is placed at my back, my hands in my lap and my knees bent.

He starts shouting from nowhere and I wince. 'I can't

believe you have made me do this!' he yells. 'Why did you have to come here today? For fuck's sake!'

He sits down so the bed bounces and I can hear heavy breathing.

'Please,' I manage, in a small voice. 'Please just let me go. My son needs me.'

He brushes my hair out of my eyes and leans down so close to me that I can smell the whisky on his breath.

'You should have thought about that before you came here,' he says and then gets up abruptly and leaves the room.

59

Angel

There's a woman muttering in a foreign language in the bed next to hers. A dinner trolley has just arrived on the ward with much clang and clatter, and the woman serving from it feels the need to deliver every word at the top of her lungs. Angel feels a sharp stab of memory: Marianne saying, 'Try to use your *inside* voice.'

She pulls the thin pillow over her head and groans. Her head is aching, and her stomach still churns. Every time she thinks about swallowing that filthy river water she wants to heave, even though she is sure all the bad stuff has now been expelled.

Her hand snakes up to her belly and she presses it against the cotton hospital gown, feeling the heat of her skin through the cloth. From nowhere, she suddenly pictures the tiny thing inside her – she sees it as a cartoon seahorse for some reason; all frilly head, curled tail and big, cute eyes. Is it even in there any more? She will find out soon enough. They are taking her for an ultrasound scan shortly. She'd had to tell them about the pregnancy when they took her for an X-ray earlier.

It would make everything much easier if it is no longer . . . there. They will shake their heads and tell her in a sad

311

voice that there is no trace of a foetal heartbeat, or words like that. Angel knows this is the best possible outcome right now. She doesn't want a baby. She can't even look after herself. So why is she crying? *Again?*

She wipes her eyes and nose on the sheet crossly and heaves a sigh.

The police left about ten minutes ago; a young male constable with a blond buzzcut and rampant hay fever, and a female PC with quick eyes and what Angel felt was an inappropriate amount of perkiness in the circumstances.

'It all happened so fast,' she'd told them, repeatedly.

It was the truth.

One minute she was walking along the towpath, and the next, she was in the water. She's 'lucky' apparently, because a passing cyclist got her out before she drowned.

Her handbag had been thrown into a hedge nearby and neither her wallet nor her mobile phone had been taken. It all seemed a bit odd. Clearly the police thought so too, because they asked if she had any reason to suspect that anyone wanted to hurt her.

She almost had to bite her lips to stop herself from telling them what she was certain was true: that Quinn had put someone up to it. He wouldn't do it himself. Too messy and public. But if she did that, she would have to tell them about her letter – and what she had threatened him with. She was well aware that this would be considered as breaching the conditions of her bail.

If Angel was going to prison, it would be at the end of the trial and not before. So, she said she had no idea whether anyone would do this out of malice and that was that. Just bad luck. The male officer gazed at her with his pink rabbity eyes and speculated, in a voice thick with snot, that perhaps the attacker panicked and ran off because he saw someone coming.

Angel can't help feeling a small sense of satisfaction that the bastard's plan didn't work. She would still get her say. Still get to tell the world all about Mr Nicholas Quinn . . .

The curtain around the bed suddenly whips back and a short, fat woman with smiley eyes and dark skin peers in at her.

'YOU-WANT-SOME-DINNER-DARLING?' she says – yells – in one breath and Angel shakes her head.

The woman is about to go when Angel calls, 'Wait!'

The nurse, orderly, whatever, stops, hand on the curtain as she regards her.

'Can you see if my handbag is in there?' Angel gestures towards the bedside cupboard. It hurts her head to move too much.

'COURSE-I-CAN-DARLING.'

She drags herself into a seated position and takes the bag, before thanking the woman.

'MY-PLEASURE-DARLING.'

She thinks guiltily of Leon, who will be doing his nut.

Angel begins to thumb through the messages. As predicted, Leon has been going crazy with worry about where she is. She needs to call him.

Then she sees a message that makes adrenaline ping in her spine. From the last person in the world she would expect to hear from.

Nina.

60

Nina

I have been drifting in and out of a sickly kind of twilight. I keep thinking I can hear the silvery, sci-fi ringtone of my phone, but I don't know where it is coming from, or whether I am imagining it.

When the bedroom door opens, I experience the strangest mix of sensations. Fear and revulsion at being near Quinn again, and intense relief that he is still here; that I haven't been left alone.

Now that I am fully awake again, my neck and back ache from being in this position and the pain in my arm beats like an internal drum. It seems to stain everything around me, as though the air itself is pulsing, angry red. When he sits heavily next to me, making the bed compress, I let out a small cry.

'What's the code for your phone?' he says. He's properly drunk now, words slurring and skidding. *Wossthecode.*

'Why?' I say. My tongue feels too big for my mouth, my voice comes out thick and muffled.

'Because you don't want your son to be worrying too much, do you?' he says and there is a sharp, malicious edge to his tone that sends a further jolt of fear through me.

Drunk, he's likely to be even meaner and less able to control himself. Breathing quickly, I force myself to try and sound calmer than I feel. I need to comply now. Get myself through this alive.

'It's 0501,' I say. January 5th. Sam's birthday.

'Ian,' he says. 'That your husband? He's asking where you are.'

'Yes,' I say through clenched teeth. 'I'm meant to be there.'

Quinn grunts then taps at my phone, breathing heavily. I can't bear to think about what he might be saying. Maybe it will be obvious it isn't me?

The very thought of Sam being given some lame excuse – of thinking I just didn't care enough to be there – is awful. I'd be lying, though, if I said it was worse than the agony radiating from my arm into my shoulder. Every breath in and out is a mist of pain. I can't even care that much about Sam right now. It is all-consuming.

'There, that should buy you some time,' he says and gets up heavily. But he has left the phone on the bed, near my knees. My heart leaps as I try to think of a way to distract him.

'When is your flight?' I say.

'I'm leaving in twenty minutes,' he says. *Twenny minutes*.

'Can I have some water please?' I say. 'I'm very thirsty.'

He makes that grunting sound again and moves towards the door. I thrust my joined hands down towards where the phone is lying and fumble to pick it up, experiencing a rush of triumph. But then the door is open again and he is roaring at me.

'Give me that fucking phone, you silly bitch!'

I scream, and he wrenches it from my fingers, throwing it hard against the wall near the door, well out of reach.

I'm sobbing now, all hope lost, and he's shouting but I

can't even make out what he is saying. There is only help-lessness and pain.

'Why can't you just—' Quinn shouts, but he doesn't get to finish the sentence because someone is banging on the door.

For a large, drunk man, he moves fast, and I barely have time to cry out before the gag has been balled up and thrust inside my mouth once again. He wrenches my hands apart and pulls them behind me to re-tie them. The pain this causes is on a whole new level now. I almost feel my mind wrenching free of its moorings. Like I will never be me, Nina, again. I am just an arm, a shoulder, and agony.

I can hear him speaking downstairs and in my dazed state it takes me a moment to realize I recognize the other voice.

It's Detective Gilbey. She's only a few feet away from me, down those stairs.

I try to cry out but all I manage is a sort of guttural rumble that hurts my throat and makes me want to be sick even more. What can I do? What can I *do*?

Gilbey's actual words are still too quiet to make out but then I hear Quinn say, 'Well, thank you for telling me, DC Gilbey. I don't understand why that young woman continues to try and cause trouble for me. I assure you that if I hear from Nina, I will get in touch with you straight away.'

Then I hear her voice, a little louder.

'What happened to your table? Looks like someone sat on that.'

He laughs, easily. 'Oh, that,' he says. 'My fault. I was bringing in a large suitcase and I knocked it over. Such a shame. Now if you'll excuse me, I do have rather a lot to do . . .'

Gilbey doesn't reply and I hear Quinn say, 'Who are you calling? What are you doing?'

My phone – lying on the carpet over by the door – starts to ring.

I strain against the gag and try to scream but it's impossible. I hear Gilbey shout, 'Stop!' and the sound of the front door opening. Then I hear another male voice, yelling, and then there is the sound of feet pounding up the stairs.

Time seems to turn back on itself. I'm in my kitchen again – that morning – as the air is suddenly filled with shouting, urgent voices.

Someone yells, 'In here, Rosie! She's in here!'

And then a red-haired figure looks down at me, her cheeks flushed with exertion.

'Hello, Nina,' DC Gilbey says breathlessly. 'Looks like you could do with a bit of help there.'

61

Lucas

Lucas wakes to a pearly, early-morning light. The room is cold. He's always cold, now.

He forces himself to pick up his phone, which is next to the bed on the floor. It wasn't charging overnight and so the battery life is low. He glances at the latest missed calls and texts from his sister and drops it back onto the carpet.

He doesn't know how to communicate with her right now. She doesn't seem to understand that he might as well be in prison. It's as good as anywhere else. Being 'free', as she calls it, doesn't bring anyone back, does it? Nothing has really changed. The only small satisfaction is the thought that Quinn is having to exist shoulder to shoulder with the kind of people he despises. No bail for him, either.

Even though the murder charge was dropped, the other charges against Lucas and Angel initially remained in place. Lucas stayed on remand for another few weeks until a hearing at which the prosecution confirmed that, after a review, the decision had been taken to discontinue the case.

They explained they didn't believe there was a reasonable prospect that a jury would convict, given the circumstances in which he had taken Zach. Also, Nina had provided a written statement seeking to withdraw her statement and saying she would only attend court as a Crown witness if compelled to do so.

Angel's charges were also dropped by the CPS.

Angel had hugged him, eyes shining, outside the courtroom. She couldn't understand why he refused to come to the pub with her.

'Don't you see?' she'd said. 'That we finally got him? You're free now!' Then she got irritated. 'Why aren't you happier, you nutter?'

Lucas had only shaken his head and said he needed a bit of time. He was just shattered, that was all. He'd be in touch.

But a week had passed now and he hadn't been able to face seeing her.

He could only sleep in short bursts. Every time he dropped off, he saw his mother's face.

Dev Shah had told him that the police were going to be looking into the case, after what Nina told them about Quinn's supposed partial confession. But he had been warned that the chances were very slim of getting a conviction after all this time.

Knowing that his mother hadn't chosen to leave them had been like a gift covered in broken glass. Something good but unbearably painful all at once.

Lucas knows he should get up now and eat something. He can't remember what he last ate, or when. The bedsit smells bad too, and he knows he hasn't washed for days. But he can't seem to get up.

He starts to cry, softly, wrapping his arms around himself.

Quinn finally did it, it seems. Managed to destroy him.

He lies there, curled in a foetal position, before his wandering thoughts tip into sleep again.

He's in the kitchen with his mother, making cakes.

Everything is golden. Sunshine fills the kitchen and Lucas feels such a lightness inside; he could just float away like an untethered helium balloon.

Marianne is singing again; some sort of cheesy pop and he joins in, singing with all his heart.

Now they are in Grandad's barn, and he can hear the sounds of animals. The old dog is nuzzling his hand. All is warm and safe.

He snaps open his eyes to the grey light of the room. And feels a loneliness that is worse than anything he has felt before.

Lucas lies there for another few minutes, listening to the tick of the water pipes and the traffic outside. Then he reaches for his phone.

Angel, he texts. Help me.

62

Nina

Four months later

My phone buzzes from where it sits on top of the packing crate.

Putting down the salad bowl I'm wrapping in newspaper, I pick it up.

What if I forget to feed it, the message reads. No question mark. It's a habit of hers.

I sigh and then laugh, despite myself. These messages are a daily occurrence at the moment. Recent queries have ranged from: What if they can't get it out to I might leave it on the bus. What then.

It looks like I have been appointed the expert on all things motherly by Angel.

Which is a little alarming, considering I have had to resort to blackmail with my own son.

When Ian and Sam came into A&E and saw me in the bed, with my arm in a cast, looking like death warmed up, Sam's expression had almost finished me off.

He hugged me, hard, and even though it hurt all my injured places I didn't say anything, just stroked his hair and let him cry for a while. But when he pulled away, his eyes were filled with something I hated to see. It was a kind of suspicion, or, I don't know, *distance*. Like his ordinary old mum had suddenly become someone else; a person who sucked in all this drama and didn't really fit with him any more.

He and Ian had waited for ages at the house. When they had received the strangely abrupt text message, ostensibly from me, Ian had known something seemed off, and put it down to the fact that we were in such a strange place with each other. But what could they do, other than go back to Laura's? I hope Sam will eventually forget what it felt like, waiting for me and thinking I just didn't care enough to be there.

I have Angel to thank for my rescue. She risked her bail by telling the police she was in touch with me and sharing her fears about where I had gone. She knew what Quinn was capable of, as well as anyone could.

I know that at some point I am going to have to stand in a witness box and describe exactly what happened in Quinn's house. It is a complicated case and I have been warned it might be well into the new year before it happens.

I still get flashbacks, especially if I awake at night to find myself lying face down on my pillow. I vividly remember the feeling of the gag; the taste of it. The utter helplessness of not being able to see him coming behind me. I'm still having physio from that bad, self-inflicted break to my arm. I had concussion from the bash against the wall, then my own attempts to be heard. I still get the odd headache from that.

I was so very lucky, though. I got away, unlike some of the other women who were unfortunate enough to come up against Nicholas Quinn.

I'm told Marina Goldman has come forward as a witness for the prosecution.

I have been working so hard at making life a bit more normal again, for Sam, but for me too.

We are moving into a ground-floor flat with a garden in a few days' time. Sam was initially upset at leaving the only house he has ever known, but now he is looking forward to it. He will be able to walk to friends' houses for the first time ever. Plus, there is a Nando's at the end of our new road. There has been rather too much excitement at this aspect of the new neighbourhood.

There's also a nice park, nearby. I expect we will be there a lot, once we have Dexter.

That's the blackmail part.

One night not long after I'd had to break the news to Sam that the house was going to be sold, I found myself looking on puppy forums.

At first, I told myself I was only browsing; not making a commitment to anything. But by the time I dragged myself off to bed, I had made an appointment to go and visit a couple in Berkshire who had Labradoodle puppies to sell.

I'm told they are less allergenic than some other breeds. I don't particularly care if Ian spends his time sneezing; he doesn't live here any more. But Sam brought this issue up and so I thought I should look willing to accommodate the other important people in his life. It looks as though this situation is the only one we have. We have to make it work; all of us.

We collect Dexter, a black Labradoodle puppy, in a couple of weeks' time. Neither Sam nor I can wait.

Ian took the news with his usual manner of late; a sort of guarded respectfulness. He still thinks I might tell Laura about what we did. But I have no wish to re-visit that night. It only happened, I think, because I was traumatized; all churned up by my recent experiences.

Still, it helped when I told Ian that I needed two thousand

pounds a couple of weeks after I came out of hospital. I think he believed I was going to treat myself to a holiday. When it didn't materialize, he didn't ask any questions. I'm grateful for that, but it isn't his business.

I needed it for a reason he would have thoroughly disapproved of.

Angel had rung me, in tears, and told me that Lucas was almost catatonic when she responded to a distress call from him.

I helped her to get him into the local psychiatric hospital, Asa House, that same day. He was a private patient there and it cost an eye-watering amount of money. But, Angel had some money saved up and with my contribution, plus the money from Ian, he was able to stay for as long as he needed.

This week he went back to his old gardening job for the council.

He sent me a thank you card the other day. Inside he had written: *If you would like help getting your new garden together, here is my number. I'm very grateful for everything you've done for me. Lucas xx*

It made me happy. I may take him up on his offer.

When he and his sister burst into my life, it was one of the worst experiences I have ever had. They broke into my home; terrorized me for hours.

Ian would think I am insane for staying in touch. I haven't mustered the energy to tell Carmen or any other friends yet, for that reason.

But life is complicated sometimes and things don't always fit into neat boxes.

I have realized it is possible for good people to do bad things with the very best of intentions. The truly wicked people are sometimes adept at hiding in plain sight.

My phone buzzes again:

What if it doesn't like me???

I laugh.

Angel becoming a mother was news that would have appalled me when I first met her, that rainy, sweaty, frightening night. I thought there had never been a less maternal woman. Worse, I thought she was a bad, violent person.

But she never was that, and anyway, pregnancy has softened her. Even the hapless Leon (who, I now realize, is rather more sinned against than sinner) is talked of a little more fondly than he once was.

When she told me, right after Lucas had been checked into Asa House, she said, 'I might be crap at all the things you're supposed to do.' There had been an embarrassed pause, and then, 'But I already love this baby. That counts for something, doesn't it?'

And I knew she and the baby would be alright.

I type out a reply.

It will, I write. You aren't that bad really. And I'm here with all my high-quality Mother Knowledge to help. I suggest blackmail when things get tough.

Seconds later a smiley emoji and a single X come back.

I grin and then put the phone down.

It's time to finish packing. Then I can leave this house behind.

Acknowledgements:

Living with a criminal lawyer can be . . . interesting. You often might not make it to the end of a television drama that plays fast and loose with legal accuracy, for example. Once, we didn't even get through the opening credits. But it also means you have a great deal of expertise on hand when you need it. So, thank you, Pete Lownds, for your invaluable input on this book and all the patient help in making sure I got my facts right. Any errors that slipped through are all my own. I'd like to thank the fantastic writer and ex-policewoman Clare Mackintosh too, for helping with a tricky scene that I was concerned about getting absolutely right. Thank you, Nic Garrett, for helping me with my gardening questions.

My kind early readers Emma Haughton and Helenanne Hansen are always a huge help when I am drafting a book. I hope I haven't yet worn out the favour quotient, ladies, because I am sure I will be back with the next one!

I feel so grateful to work with a talented team of people in writing these books, from my stupendous agent Mark Stanton (Stan) at the North Agency, who does so much patient hand-holding and reassuring when I have my (many) wobbles, to brilliant Sarah Hodgson, my editor, who has been such a delight to work with on this book and the ones before. Finn Cotton and Emilie Chambeyron at HarperCollins have been so wonderfully supportive too, and make me feel really well looked after. Thanks to Rhian McKay for her forensic eye on copy edits.

I'm immensely grateful to all the people who have read and reviewed my books and who write to tell me what they think. Every time I hear from one of you, it makes all the hard bits of writing (spoiler: there are LOADS of these) much, much more bearable.

I'm writing this on the 100th anniversary of the day some women got the vote in the UK. This is a cause to celebrate, of course, but let's not forget that two women a week are still being murdered by partners or ex partners. Changes to government funding mean that vulnerable women and children are being turned away from refuges all the time. This is a national disgrace.

There are far too many women who, like Marianne in my book, didn't get away.

If you are concerned about anyone you suspect may be a victim of this kind of violence, the 24-hour National Domestic Violence Freephone Helpline number is 0808 2000 247.

Thank you.

Caroline Green. London. Feb 2018